LARGE
PRINT
EDITION

RANDOM
HOUSE

Anything Considered

—

PETER MAYLE

Published by Random House Large Print
in association with Alfred A. Knopf, Inc.
New York 1996

Library of Congress Cataloging-in-Publication Data

Mayle, Peter.
Anything considered / by Peter Mayle.
p.   cm.
ISBN 0-679-75882-8
1. Truffles—Marketing—Fiction.
2. British—Monaco—Fiction.
3. Large type books. I. Title.
PR6063.A8875A59   1996   95-50060
823´. 914—dc20   CIP

Random House Web Address: http://www.randomhouse.com/
Printed in the United States of America
24689753

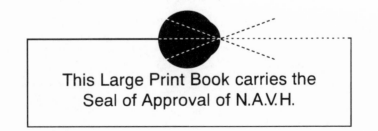

This Large Print Book carries the
Seal of Approval of N.A.V.H.

For Jeremy

AUTHOR'S NOTE

I would like to thank Elizabeth O'Hara-Boyce and Richard La Plante for their generous help in providing me with information about truffle production and karate. Any inaccuracies are mine, not theirs.

This is a work of fiction. The characters and their names are inventions, and have nothing to do with real life, with the possible exception of Lord Glebe.

Anything Considered

1

SOMETHING would turn up, Bennett kept telling himself. On the good days, the days when the sun shone and no bills arrived, he found it easy to believe that this sudden poverty was a temporary blot on the landscape of life, a hiccup of fate, no more than a passing inconvenience. Even so, he couldn't ignore the facts: his pockets were hollow, his checks were prone to bounce, and his financial prospects generally—as his bank manager had pointed out with the gloomy relish that bank managers convey when imparting bad news—were vague and unsatisfactory.

But Bennett suffered from optimism, and he was unwilling to leave France. And so, with scanty qualifications, other than a good amateur eye for property and a pressing need for sales commissions, he had joined the roving band of *agents immobiliers*—some of them no better qualified than he—who spend their lives rooting through the Provençal countryside. Like them, he passed his days searching for ruins with character, barns with potential, pigsties with promise, sheep hangars with personality, disused *pigeonniers,* and any other tottering edifice that might, with massive applications of imagination and even more money, be suitable for transformation into a desirable residence.

It had not been easy. Competition was intense; indeed, there were days when Bennett felt that property agents were thicker on the stony ground than clients. The market had gone soft, and the culprit was the French franc. It was too strong—particularly for the Americans, the British, the Dutch, and the Swedes. The Swiss had the money but were waiting, prudent and patient as ever, for the franc to drop. The few clients were either Germans laden with marks, or Parisians looking to invest cash they had discovered under Grandmama's mattress. But even they were scarce.

And then, the previous summer, a few flippant remarks—a joke not in the best of taste, Bennett had to admit—had led to a minor but potentially rewarding sideline to augment his qualifications as purveyor of real estate to the English gentry.

He had been a guest at one of the parties thrown by members of the expatriate community that descends on Provence each year for its annual ration of sun and garlic. As a permanent resident, with the useful social advantages of being a presentable bachelor who spoke English—in other words, an invaluable Spare Man— Bennett was never short of invitations. He endured the gossip in exchange for a full stomach.

Boredom was the occupational hazard, and mischief was the antidote, as it had been on that luminous August evening, the flagstones on the terrace still warm from the day's sun, the view extending across the valley to the medieval skyline of Bonnieux. Slightly tipsy, and numbed by the other guests' endless speculations about the future of British politics and the employment prospects for junior members of the royal family, Bennett had diverted himself by inventing a fresh nightmare for the prosperous owners of holiday homes. It would be a change for them, he thought, something different to talk about when they got home, an exotic addition to their normal complaints about burglars, frozen pipes, swimming pool vandals, and light-fingered staff.

Bennett's warning, which he delivered with tongue in cheek between mouthfuls of smoked salmon, struck at the very heart of rural domestic life: the plumbing. He claimed to have heard of a new and malevolent strain of dung beetle that had recently been observed in the region, invading any septic tank that was left unused and creating unsavory chaos throughout the plumbing system. Naturally, he said, the authorities were trying to hush it up, as dung beetles and tourists were not a happy combination. But the beetles were there, all right, biding their time until houses became empty and they could have the run of the pipes.

His audience, two sisters from Oxford with matching pink-cheeked husbands, had listened to him with mounting dismay. To his surprise, he realized they were taking him seriously.

"How absolutely *ghastly*," said one of the sisters, in the precisely tailored accent of the English Home Counties. "What does one do? I mean, our house stays empty for *months* in the winter."

"Well," said Bennett, "the only thing that works is regular flushing, at least twice a week. Drown the little devils, that's the answer. They're not amphibious, you see. Does anyone want that last shrimp? Pity to waste it." He smiled, excused himself, and made his way across the terrace toward a pretty girl who he was sure needed rescuing from a notoriously boring local interior decorator. As he came closer, he heard the drone of a familiar mantra about the charm, the ageless charm, of distressed chintz, and plunged in to bring some light relief.

Unknown to Bennett, the sisters from Oxford were spreading news of the dung beetle invasion throughout the party, and by the end of the evening it had reached the status of a full-scale epidemic that threatened the sanitary arrangements of every unattended house between Saint-Rémy and Aix. Faced with this common menace, half a dozen anxious home owners formed an instant coalition and waylaid Bennett as he was about to leave.

"This beetle business," said the group's spokesman, an ex–cabinet minister resting between elections, "sounds as though it could be rather nasty." Solemn, sun-flushed faces nodded in agreement. "And we were all wondering if you wouldn't mind keeping an eye on things for us when we leave. Be our man on the spot, as it were." He dropped his voice, in the way of the English when obliged to discuss a vulgar subject. "We'd make it worth your while, of course— proper commercial basis for services rendered. Wouldn't dream of asking you to take it on otherwise."

Bennett looked at them—middle-aged, wealthy men who doubtless had many middle-aged, wealthy friends—and came to an instinctive decision. "Of course," he said. "I'd be delighted to help out. But I won't hear of being paid for it." He waved their gratitude aside. Favors had a way of turning into introductions and then into sales, as he knew from listening to other agents. Most of them performed a variety of chores for their absent clients, from stocking the refrigerator to firing the alcoholic gardener. But none of them, he was certain, had received this ultimate mark of trust, or the position that went with it: official flusher, guardian of the septic tank, *inspecteur sanitaire*. In the quiet winter months that followed, it amused him to take his task seriously.

———

He pressed the porcelain-clad lever, listened approvingly to the vigorous rush of water, and put a tick against a name on his clipboard: Carlson, the mustard tycoon from Nottingham, who had often been heard to boast that his fortune had been made from what people left on their plates; a rich man, and not afraid to show it, particularly in the matter of bathrooms, where his taste leaned toward the grandiose. Bennett stepped down from the raised throne, crossed the mosaic floor, and washed his hands at a basin sunk into a slab of polished granite. He looked through the window at what Carlson, with mock humility, called his little patch of garden—a dozen acres of groomed terracing, thickly studded with mature olive trees. Imported from Italy, Carlson had told him, not one of them less than two hundred years old. Bennett had once estimated their cost and had arrived at a figure that would have paid for a small house.

He went downstairs, through gray humps of furniture shrouded in dustcovers, and set the alarm system before letting himself out. Standing on the raked, weedless gravel of the drive, he took a deep breath of crisp air and considered the morning. It was sending a clear signal of spring, with mist burning off in the valley below and almond blossom bright against a clean blue sky. How could he think of living anywhere else? He remembered the comment of a friend, all those years ago when he'd moved to France. *Wonderful country, old chap. Pity about the people. Absolutely impossible. You'll be back.* As it happened, he had become fond of the French, and he had stayed.

But how much longer could he hang on? The contacts and sales that he had hoped to make as a result of helping out his nonpaying clients had not materialized. They'd been grateful. They'd sent Christmas cards, photographs of their children on ponies, puddings from Fortnum & Mason, the odd bottle of port. But so far, no customers. Soon it would be Easter. Soon the dustcovers would come off the elaborate furniture, and the home owners would return to do for themselves what Bennett had been doing for them with such diligence all winter. Well, something might come of it once the season got under way.

But there was nothing immediate, and as he drove back to the tiny house in Saint-Martin-le-Vieux, he went through his options. The prospect of going back to producing television commercials, as he had done for ten years in London and Paris, was not attractive. He'd escaped just as the business was being taken over by unshaven young men with earrings, delusions of creativity, and that badge of the artistic temperament, the ponytail. He no longer had the patience to humor them. He'd been spoiled, having worked with some genuinely talented directors who had now graduated to Hollywood. The new breed, arrogant and ill-mannered, used special effects to disguise a lack of ideas, and lived in hope of a phone call offering them a rock video to shoot. No, he couldn't go back to that.

He could, he supposed, try to scrape the money together to go off and look for the little bastard who had stolen his boat, but the Caribbean was a big place, and both the boat and Eddie Brynford-Smith might easily have different names now. He remembered the euphoric evening at the Blue Bar in Cannes when, in a haze of champagne, they had christened the elegant forty-five-foot yacht the *Floating Pound* and made their plans. Bennett had put up the money—all that he'd ever made from the production business—and Brynford-Smith was to take care of the chartering. He'd set off for Barbados with an all-girl crew, and hadn't been heard from since. Bennett's letters had gone unanswered, and when he'd called the Barbados Yacht Club, they'd never heard of the boat or its skipper. Fast Eddie had disappeared. In his darker moments, Bennett hoped he'd gone down nosefirst somewhere in the Bermuda Triangle.

And that, Bennett had to admit to himself, was the sum total of his current business opportunities: a backward step into commercials, or an expensive hunt for a floating needle in a watery haystack. It was time for some concentrated thought about his future. He decided to spend the rest of the day working on it at home, and cut across the N100 to take the steep, winding road that led up to the village.

Saint-Martin was saved from being chic by its mayor, an old Communist with a deep distrust of government, the middle classes, and progress. It had been the last village in the Lubéron to have paved streets and water mains, and applications from eager foreigners to restore the crumbling, faded stone houses, some of them three or four hundred years old, were resisted with all the considerable influence that the mayor could bring to bear. Bennett would have voted for him just for that. He enjoyed living in a picturesque anachronism, virtually untouched by the hand of architect or decorator, the houses innocent of chintz, silk-covered walls, or lavatories on plinths. Winters in Saint-Martin were cold and quiet; in summer, the scent of thyme and lavender struggled against a persistent whiff of drains. Tourists came and went, but never stayed. There *was* nowhere to stay.

Bennett's house, in a narrow stepped alley at the end of the main street, had the overwhelming attraction of being almost free. It belonged to the village doctor, another bachelor, whom Bennett had met at a dinner party and who shared his interest in young women and old wines. The two had become friends, and when the doctor accepted a three-year posting to Mauritius, he had offered Bennett the house. The one condition was that the *femme de ménage,* a stalwart lady named Georgette, should continue as housekeeper.

Bennett opened the scarred oak front door and flinched at the blare of Radio Monte Carlo coming from the kitchen—pop music seemingly imprisoned in the seventies and wailing to get out. His efforts to introduce Georgette to the joys of Mozart and Brahms had been decisively dismissed. Georgette liked *le beat* while she worked.

All the furniture—simple, heavy, and dark—had been pushed back against the walls of the living room, and Georgette, on hands and knees, her rump swaying in time to the music, was attacking the already spotless floor tiles with a mixture of water and linseed oil. To her, the house was not so much a job as a hobby, a jewel to be scrubbed and polished and waxed and buffed. Dust was forbidden, untidiness a crime. Bennett had often thought that if he stood still long enough, he would be folded up and tucked neatly into a closet.

He bellowed to be heard over the radio. "*Bonjour,* Georgette."

With a grunt, the kneeling figure stood up and turned to inspect him, hands on hips, a lick of black, silver-streaked hair escaping from the bright-yellow Ricard baseball cap that she wore for strenuous housework. Georgette was what the French would gallantly describe as a woman of a certain age, somewhere in that mysterious period between forty and sixty. She matched the furniture in the house: low, heavyset, built to last. Her brown, seamed face was set in an expression of disapproval.

"You've been drinking cognac in bed again," she said. "I found the glass on the floor. *En plus,* underwear and shirts thrown in the bidet, as if I haven't got enough to do." She flapped a hand at him. "Don't stand there on the wet floor. There's a *tartine* and coffee in the kitchen."

She watched as he tiptoed across the living room and into the gleaming microscopic kitchen, where a tray had been laid for breakfast: starched linen cloth, white coffee bowl, lavender honey, and a baguette sliced in half and spread with pale Normandy butter. Bennett switched on the percolator, modified the radio to a bearable volume, and bit into the warm crust of the bread. He poked his head through the kitchen door.

"Georgette?"

The baseball cap rose from its examination of the floor. "Now what?"

"How long are you going to be? I was thinking of working at home today."

Another grunt, as Georgette sat back on her haunches and looked at him. "*Impossible.* Do you think the house cleans itself? It must be prepared for spring. Josephine is coming this morning to help with the turning of the mattress. Also Jean-Luc, with his ladder for the windows. Then there is the beating of the carpets."

She wrung out the floor cloth as though she were throttling a chicken. "You would be inconvenient. Besides, you can work in the café." She frowned at Bennett's feet and sniffed. "Drop your crumbs on the floor there."

Bennett withdrew, wiping his mouth guiltily. He knew himself to be a daily challenge to Georgette's sense of neatness and order, but her liking for him was obvious from her actions. She might bully him as if he were a grubby schoolboy, but she took care of him like a prince—cooking for him, mending his clothes, fussing when he came down with flu—and he had once overheard her refer to him as "my little English *milor.*" Kind words and compliments addressed directly to him, however, were not part of the service, and when he left the house after breakfast, she shouted at him not to be back until the late afternoon, and to be sure to wipe his feet before coming into the house.

He walked down the main street to the bakery, with its gleaming iron-and-brass bread racks, which antique dealers were always trying to buy. He knew they wouldn't succeed as long as Barbier was the baker—a proper baker, possessed of a baker's stoop, a permanent flour pallor, and a stubborn attachment to the old ways of doing things. The thought pleased Bennett, and he stopped to take in the smell of fresh loaves and almond cakes.

"Jeune homme!"

Madame Joux beckoned to him from the open door of the *épicerie* next door. He obeyed the insistent finger, preparing himself for the worst. His account, a dispensation that he had been able to establish only after Georgette had bullied Madame Joux into accepting such a modern notion, was overdue. Credit facilities, always regarded with distrust in any self-respecting French village, were about to be withdrawn. He could sense it coming.

He took the sturdy hand of Madame Joux and bent

over it politely, inhaling the aromatic traces of Roquefort and smoked sausage that clung to her fingers. "Madame," he said. "As always, you add to the beauty of the morning." He was encouraged to see the beginnings of a simper cross her face, and decided it was safe to broach the subject of his account. "I am desolated. I've run out of checks. You have no idea how inefficient these banks are nowadays. I myself . . ."

Madame Joux stopped him with a playful backhand to the chest. "A detail," she said. "I trust you like a son. *Écoute*—my little Solange is coming this weekend from Avignon. You must join us for dinner *en famille.*"

Bennett's smile slipped fractionally. Madame Joux had been trying to engineer a romance between him and little Solange for several months. He had nothing against the girl—she was quite sweet, in fact, and there had been a moment at the village fete last summer when he had almost been carried away during a *paso doble* under the trees—but the thought of being an appendage to the Joux dynasty had saved him.

"Madame," he said, "nothing would give me more pleasure. If it wasn't for my old aunt . . ."

"What aunt is this?"

"The one in Menton, with the varicose veins. I must be at her side this weekend. There is talk of an operation."

Madame Joux was a connoisseur of other people's operations, ever hopeful that some fascinating complications might develop. She pursed her lips and nodded. Patting her on the shoulder, Bennett took his leave before Madame Joux could suggest that the fictitious aunt should be brought to Saint-Martin to convalesce. He'd have to lie low during the weekend, and be prepared for many questions of a surgical nature during the following week. As he continued down the street, he reflected on the complexities of village life, realizing how much he enjoyed them.

He ducked through the narrow door of the post office. Saint-Martin—or rather the mayor—had declined a delivery service as being elitist and unnecessary, so villagers were obliged to collect their mail from the mayor's brother-in-law, Monsieur Papin, who took a close interest in all incoming communications; he was widely believed to steam open letters that looked in any way personal. He greeted Bennett with small clucking sounds and shook his head.

"No love letters today, monsieur. No *billets-doux.* Just two bills." He slid the drab envelopes across the stained plastic counter. "Oh, and your newspaper."

Bennett slipped the bills into his pocket, nodded to Papin, and took his *International Herald Tribune* next door to the Café Crillon, center of Saint-Martin's social life, headquarters of the village *boules* club, and the setting, every day at noon, for a fifty-franc lunch. The room was long and dark, with a pockmarked zinc bar to one side, tables and chairs scattered at random across the bare tiled floor, and a video-game machine, which had lost an argument with an overenthusiastic player two years earlier and had been out of order ever since.

What ambiance there was came from Anne-Marie and Léon, the young couple who had exchanged office life in Lyon for, as Anne-Marie put it, a career in hospitality. They were regarded in the village with some suspicion, being considered foreign and unnaturally cheerful, and it would be twenty years or so before they were accepted. Bennett, another foreigner who hadn't learned enough about life to lose his optimism, found them a delightful change from the monosyllabic peasants who played cards each day in the back while they waited for the crack of doom to sound.

Léon looked up from the copy of *Le Provençal* that was spread over the bar. *"Bonjour, chef. Du champagne?"* He shook Bennett's hand and raised his eyebrows. *"Bière? Pastaga?"* Léon's idea of a good client was one who started drinking shortly after breakfast, and it was with an air of disappointment that he took Bennett's order for a coffee. "With a little something, perhaps? I have some homemade *Calva.*"

Bennett shook his head. "Maybe after lunch. What's Anny cooking today?"

Léon's rosy moon face beamed, and he kissed the tips of his stubby fingers. "A triumph—lentils, bacon, and Lyonnais sausage. Too good for fifty francs." He shrugged. "But what can you do? Here, they expect a banquet for nothing."

"It's a hard life, Léon."

"*Bien sûr.* And then you die." He grinned and poured himself a beer, as Bennett took his coffee to a table by the window, where he unfolded his paper.

The *Herald Tribune* was Bennett's small daily indulgence. He liked its manageable size, the balance of its editorial content, and its restrained treatment of the recurring political indiscretions that turned newspapers on the other side of the Channel into shrill scandal sheets. He had given up reading the British press once he realized that he no longer recognized the names of the people being pilloried in its pages.

Sipping his coffee, he reviewed the state of the world as shown on the front page. Unrest in Russia. Bickering in the European Community. Squabbling in the U.S. Senate. The death of a venerable Hollywood actor. Not one of the *Tribune*'s jollier days, he thought, and stared through the window at the little village square, where miniature French flags snapped in the breeze above the war memorial. The sun was higher now, the sky a deeper blue, the mountains gray-green and hazy in the distance. He would hate to leave this place for the grind of an office in a morose northern city.

But the question nagged away at him: How could he afford to stay? He started to make notes on the back of an envelope. Current assets: excellent health, colloquial French picked up during his years in Paris, no family ties, a small wardrobe of old but good clothes, a Cartier watch that had so far avoided the pawnshop, a secondhand Peugeot, and approximately twenty thousand francs in cash, the residue of a split commission from a house sale. Current liabilities: domestic bills, Georgette's wages, and a dispiriting absence of brilliant moneymaking ideas. He had enough to get by on for another two or three months, providing he was frugal. But economy had never been one of his vices, and ten years of expense account life in the production business hadn't helped.

Sod it. He'd think of something. He always had before. He pushed the envelope away and went over to the bar.

"Léon? I'd like a glass of champagne. But a good one. Not that vinegar you were selling on New Year's Eve." He slid a hundred-franc note across the zinc.

Léon's amiable expression didn't change. "It was cheap."

"My friend, it was terrible."

"Of *course* for ten francs a glass it was terrible." Léon held up a finger. "I will find you a treasure." He went through a door behind the bar, and reappeared cradling a bottle with exaggerated care, which he held out for Bennett's approval. "*Voilà.* The 1988 of Perrier-Jouet." He set the bottle down and undressed the neck. "Are you celebrating?"

Bennett watched him twist the cork until it came out

with a muffled sigh, and he savored the familiar flicker of hopeful well-being that champagne always gave him. "I'm about to have a good idea."

Léon, nodding, filled the tall, narrow glass. Bennett listened to the delicate hiss of the wine, bent his head to inhale its toasty bouquet. The old peasants in the back turned to look at this new example of foreign extravagance, shook their heads in disapproval, and returned to their cards and the tumblers of *rosé* they would nurse throughout the morning.

Bennett felt the cool rush of bubbles on his tongue, then turned to the section of his newspaper marked "International Classified," where tax havens and business opportunities were advertised next to services of a more personal nature. On the left side of the page, a worldwide exclusive marriage agency offered—"for responsible people"—introductions to elite industrialists with alpha personalities. Over on the right of the page, just in case things didn't work out, was a number to call if you wanted a fast divorce for $495. As he looked through the selection of tax-free cars, apartments of *grand luxe* in Paris, and escort agencies everywhere from Mayfair to Wiesbaden, Bennett did indeed have an idea.

Why wait for something to happen, hoping that fate would be kind to him? He would take the initiative and make his own luck. He would advertise himself.

After a little rewriting and editing, and a second inspirational glass of champagne, he sat back and reviewed his efforts:

UNATTACHED ENGLISHMAN
Mid thirties, personable, fluent French, seeks interesting and unusual work, preferably in the Aix/Avignon area. Anything considered except marriage.

In the afternoon, he would call the *Herald Tribune* and place the ad. The season was about to start. There were bound to be dozens of replies. His blood quickened with a sense of impending adventure, and his appetite bloomed. Bennett turned his attention to Anne-Marie's cooking.

2

"THESE won't do for another summer," said Georgette, holding up Bennett's last remaining pair of white cotton trousers. "They are exhausted. *Fini.*"

"They look fine to me, Georgette. Worn in. I like old clothes."

"*Non.* They have suffered. These I have scrubbed too many times. Wine, soup, sauce—every time you eat, you make a catastrophe. Don't the English ever use napkins?" She shook her head, tossing the retired trousers onto a pile of shirts and shorts that had failed to meet her sartorial standards. Later, they would be taken to the mission of the *Pénitents Blancs* for distribution to the poor.

"Georgette, it is impossible to eat *écrevisses* with your clothes on without some trivial accident. Unfortunately, even in France, one is not permitted to dine naked."

Georgette shuddered. "*Quelle horreur.* Imagine Papin. Or Madame Joux."

"There's no need to bring personalities into it, Georgette."

"*D'accord.* The trousers go."

Bennett sighed. It was true that he was prone to the occasional mishap at the table. It was also true that the white trousers seldom survived a meal unsoiled; indeed, in the enthusiasm of the moment, they very often didn't make it through the first course. But in his current circumstances, more clothes were out of the question. He made a last plea for the trousers. They had a sentimental value, having been bought for him in Saint-Tropez by one of the girlfriends he still remembered fondly. Surely they could survive for one final summer.

Georgette leaned toward him and poked his chest repeatedly with an iron finger. "*Non, non, et non.* Would you walk around in rags and disgrace me in front of the village? Eh?"

Bennett had endured one of Georgette's sulks before, over the matter of the ancient tweed jacket that he had insisted on keeping against her wishes. She had punished him with a week of silence and had deliberately overstarched his underwear. He wasn't prepared to repeat the experience.

"Very well, Georgette. I shall have my chauffeur drive me up to Paris next week and buy a complete summer wardrobe. From Charvet."

"No doubt," she said. "And I shall win the Tour de France." Scooping up the pile from the floor, she disappeared, cackling in triumph, to the kitchen.

Bennett looked at his watch and saw that it was

eleven o'clock. The post should have arrived by now, and replies were due. His advertisement had run more than two weeks ago, and he had spent the period since then mostly with a client from Zurich, who had finally decided that his idea of rural bliss was not Provence but an apartment in Geneva. As Georgette cranked the radio up to working level in the kitchen, Bennett let himself out and made his way down the street toward what he hoped would be a sackful of replies and a glittering future.

Monsieur Papin peered at him through the window of the *guichet,* nodded good morning, and retrieved a newspaper and a large brown envelope from a cubbyhole behind him. He surrendered the newspaper, weighed the envelope in his hand. "An important packet," he said, "from Paris."

"Ah bon," said Bennett.

"Seven francs fifty to pay, for insufficient postage. Or if you wish, I can send it back."

This was known in the village as Papin's *pourboire,* the little extra he added on when he thought the market would bear it. Three francs here, five francs there—it came to enough to buy himself a few good bottles at Christmas. Bennett handed over the seven francs fifty and asked for a receipt. Papin, scowling, said he would eventually prepare one. The two men parted in an atmosphere of chilly politeness. Bennett rarely disliked anyone, but for Papin he could make an exception.

The café was quiet, the only sounds coming from the wheeze of the refrigerator and the slap of cards from the table in the back. The old men turned their heads in unison as Bennett came in. He nodded. The heads turned back. Bennett took his glass of *rosé* and settled at a window table. The envelope felt bulky and promising, and before opening it and tipping out the contents, he offered up a silent toast to the patron saint of impoverished Englishmen.

An invitation to invest a quarter of a million francs in Pizza Sympa, the fastest-growing chain on the Côte d'Azur, was the first to be put to one side as a non-starter. It was followed by a letter, written in lavender ink, from a man in Neuilly in search of a younger companion to share nature pursuits. An escort agency in Cannes promised substantial remuneration for gentlemen of taste and breeding, and requested a nude photograph for their files. Bennett thought of giving this to Papin.

Here was a job he could at least do with his clothes on. A Saudi prince needed a chauffeur-interpreter for the summer—based on Cap Ferrat, choice of three Mercedes, free lodging, uniform allowance, references essential. That might do, Bennett thought, if only he could manage the references. Georgette? Léon? His septic tank clients? He still had a small supply of crested House of Lords writing paper, left behind by an earl who had rented one of the houses last summer. He could use that and write his own reference. The princely letter went to start a pile of possibles.

But the pile failed to grow, as Bennett sifted through the next batch of replies. He decided against becoming a Jehovah's Witness, a tour guide, a part-time instructor at a language school, or a tout for a pleasure boat operator in Antibes, memories of the boat business still being too fresh and painful. Finally, a single envelope—the envelope Bennett had saved until last—remained.

Of that rich, self-confident true blue favored by the English establishment, it made Bennett think of Smythson's in Bond Street, where pinstriped men gather to brood over such arcane but vital details as blind embossing and deckled edges. He opened the envelope carefully and saw that it was lined with darker-blue tissue, a shade that matched precisely the brief printed heading at the top of the letter.

DOMAINE DES ROCHERS

I write in response to your advertisement. It is possible that we might find an area of mutual interest. If you would like to discuss it, please telephone me at 90.90.00.77.

Julian Poe

Bennett studied the bold, angular handwriting in deep-black ink. He held the paper up to the light and saw the edge of a watermark. Everything about the letter suggested taste and affluence, and Bennett was out of his chair and halfway to the bar to use the café phone when he realized that it was almost noon. Did people like Julian Poe sit down for lunch at twelve on the dot? Disturbing him at the table would be a bad start. Bennett dithered for a moment, then decided to take a chance.

The voice at the other end of the phone was French, reserved and impersonal, a servant's voice. Bennett asked for Monsieur Poe.

"De la part de qui?"

"Bennett. No, wait a minute. Say it's Box Eighty-four, from the *Herald Tribune*."

The line clicked to hold, and Bennett signaled Léon for another glass of wine. He felt unreasonably hopeful, sure that this would lead to something. Such is the effect that opulent writing paper can have on a man who has just lost his last pair of white trousers.

The line clicked again.

"This is all very clandestine. Shall I call you Box Eighty-four, or do you have a name?" The voice matched the writing paper—smooth and rich and assured. A toff's voice. With the instinctive English habit of classifying people by their accents, Bennett placed Poe at the top end of the social order. Probably an Old Etonian, like that little turd Brynford-Smith.

"Yes. Sorry. It's Bennett."

"Well, Mr. Bennett, we should meet. I take it you're not too far from Bonnieux?"

"Saint-Martin-le-Vieux, actually. About half an hour away."

"Splendid. Why don't you come over this evening, about six. If we don't instantly loathe each other, we can dine together."

Bennett took down the directions to Poe's house, treated himself to lunch, and went back over the brief conversation. Poe had sounded pleasant and relaxed, and from what he had described of his property, it seemed as though he owned the major part of a mountain above Bonnieux. Bennett wondered what the job was, and what would be appropriate dress for the interview.

He stood in front of the mirror in his bedroom, trying to gauge the effect he would have on a prospective employer. He was an inch under six feet, and lean, as bachelors with irregular eating habits often are. His face was long and tight-skinned, with sun wrinkles around the blue eyes and well-defined lines on either side of his mouth. His hair, straight and dark brown, was a little long, but it shone, Georgette having long ago convinced him of the benefits of Savon de Marseille on the scalp.

From the neck down, he was irreproachable. A pale-pink shirt, a navy-blue knitted silk tie, a blazer and gray flannels that Hayward had made for him in

London long ago, when the money was coming in, and cordovan shoes from St. James's. He had always bought the best clothes that he could afford, classic rather than fashionable, following the principle that a prosperous appearance was a business asset, particularly when business wasn't going too well. Millionaires could afford to dress like their gardeners. Bennett didn't have that luxury. In fact, he enjoyed the feeling of well-made, well-fitting clothes that seemed to improve with age.

He chose a silk handkerchief from the drawer, and was tucking it into the top pocket of his blazer when he felt a small obstruction. Smiling to himself, he pulled out a sachet of dried lavender. Georgette had developed the habit of seasoning his clothes, and he was constantly finding sprigs of thyme and rosemary or small tablets of mimosa soap among his socks and underwear. The lavender sachets were new. He was grateful that she'd decided against garlic as the flavor of the month. With a final tweak of his pocket handkerchief, he left the house and headed for the Domaine des Rochers.

———

The D36 twists south from Bonnieux, becoming the D943 as it continues down through the Lubéron toward the flatter, less savage country around Lourmarin. It is a narrow corkscrew of a road, cut through rock, the perfect setting by night for the twentieth-century highwayman. Rumors of armed robberies had been circulating recently in village cafés, and the story was always the same. A car, seemingly broken down, blocks the road, with a lone figure standing beside it. The unsuspecting motorist stops to offer help. Friends of the lone figure then jump out from their hiding place in the bushes, often with guns. The helpful motorist is left with a ten-mile walk to civilization, while his car is being processed for resale in a backstreet Marseille garage.

But on a fine spring evening, with the sun still catching the high limestone peaks, the road offered some spectacular views, and Bennett was in the best of spirits as he slowed down to go through the iron gates that marked the entrance to Poe's property. The coarse gravel track was smooth and well maintained, curving to follow the contours of the land, always rising. Poe had apologized over the phone for its length, which was nearly ten miles, but had said that the destination was worth the drive.

And so it was. Bennett came around the final sweep of gravel, and stopped the car to look, astonished, at the view before him.

It was as though the crest of the mountain had been sliced off to form an immense plateau level enough to build on. Immediately in front of Bennett's car, a broad alley of stout old plane trees led, in two perfectly straight lines half a mile long, to a massive arch that pierced a high stone wall. Behind the wall, Bennett could see the slopes of roof tiles, a warm, faded terra-cotta in the evening sun, with the tower of a *pigeonnier* at one corner of what appeared to be a court-yard. In the distance beyond the buildings, the Grand Lubéron stretched away to the eastern horizon. To the north, the bald white cap of Mont Ventoux; to the south, the plains leading to Aix, Marseille, and the Mediterranean. Nowhere, in the entire sweep of the view, was there any sign of a power cable, a pylon, or another building. It was the most perfectly sited property Bennett had ever seen.

He drove slowly down the alley of plane trees, wondering what the owner of such a place did if he ran out of milk or cigarettes on a rainy night, with the nearest village fifteen miles away. But then, of course, people like Poe didn't run out. Servants made sure of that.

With a heightening sense of anticipation, Bennett drove through the arch and pulled in next to the dark-green Range Rover and the long black Citroën that were parked to one side of the huge courtyard. He walked toward the house, past a fountain that would have done credit to a medium-sized village with its three great stone gargoyles spouting water into a circular *bassin,* and was searching for something as modern as a bell when the high carved double doors swung open. A man in a black suit, tall for a Japanese, bowed his head.

"Monsieur Bennett?"

Bennett bowed back.

"Please follow."

They went down a long hallway, polished flag-stones softened by the subdued gleam of Iranian rugs. Bennett ran a surreptitious finger along the top of an antique oak game table. Not a speck of dust. Georgette would have approved, he thought, and then whistled softly to himself as they entered a space that was big enough to have kept her busy until she qualified for her pension.

The low ceiling of the classic Provençal farmhouse had been removed, probably at the cost of several up-stairs rooms, and the traditional small windows re-placed by high, wide slabs of plate glass set into the stone walls, which had the effect of bringing the view into the house. Beyond the rows of lavender and groups of olive trees, Bennett could see the post-and-rail fencing of a paddock, with a chestnut horse con-templating the sunset. The scene might have been arranged for a photographer, he thought, and turned to look at the equally photogenic interior.

The flames of a log fire danced and sputtered in a cut-stone fireplace with a mantel the height of a stand-ing man. Arranged on the putty-colored plaster walls around the room were dozens of paintings and vintage black-and-white photographs in a variety of frames and styles, Sisley next to Hockney, Hopper next to Lartigue. The furniture was large, soft, and covered in those artfully faded materials that make interior decorators giddy with delight. It was a comfortable, stylish room, and standing with his back to it, silhouetted against the plate glass with a portable phone held to his ear, was the figure of a man who Bennett assumed was Julian Poe.

"Monsieur?"

Bennett turned abruptly, and would have knocked the glass of champagne off the tray if the Japanese hadn't swayed backward, smooth as a boxer avoiding a punch. He nodded at Bennett. "Perhaps you would like to sit."

Bennett took the champagne and smiled at him. "Thanks. No, I think I'll stand, actually. Stretch the legs."

The Japanese inclined his head again, and retired on noiseless feet as Bennett went over to the fireplace for a closer look at the paintings. One or two of them, he was sure, he'd seen in museums in Paris. Had Poe lent them? Could they be fakes? They certainly didn't look it, although you never knew nowadays. He was wondering if the subject was too delicate to raise, when he heard footsteps behind him, and turned to see the smiling face and outstretched hand of his host.

"Box Eighty-four, I presume?"

3

BENNETT'S first impression was that he was meeting someone who had strayed from the pages of a magazine article about men of distinction. Julian Poe was glossy, from the top of his immaculately barbered graying head to the radiant toe caps of his dark-brown shoes, which had the deep, well-established glow that can only be achieved by years of diligent polishing. A black cashmere cardigan was slung around his shoulders, over a heavy silk shirt the color of clotted cream. The trousers were light-tan gabardine. Bennett was glad he'd dressed up for the occasion, and made a mental note to pay his tailor's bill as soon as he was in funds again.

"I see Shimo's already given you a drink. I wonder if he's got one for me." Poe looked around as the Japanese glided toward him. "Ah, splendid." He took the glass and handed his phone to Shimo. "Your health, Mr. Bennett."

Bennett raised his glass, watching as Poe took his first, reflective sip. Bennett put his age at a well-preserved fifty, the tanned face barely lined, the body upright and trim, the stomach flat.

"That's better." Poe smiled at Bennett. "I find if I drink at lunchtime, the afternoon's a blur; if I don't, I'm gasping by six. I hope you had no trouble finding us?"

Bennett shook his head. "I must say, you have a wonderful place here. I know the Lubéron pretty well, but I've never seen anything like it."

"There isn't anything like it. I spent five years looking for it, and almost as long licking it into shape." He turned toward the window. "Why don't we pop outside and see the last of the sun." He took a small black wafer the size of a credit card from his pocket and aimed it at the plate glass, which slid back into the wall. The two men walked across the terrace and down toward the paddock.

"On the way up the drive," said Bennett, "I was wondering what you do about all those practical things—electricity, the odd loaf of bread. You're not exactly next door to the supermarket."

"Oh, we muddle along," said Poe. "There are two generators in that barn, half a dozen live-in staff, and we stock up once a week in Nice. It's a forty-five-minute hop. Look over there, at the stand of cypresses. You can just see it."

Bennett followed the direction of Poe's casual nod and saw the helicopter, squatting like a giant dark-green grasshopper behind the screen of the trees. He was starting to make polite helicopter conversation when the hurried thud of hoofbeats made them turn their heads. Two horses and their riders appeared from the trees below the paddock, galloping hard as they came out of a shallow depression in the meadow. Bennett heard a girl's laughter, and then a shout as the horses changed direction and came up to them.

The girl swung down from the saddle, easy and supple. Her companion, a heavyset man with a dark, Gypsy face, touched his cap to Poe and led both horses off toward the small block of stables beside the paddock.

Poe was beaming, and Bennett could understand why. The girl must have been six feet tall, with tangled shoulder-length brown hair, a wide, full mouth, and a flush that set off high, prominent cheekbones. Her riding breeches were tight enough to show that she didn't have a weight problem, and as she ran toward them it was delightfully apparent to Bennett that she didn't believe in bras. He was sure he'd seen her before, and couldn't imagine that he'd forgotten where.

"Salut, chéri." She offered Poe both cheekbones to be kissed, and turned to look at Bennett with feline, slightly slanted green eyes under raised eyebrows.

"Chou-Chou, this is Mr. Bennett. He lives over in Saint-Martin."

Chou-Chou extended a gloved hand. Bennett would

have preferred the cheekbones, and wondered if this was Poe's daughter or another perfect accessory. *"Enchanté."*

Poe slipped an arm around Chou-Chou's waist and let his hand rest on her hip. It was a possessive rather than a paternal gesture, Bennett thought, and regretfully dismissed the daughter theory.

"It's turning chilly," Poe said. "Let's go inside and have a chat."

Chou-Chou made her excuses, and went upstairs to bathe and change. The two men settled in front of the fire, their glasses refilled by the hovering Shimo, and Bennett noticed, with a certain wry amusement, that they had automatically adopted the rich man/poor man positions, Poe leaning back in his chair, Bennett leaning forward in his.

"I was intrigued by something in your advertisement," Poe said. "You remember? Anything considered except marriage. You don't look like a man bearing the scars of matrimony." He cocked his head. "Or have they healed now?"

Bennett shrugged. "No. I've never tried it. My parents rather put me off." And with occasional smiles and nods of encouragement from Poe, he described his abbreviated family tree. His mother was Italian, a competent soprano with a diva's ego; his father was one of those eccentrics that England specializes in producing—part writer, part explorer, a misfit born in the wrong century. He was constantly away, bicycling through the Himalayas, studying flora in the Andes, living with nomads in the Hindu Kush. He was drawn to high, lonely places, returning to London as little as possible, but it was on one of these visits that he and Bennett's mother, singing a minor role at Covent Garden, had met. Led astray by passion, and mistaking it for love, they had married. Bennett was the result, but domestic life had no appeal for either parent. The infant was farmed out to a distant relative in Dorset, then sent to boarding school. His father disappeared, clutching a rucksack and a Bantu phrase book. His mother absconded to Milan with a young tenor who had a good leg for tights. Bennett grew up in the company of other boys with wandering parents.

Bennett paused for breath and champagne. Poe nodded. "Yes," he said, "I can imagine that would give you a jaundiced view of the joys of family life. Do you ever see them—your mother and father?"

Bennett thought back over the years. He wouldn't know his mother if they passed in the street. The last time he'd seen his father, he'd been eighteen, and he had been bidden to lunch at his father's London club to discuss his career. He remembered it well—nursery food, pallid and bland, excellent wine, his father's gaunt, rutted face with the distant, mad eyes of a man addicted to hundred-mile views and uncomfortable in the proximity of people. Over coffee, he had delivered his career advice to Bennett: "Don't care what you do really, as long as you're not a ballet dancer." This jewel of wisdom had been accompanied by a check for a thousand pounds and a glass of port. Since then, Bennett hadn't seen his father, although he had received a postcard from Kashmir, wishing him a happy twenty-first birthday. He'd been twenty-four at the time.

Poe was laughing. "Forgive me," he said, "but it's not without its funny side." He looked at his watch. "I hope you can stay for dinner. I'd like to hear more, and we're having the last winter menu tonight. I think you'll find it's one of the more enjoyable aspects of domestic life."

Bennett was happy to accept. He had obviously passed the first test, and he found himself liking Poe, as people always tend to like a good listener. He finished his champagne, and wondered if Chou-Chou was going to slip into a little *décolleté* number for the evening. Things were looking up.

"If you'd like to wash your hands before dinner, it's through there, just off the hall." Bennett, by now a keen judge of bathrooms and lavatories, took the opportunity to pay a nonprofessional visit, and found himself in a room that resembled a miniature photographer's gallery with plumbing. The walls were covered with souvenirs of the sporting life—Poe on skis, on boats, with guns and various dead creatures, presumably in Africa, or standing beside monstrous fish suspended from winches. Poe's living companions were all men, all bronzed, all smiling in the perpetual sunlight that brightens the lives of the rich and privileged. Bennett, wondering what Poe did to pay for it all, dried his hands on a discreetly monogrammed towel, then went back to join his host.

Poe was once again on the phone, and Bennett was about to resume his study of the pictures around the fireplace when Chou-Chou came into the room, moving with the swaying strut of a catwalk model. The dress was fashionably skimpy, the legs were long, the heels were high. Bennett instinctively straightened his tie.

Chou-Chou smiled. "Julian's always on the phone when I need him. Can you help me?" She handed Bennett a heavy chain of gold links. "It's a very complicated fastening." Turning her back on him, she swept up her hair. Bennett stood on tiptoe and inhaled the scent, musky and expensive, coming from the exposed nape of her neck as he fumbled with the catch.

"Sorry," he said. "I haven't had much practice with necklaces. But if you ever need a hand with a bow tie, I'm an ace. There." He stepped away, the curtain of hair came down, and his pulse rate returned to normal.

"Thanks," said Chou-Chou. "Julian usually takes much longer to do it."

Can't say I blame him, Bennett thought. "Tell me something," he said. "I know we haven't met before, but I'm sure I've seen your face. Do you do any modeling?"

She shrugged. "Not anymore. Julian—"

"Let me hear nothing but good about Julian." Poe had finished his call and was looking at them, a half-smile on his face. "You must forgive the phone calls. Those people on Wall Street have no respect for European hours. I often think they wait until they know I'm about to have dinner. Let's go in, shall we? I'm famished."

Chou-Chou led the way, with Bennett, who counted walking behind pretty women as one of the small rewards of life, doing his best to keep his eyes off the undulant hips and the impressive length of her legs. She had to duck to go through the low doorway and into a smaller, vaulted room lit by candles, where Shimo ushered them to their seats and nodded to the young serving girl standing in the corner. Poe shook out his napkin and tucked it into the collar of his shirt, and Bennett, remembering Georgette's comments on the English and their napkins, did the same.

Poe rubbed his hands. "You're in luck tonight, Mr. Bennett. We're having the last of the truffles. They're a weakness of mine. You know all about them, I'm sure."

"A bit. They're a little beyond my budget at the-moment."

Poe nodded in sympathy. "This past season, they were going at four thousand francs a kilo. My American friends find it hard to believe—four hundred dollars a pound. And that's what the old rogue in Carpentras calls a friend's price. Double that in Paris.

The whole business is full of scoundrels. Fascinating. Ah, thank you, Shimo." Poe lifted the wineglass, inspected the color, presented the glass to his nose and breathed in. Bennett imagined he was the sort of man who sent the wine back in his own house if it didn't come up to expectations.

"Now then. Where were we in the Bennett life story? I seem to remember you'd been put off the idea of becoming a ballet dancer, but I'm sure you managed to overcome the disappointment. What happened next?"

What happened next had been an extended period of drifting, from job to job, from country to country. He had taught English literature with little satisfaction in a small private school in Connecticut, and then tried his hand at public relations in New York before taking a job with a film production company in London. That he had liked, and he'd been good enough at it to be sent to Paris as the head of the French office. He'd built the business up, acquired shares in it, and prospered.

Poe held up his hand. "Let's leave you there prospering while we deal with these. It wouldn't do to let them get cold."

The serving girl had placed large white plates in front of them. On each plate, incongruous against the plain elegance of the porcelain, was a foil-wrapped packet a little smaller than a tennis ball.

"The presentation is a little homespun," said Poe,

"but it's practical. Inside the foil is a single truffle and a slice of foie gras. As the truffle is warmed, the foie gras melts into it." He unwrapped the foil and bent his head in appreciation. "Mmm. Smell that."

Bennett followed instructions and took in the complex, ripely aromatic puff of warm air that escaped from the open foil. The black, lumpy shape of the truffle glistened with melted fat, ugly, delicious, and outrageously expensive. Bennett judged his to be a good quarter of a pound: a hundred dollars—at friend's prices.

"Wonderful, isn't it?" said Poe. "Now put a good pinch of that on it." He pointed to a small silver dish in front of Bennett's plate. "It's *fleur de sel,* comes from the Guérande. They harvest it every summer. Best salt in France."

Bennett sprinkled the coarse grayish-white salt over the truffle, cut off a slice, and bit into it. He'd eaten truffles before, but never anything this big, this rich, or this self-indulgent. He loved it, and he noticed that Chou-Chou was attacking hers as though she hadn't eaten for a week, mopping up the melted foie gras with scraps of bread.

Bennett and Poe finished, and both took mouthfuls of wine.

Poe dabbed his lips with his napkin and leaned back. "So. You prospered?"

He had, for some years. But with a certain amount of success and financial security, Bennett had started to suffer from the malaise of the business. He became restless, bored, irritated by the constant need to stroke his clients, to feign interest in their views on film and the creative process over endless lunches, to pacify directors and models. He felt he had turned into a highly paid nursemaid. And so, one fine day in April when the thought of spending another long summer working in Paris was weighing on him like a penance, he had quit. He sold his shares, sold his apartment, and headed south. It was there, in a harbor bar in Antibes, that he had met Edward Brynford-Smith, one of Eton's less distinguished alumni.

At the mention of Eton, Poe smiled. "I was there myself—a little before your friend's time, I imagine. Although there are so many double-barreled names there, it's hard to keep track. I'm sorry. Do go on."

Brynford-Smith liked to describe himself as a remittance man. He lived on sporadic checks received from a family trust, the occasional shifty deal in real estate, and his fees as a freelance charter boat captain. He was short, affable, and amusing, qualities that were immediately obvious. His eye for the main chance and his unscrupulous dishonesty were less evident, and Bennett found himself nodding in agreement one night as Brynford-Smith outlined a scheme that would provide them both with a comfortable life in the sun— summers on the Côte d'Azur, winters in the Caribbean. All it required was a boat.

Bennett loved the sea—to look at, to swim in, to listen to. But he loathed boats. He found them uncomfortable and claustrophobic. He hated the lack of privacy, the fact that you couldn't get off, and the personality change that transformed the skipper from a normally pleasant man into a bellowing paranoiac, a modern Captain Bligh, as soon as land was out of sight. Nevertheless, as Brynford-Smith pointed out, a boat that could pick up ten months' chartering a year—"absolutely guaranteed, old boy"—was an attractive business opportunity. Bennett had taken the bait, put up virtually all his money for the boat, and arranged to fly out later and meet Brynford-Smith in Barbados. And then Brynford-Smith had vanished.

Poe's brow was furrowed, either in sympathy or in disapproval of such slapdash commercial behavior. "You must have had some kind of legal agreement, surely?"

"Pages and pages," said Bennett. "But legal agreements are designed for law-abiding people. They're not much use if your partner does a bunk with the assets and you don't know where he is."

Chou-Chou had been listening attentively, toying with the gold chain around the slim column of her neck. "Can't you go and look for him? How can he hide a big boat?"

"You can hide a small navy in the Caribbean. Besides, to be quite honest with you, I'm skint."

"Skint?" Chou-Chou's English failed her. "What is skint?"

"*Fauché,* my dear," said Poe. "Broke. Well, Mr. Bennett, we must see what we can do about that. At least we can make sure that you don't go hungry tonight."

The next course was served, a dense, dark stew of beef and wine and bacon, onions, carrots, herbs, and olives, steaming, fragrant, the meat almost black.

"The cook's winter specialty," said Poe. "A four-day *daube*. It's been marinating since the weekend. She steals my best wine for it, too, the wicked woman. You'll find it's terribly good."

Bennett tasted the tender, piquant meat and wondered why the English of a certain class so often qualify their praise or approval with an ominous prefix—frightfully pretty, horribly clever, awfully nice. He put the question to Poe, who took a thoughtful sip of wine before replying.

"Interesting, isn't it? You'd never hear a Cockney talk like that, or a Yorkshire farmer. Bernard Shaw would have had an answer for you. Maybe the English middle-class horror of unqualified enthusiasm has something to do with it." He smiled. "But it *is* terribly good, don't you think?"

Bennett felt that the evening was going well. Poe was a congenial companion and seemed to like him. But other than the reference to Eton, he had revealed very little about himself, and even less about the job. Bennett was about to bring up the subject of his future, when Shimo appeared behind Poe's chair and whispered in his ear. Poe frowned, then nodded and stood up.

"Excuse me. Another of those wretched calls."

Bennett was left alone with Chou-Chou, who had demolished a serving of *daube* that would have defeated a lumberjack. He'd known French girls like her before—beautiful, slender, with appetites that could put a Michelin inspector under the table. Something to do with Gallic genes. He went back to their earlier, interrupted conversation.

"You were telling me about your modeling."

"Oh, I was the girl for Étoile. You know? The big cosmetic company. They own your face for three years, exclusive. They pay you *une grosse fortune,* and then you can buy a horse farm and retire." She smiled. "Except it didn't work like that."

"What happened?"

Chou-Chou took a cigarette from the silver box beside her, and lit it before Bennett had a chance to be gallant and possibly dangerous with one of the candles. She blew smoke up to the vaulted ceiling. "I met Julian when I was six months into the contract. He didn't like me working."

"So?"

"So he went to see the directors of Étoile. *Et puis voilà.*"

"What do you mean?"

"He bought the contract."

Bennett's estimation of Poe's wealth, already high, went up by a few million. Top models with exclusive contracts, he knew from past dealings with them, made a comfortable seven figures a year.

"He seems to be a man who gets what he wants."

Chou-Chou nodded. "Always."

The serving girl came in to clear away, and by the time Poe returned to the table, Bennett, replete after fresh goat's cheese and pears, was listening with fascination to Chou-Chou's gossip about her old colleagues in the modeling business, most of whom seemed to be addicted to either heroin or their dermatologists.

Poe listened for a few moments, then looked at his watch. "Darling, I hate to interrupt this riveting catalogue of vice, but Mr. Bennett and I need to talk." He smiled at her and brushed her cheek with the backs of his fingers. "I'll see you later." He turned to Bennett. "We'll be more comfortable in the sitting room."

Bennett stood aside to let Chou-Chou through the door. "My regards to your dermatologist. He's not called Monsieur Peau, is he?"

She giggled. "Good night, Mr. Bennett. I hope we meet again."

Poe winced at the pun and led the way back to the sitting room, pausing at a table behind the couch. "Coffee? Cognac? Help yourself, and the same for me." While Bennett busied himself with coffee cups and brandy balloons, wondering if his host ever did anything for himself, Poe went across to a large humidor in the corner. "Will you take a cigar? I can recommend them. They're Cohibas—Castro's favorite, before he gave up smoking."

"I'd love one," said Bennett. "Can you get them here?"

"I've no idea. Fortunately, he sends them over. We do business together from time to time. Cuba's changing. Interesting place." He clipped two cigars and handed one to Bennett.

The two men settled in their chairs. Smoke drifted upward, blue wreaths against the firelight, and there was a contented moment of silence as the first sip of cognac slipped down, warm and smooth.

"One last question," said Poe. "If we're going to work together, I think we can dispense with the formalities. I can't keep calling you Mr. Bennett. What's your first name?"

"Actually, I never use it." Bennett blew gently at the glowing tip of his cigar. "It was my mother's bright idea. Bloody embarrassment at school, and I dropped it."

"Let me guess," said Poe. "Something Italian and inappropriate?"

"Luciano."

"I see. Well, we'll stick to Bennett." Poe put down

his brandy. "Now then. What I have in mind is not exactly conventional employment, but from what you've told me about yourself, I don't think that will bother you. Don't worry—it's not seriously illegal." Poe paused, and smiled. "Not from your point of view, at any rate."

4

"THERE'S an interesting statistic," said Poe, "that has a bearing on what I'm going to suggest to you. It's this: something close to forty percent of the French labor force is employed by the state. You're familiar, I'm sure, from your time in Paris, with what this means to honest workingmen like you and me."

Bennett nodded. He remembered the torrents of complicated forms—paper diarrhea, he used to call it—the sullen laziness of self-important bureaucrats, the hours spent in poky offices, disputing the latest fiscal assault on his company's income. "Yes," he said. "It was one of the reasons I left; I was being buried in bureaucracy."

"Exactly. And all those millions of irritating little paper-shufflers have to be paid, given subsidized medical care, five-week vacations, and index-linked pensions." Poe tapped the ash from his cigar. "A delightful system if you happen to be one of the beneficiaries, but damned expensive for the rest of us. You're aware of the French rates of tax if you commit the crime of making a decent income? Sixty, seventy percent. Sometimes more." He paused to nuzzle his brandy.

"That's true," said Bennett, "but everybody cheats."

Poe smiled. "Quite. And with your help, I'm going to join them. Another cognac?" Bennett fetched the decanter, and watched the pale-golden liquid swirl into the bottom of the glasses. The thought of an almost destitute ex–house-sitter being in a position to help a man like Poe was strangely satisfying, and Bennett decided there and then to take the job, whatever it was.

Poe thanked him for the cognac and continued. "For some years now, I've kept a little place in Monaco, where the authorities take a much more intelligent view of income tax. But there are two snags. First, I feel about Monaco very much how you feel about boats—cramped and much too crowded. And second, despite all the bureaucratic nonsense, I love living in France. It's tiresome and inconvenient to have to limit my time here to six months a year."

Bennett's knowledge of the tax restrictions on the rich was sketchy. "Why six months a year?"

"Anything over six months—even a day—and you're assessed as a French resident for tax purposes, whether you like it or not." Poe took a long draw on his cigar and blew a smoke ring. Bennett noticed, without surprise, that it was perfect. "Which brings me to my harmless little deception. As you know, there's no official border between Monaco and France—no customs, no passports, no immigration checks. So it's difficult for the authorities to know exactly how long you spend there."

"And they're not prepared to take your word for it, I suppose."

Poe got up, stood with his back to the fire, and looked down at Bennett, shaking his head slowly. "It doesn't work like that. You see, it's not up to them to prove you haven't been living in Monaco; it's up to you to prove that you have. And in true French fashion, they will always give themselves the benefit of any doubt. You see the problem?"

"Sure," said Bennett. "But how do you prove that you're living there—call in to Prince Rainier? Report to the police station every day?"

"Luckily, it hasn't come to that yet. But you do need to lay a fairly conspicuous trail—restaurant bills, parking tickets, receipts from service stations, dry cleaners, wine merchants, that kind of thing—and you need to run up a healthy phone bill. You know how the French authorities love phone bills. In other words, you need to establish a permanent paper presence."

"Ah," said Bennett.

"I see the penny's dropped."

"I think so. You want me to be you."

"On paper. For the next six months, and then we'll see how we go from there. I'll pay you in cash every month, which will avoid any tax problems for you. Of course, you'll live in my apartment in Monaco. You'll drive my car, set up accounts in my name with the local tradesmen and two or three restaurants, sign for everything. I'll give you a specimen signature. You'll find it's easier to fake if you turn it upside down. You'll get the hang of it in a few hours." Poe grinned at Bennett and spread his hands wide. "Not too taxing, is it? I think that's the appropriate word."

Bennett finished his brandy, resisted the temptation to have another one, and tried to conceal his excitement at the prospect of being paid to live like a millionaire. Of course it was a scam, but it was a scam with a deserving victim.

Poe sabotaged Bennett's good intentions by pouring another tot of brandy into his glass. "How does that appeal to you? Questions? Reservations?"

"Well, I must admit there are one or two. I mean, you've only just met me, and here you are making me an accomplice in a tax dodge."

"Does that bother you? You said yourself that everybody cheats. Is this really going to affect anyone except you and me? Will France collapse? Will old pensioners be thrown out of their homes? Will hospitals close down? Will there be nationwide suffering, and a run on the franc? Will the president of the Republic have to give up his four-course lunches at Lipp, or wherever he goes nowadays?"

"No," said Bennett. "Put like that, I suppose not."

"So if we assume that our social conscience is clear,

what else should we worry about? The risk of discovery?"

"There's always that chance."

"Minimal," said Poe. "Unless, of course, one of us is indiscreet." An eyebrow went up, and he smiled. "I can promise you it won't be me."

"But supposing—just supposing, only a hypothetical possibility in a situation like this—*I* turned out to be less than discreet. In fact"—Bennett was by now made bold by brandy—"supposing I did the six months and then . . . well, screwed you. Blackmailed you, or something. How could you trust me not to do that?"

Poe sighed, as if explaining a simple concept to a dense child. "Business dealings should never be dependent on trust, as I'm afraid you learned with your friend Brynford-Smith." He looked at Bennett for a moment, letting the thought sink in. "I know we're talking hypothetically, so you mustn't take this personally. But if you were to do anything . . . embarrassing, I would deny ever having met you, and sue you for forgery, theft, and criminal impersonation. It would be tedious for me, but much worse for you. My lawyers are not kindly people, and French prisons are extremely disagreeable. Or so I'm told."

Bennett blinked. "I could skip the country."

"And I could find you. Or rather, Shimo could find you. He's a very resourceful man."

Bennett had a sudden mental picture of what the

noiseless Japanese would do to him, and it wouldn't be to give him a glass of champagne. He looked at Poe's amiable, relaxed expression. The man had a friendly, understated way of imparting a threat that Bennett found infinitely more believable than bluster.

Poe laughed, and came across to clap Bennett on the shoulder. "But let's not spoil a pleasant evening. This can be our little secret, an arrangement of mutual convenience. Think about it. You will spend the summer in great comfort, with money in your pocket; I shall stay here, which is where I want to be. The only one to suffer will be the taxman, and I feel we've both been more than generous to him in the past." Poe took a final puff of his cigar and tossed the butt into the fire. "And who knows? I might be able to help you find your vanishing sailor friend. I know a few people in the Caribbean."

Bennett could see himself in Monaco—solvent, well fed, with time on his hands to work out the rest of his life. What were the alternatives? An office job, if he could find one. Driving a Saudi prince up and down the Croisette. Or another summer of living from hand to mouth in the Lubéron. Shit. Wasn't this the kind of chance he'd hoped for when he ran the ad? Why not take it? Why not live soft for a change?

He looked up at Poe. "OK. I'll do it."

"I'm delighted." Another clap on the shoulder. "Leave your address, and I'll send Shimo round in the morning with the details." Poe stretched and yawned.

"You'll have to forgive me, but I need my eight hours."

They walked out into the quiet chill of the night, the vast blackness of the sky pricked with stars. Bennett glanced back from his car and saw Poe's figure framed in the lighted doorway, one hand raised in farewell. He drove out of the courtyard, and the great gates slid shut behind him. From start to finish, it had been a perfectly orchestrated evening, as all evenings were, Bennett imagined, *chez* Poe.

———

Shimo parked the big Citroën in the village square and walked up the street, his exotic appearance and formal black suit attracting undisguised stares from a group of women chatting outside the épicerie. They stopped talking as they watched to see where he was going, and nodded to each other when he turned up the alley that led to Bennett's house. Later, they would ask Georgette what business such a visitor had with her Englishman. Shimo paid them no attention. He was used to being stared at in that impolite, gaijin way.

He knocked at the door. Bennett opened it, and the two men exchanged solemn inclinations of the head.

"Bonjour, Monsieur Bennett."

"Bonjour, Monsieur Shimo."

"Bonjour, bonjour." Georgette appeared from the kitchen, eyes bright with curiosity under the peak of her cap. *"Alors, un petit café?"* She returned to the

kitchen and turned off the radio, the better to eavesdrop. Bennett scratched his head, while Shimo looked at him impassively. To have Georgette as an unofficial member of the meeting, and subsequent reporter to her friends in the village, would give the proceedings the secrecy of a news broadcast. Going down to the café would be almost as bad. Bennett decided to change languages.

"I seem to remember you speak English."

The faintest shadow of a smile. "Of course. I speak all the European languages."

Bennett grinned with relief. "We'll speak English, then." He nodded back toward the kitchen. "She can't understand a word. Let's sit over here."

"You may wish to make notes," Shimo said. "And before we start, I must ask you to give me the letter you received from our mutual friend."

Bennett went to fetch a notepad and Poe's letter, as Georgette came in with coffee, tried to engage Shimo in conversation, and retired in a huff when he thanked her in English.

"There you are." Bennett slid the blue envelope across the table. Shimo checked that the letter was inside before putting it in his pocket, lit a cigarette, and began to speak in a low monotone.

"The address is the Residence Grimaldi, Avenue de Monte Carlo, just off the Place du Casino. The top two floors. The car is a dark-blue Mercedes 380 SL, with Monegasque plates. It was serviced last week. You'll find it in the underground garage. There's a spare place next to it for your car. Accounts have been opened at three restaurants—the Coupole, the Louis XV, and the Roger Vergé Café. Sign for your meals. When you receive the bills at the end of the month, call me with the amounts. Checks will be sent to you, which you will then mail from the Monaco post office. The same system with the phone and electricity bills, and with parking tickets. Be sure to get three or four of those a month. Are you clear so far?"

Bennett looked up from his scribbling. "It doesn't sound too arduous. Tell me, does anyone come into the apartment to clean?"

Shimo stubbed out his cigarette. "The previous *femme de ménage* has been sent back to the Philippines. You will hire another one." He made a slight motion of his head toward the kitchen. "Not her. Pay in cash."

"Ah," said Bennett. "That's the other thing I was going to ask you. I'm a little short at the moment. Bills to pay here . . ."

Shimo held up his hand, and Bennett noticed for the first time the pronounced bulge of the knuckles of his index and second fingers, and the ridge of hardened skin that ran like a carapace down the side of his palm. So useful for breaking bricks, or necks. "Twenty thousand francs will be delivered to the apartment on the fifteenth of every month." He took a plain brown envelope from his pocket. "Here is the first payment.

The keys to the car and the apartment are also in there, and our friend's signature. I will call you in Monaco at eight tomorrow night to make sure you've settled in without any problems." He looked at his watch. "Any questions?"

Bennett studied his notes for a moment, then shook his head. "No. It seems pretty straightforward."

Shimo stood up, and Bennett followed him to the door. The Japanese turned and bowed. "I wish you a pleasant stay in Monaco." He managed to make it sound like an order.

Coming back to the living room, Bennett found the inquisitor in the baseball cap, her feathers still ruffled, putting the coffee cups on a tray and looking with disapproval at the mashed remains of Shimo's cigarette. "So," she said. "A Japanese. No doubt you had business with him."

Bennett thought for a second. "As a matter of fact, Georgette, I'm thinking of buying a car. A Toyota. Very good cars, Toyotas. Very reliable."

"But not cheap." Georgette cocked her head, waiting for further information.

Bennett took a deep breath. "Absolutely. But I'll be doing this job for the next few months, a lot of traveling. In fact, I've got to leave tomorrow." He saw Georgette's eyes narrow. "Don't worry, though. I'll see that you get your money."

"And who will take care of your clothes? Who will scrub and darn? Who will treat your shirts like babies? Eh?"

"Don't you worry about that, either. I'll be staying in hotels."

Georgette blew an expressive gust of air through pursed lips. "Those barbarians. They use starch like jam. This I have been told."

———

That evening, while Bennett was preparing for his extended absence, Georgette went into the Café Crillon for her daily dose of pastis and gossip. Monsieur Papin, as usual, was recovering at the bar from an exhausting day of petty extortion and steaming open envelopes. Three of the village ladies had already told him about the foreigner who had paid a call on Bennett—most unusual, a *Japonais* in a suit—and he sidled up to stand beside Georgette, ready to gather intelligence.

"Et alors, ma belle," he whispered confidentially, as though he were proposing an assignation behind the café. "You had a visitation today?"

Georgette, not wishing to admit she knew nothing of what had been discussed, and particularly not to Papin, whom she detested, took her time before giving him a knowing, sideways look. "None of your business. Certain things are private." She took a deep swallow of pastis, and shuddered with pleasure as it went down.

"The Japanese had a very important car. *Une grosse*

Citroën. And a suit. He was obviously a serious man. A friend of Monsieur Bennett's, perhaps?"

"Papin, this I will tell you, and no more. Monsieur Bennett is leaving the village tomorrow, for certain reasons. I am not permitted to say what they are."

Papin nodded, and tapped the side of his nose. "He will want his letters forwarded."

"Yes," said Georgette. "To me. Unopened, if possible." She emptied her glass, banged it on the bar, and left the café in a mood of considerable satisfaction. That little *salaud,* trying to poke his nose in her affairs. Well, not exactly her affairs, but almost.

5

GEORGETTE had insisted on taking charge of Bennett's packing, putting each shoe in a separate plastic bag, swathing his shirts in tissue paper, arranging socks and underwear and ties just so, all the while muttering about the brutal incompetence of commercial laundries and the ever-present danger of voracious moths in strange, and doubtless poorly cleaned, hotel closets. Bennett wished he could take her with him. She had never been farther from the village than Avignon, an hour's drive away, and a duplex in Monaco would seem like a different world to her.

"I'm going to miss you, Georgette."

"Pouf."

"No, really. But I'll keep in touch. I'm sure I'll get back from time to time."

Georgette sniffed, smoothed a final layer of tissue paper over a trio of sweaters folded shoulder-to-shoulder, and closed the scuffed leather suitcase with a grunt of satisfaction. *"Voilà."*

Bennett checked his jacket pockets, feeling the reassuring swell of cash. Keys. Passport, just in case. He was ready to go.

"Well," he said. "Take care of yourself."

"And if someone should ask for you? What shall I tell them?"

"Say I'm traveling." He picked up the suitcase. "I'll send you a postcard. Lots of postcards."

Georgette abandoned any further attempts to pry information from Bennett, sniffed again, and patted him roughly on the arm. "Remember to change your socks."

————

Bennett kept his little car at a steady seventy-five on the autoroute, pulling over to let the BMWs and Mercedes hurtle past, with disdainful snorts from their exhaust pipes. Even this early in the season, cars with German and Swiss plates were plentiful, their drivers impatient to reach the sun after a long northern winter. A week, two weeks, and then they'd rush back, skins lightly toasted, to their Munich offices or their Geneva clinics, and start making plans to do it all over again in August. Bennett was beginning to appreciate the luxury of his own situation, and felt any misgivings about his decision to work for Poe melt away in the face of six months of paid sunshine. What had Poe called it? *A harmless deception. The only one to suffer will be the taxman.* It was a seductive argument, and to Bennett it was no worse a crime than many of the creative financial adjustments practiced every day by big corporations in the sacred cause of increased dividends and satisfied shareholders.

He glanced at his watch as he passed the signs for Cannes and Antibes. Too late for lunch. Anyway, he was anxious to see his summer lodgings, to take in the rarefied air of the place that Brynford-Smith had always called, with a hint of envious resentment, Millionaires-sur-Mer, and to start living life according to Poe. He turned off the autoroute at Nice and took the road that curls along the coast, past Villefranche, Beaulieu, and Éze, remembering all the good times he had spent with various girls in various hotels in the days when the fitting end to a successful shoot in Paris had been a weekend on the Riviera. Scouting for locations, they'd called it, until the company accountant had put his foot down when Bennett tried to justify the purchase and consumption of a magnum of '73 Margaux as refreshments for the crew.

He came into Monaco, feeling suddenly shabby in his small and dusty car, turned right to take the road down to the port, and then stopped to get his bearings.

Monaco is tiny. The entire principality would fit comfortably into New York's Central Park, and so expansion and development over the years has been upward, with most of the twenty thousand or so residents living in scaled-down skyscrapers. The senior resident, being a prince and the current representative of the world's oldest ruling family, has more spacious quarters—a palace, complete with a band, a palace guard, and a battery of antique cannons to repel any invaders prepared to drag themselves away from the gambling tables. Police are faultlessly dressed and numerous. Crime is something one reads about in the foreign press. It is a place where a man can be at peace with his money.

Bennett drove slowly around the port, turned up the hill that lead to the casino, and found the ramp descending to the parking area beneath the Residence Grimaldi. He used his key to operate the security barrier, made his way cautiously past the protruding snout of a white Rolls-Royce, and pulled into the vacant space next to Poe's Mercedes. It was all as Shimo had said it would be. He got out and eased his back, while he looked around what could have been an underground showroom for the better class of automobile. His Peugeot was by far the smallest and easily the dirtiest car to be seen. He wondered if they fined you in Monaco for being in possession of an unwashed vehicle.

The elevator was carpeted and mirrored, and it took him up to the penthouse with a resigned hydraulic sigh, as if unused to carrying such an elderly and travel-worn suitcase. Bennett crossed a small hallway, and unlocked the door, blank except for the round black eye of a peephole.

Poe was clearly a man who liked the grand view. Through the glass wall of the sitting room, beyond the terrace, with its tubs of geraniums and oleanders, Bennett could see the rippling shimmer of the Mediterranean in the afternoon sun. The room itself was cool and modern, glass and brushed steel and leather, impersonal except for a few books, a stack of CDs by the stereo, and a collection of framed, signed travel posters from the thirties, promoting the winter delights of Cannes and Monte Carlo. In the far corner, a spiral staircase led to the lower level, where Bennett found that the entire floor had been gutted to make one enormous master suite of bedroom, dressing room, and bathroom, a supremely selfish and comfortable arrangement. There was no provision for any overnight guest who wasn't prepared to share Poe's bed. Bennett put down his suitcase, opened the sliding doors, and stepped out onto a second, slightly smaller terrace, facing due east. A sunrise terrace. The air was soft, a good ten degrees warmer than in the Vaucluse, and as he looked down at the small sailboats tacking their way across the sheen of the bay, Bennett felt that his luck had changed. Summer here was not going to be a hardship.

Unpacking could wait. There were errands to do, the Mercedes to be exercised, parking tickets to be gathered. He took the elevator down to the garage and spent a few minutes sitting in Poe's car, adjusting the seat and mirrors, enjoying the scent of leather, the solid, bank vault sound of the door closing, the growling echo of the engine as he started her up. It was

a different world from the baby Peugeot, and encouraged a different, more relaxed style of driving. A
right-of-way seemed to come with the car, and Bennett noticed an unusual deference from other drivers.
Or perhaps it was just that traffic squabbles, like
crime, poverty, and income tax, were not permitted to
disturb the orderly, agreeable rhythm of Monegasque
life.

Bennett made several stops—for wine, bread, coffee, milk, and a celebratory pair of Armani sunglasses—but failed to pick up a ticket. Was a
Mercedes immune? He decided to test the forbearance
of the police, and left the car beside the steps to the
casino while he went across the road to the Café de
Paris, stopping at the entrance to buy a copy of Gault
Millau's restaurant bible. He chose a table on the terrace and ordered a beer from a waiter who was still
displaying the early-season smile that would turn into
an overworked scowl by August.

From his seat in the sun, Bennett enjoyed a view
deluxe. To his left, the Rococo pile of the casino, once
known to its less fortunate patrons as the cathedral of
hell; to his right, the sculptures and meticulously
clipped and watered casino gardens, a platoon of gardeners moving slowly through the palm trees in search
of any weed foolish enough to try its luck in such exalted surroundings; directly opposite, the Hôtel de
Paris, birthplace of the *crêpe Suzette*, and conveniently placed for any guests with an urge to invest in

roulette and blackjack. Bennett watched the obsequious flurry at the hotel entrance as an extremely old man, accompanied by an extremely blond girl, emerged and frowned up at the sun before inching his way across to the casino, where willing hands massaged him up the steps and into the permanent twilight of the gaming rooms.

The beer arrived, and with it a ticket informing Bennett that it would cost him thirty francs, exactly three times what Léon charged him in the café at Saint-Martin. But what the hell, Bennett thought. Tonight he'd be signing rather than paying, and he turned to the pages of his Gault Millau for inspiration. He studied the descriptions of the three restaurants that Poe had designated, and decided to start at the top, with the cooking of Alain Ducasse at Louis XV, one of the dozen restaurants in France to be given a rating of 19 out of 20, and almost certainly more expensive than anywhere he had eaten in years. He was glad he'd missed lunch.

The thought of dinner reminded him of his homework—a little light forgery, the training of his hand in the peaks and swoops of the Poe signature. He tipped the waiter, received a nod in return, walked over to the Mercedes—to find, at last, a parking ticket. He slipped it into his pocket with the sense of a mission accomplished, and drove around the corner to his new home.

The evening sun was still on the terrace, its residual glow gilding the walls of the living room. Bennett looked through Poe's musical library, mostly opera—he wondered idly if his mother was anywhere to be heard in the chorus—and chose a selection of arias sung by Freni. Music to forge by, he thought. Did this constitute a crime, or did the permission of the signature's owner excuse any wrongdoing? Well, it was academic. Here he was, and Poe he'd be. He settled on the couch in front of the coffee table with a pad of paper and the specimen signature, turning it upside down, as Poe had suggested, for the first few attempts. It reminded him of school punishments: write one hundred times *I must not chatter in class. A prolix boy is an ignorant boy.* Copying a mere four letters was easier, and within an hour, his version of *J. Poe* resembled the real thing closely enough to pass the scrutiny of a bored waiter.

His eye was caught by one of the books on the table—a square black volume with a photograph of a rough, grimy hand holding a pockmarked black lump. The title, reversed out in white, read: *La Truffe: The Mysteries of the Black Diamond.* He flicked through it. There were photographs of dogs digging in the earth, of more grimy hands holding truffles, or wads of banknotes, of creased and weather-beaten faces. And at the beginning of a chapter headed "Truffle Swindles," there were several sheets of paper covered with notes and figures in Poe's bold black handwriting. Curious, Bennett took them out to read over dinner.

His own knowledge of truffles was not altogether limited to the occasional extravagant meal. It was impossible to live in France for any length of time without becoming aware of the importance—indeed, reverence—with which these pungent fungi were regarded; they were the black, misshapen jewels in the crown of *la France gastronomique.* Their prices were reported in newspapers. Their quality, which varied from year to year, was discussed in bars and restaurants all over the country. Their superiority over the white Italian truffle was proclaimed by patriot gourmets from Lille to Carcassonne, and God help anyone who disagreed. In Anglo-Saxon countries, cleanliness is said to rank next to godliness; but the French give the stomach precedence over soap and water, and the truffle is an icon. In fact, it was not unknown for the village church at Saint-Martin to hold a truffle Mass in celebration of a particularly good season. In other words, truffles were very close to being sacred objects—with the added allure of being impossibly, riotously expensive. Or, with the right connections, free.

Bennett had once spent a bitter January day on the slopes of Mont Ventoux in the company of Georgette's uncle Bertrand, whose winter occupation was *braconnage,* or poaching, of truffles. The whole village knew about it but kept their silence, bribed by Bertrand's judicious distribution of the spoils. He never sold them. The thrill of finding them, the joy of not paying for them, the delight of eating them, these were reward enough. Uncle Bertrand worked with a low-slung, muscular dachshund bitch, and Bennett could still picture the two of them, the man on all fours probing gently with his truffle pick, the dog, taut with excitement, looking on. It had been a good day, ending in Bertrand's kitchen with the best omelet Bennett had ever eaten. The thought of it made him reach for the phone.

He made his reservation at Louis XV, and checked that the account had been opened. *"Bien sûr, Monsieur Poe, bien sûr. À très bientôt,"* said the professionally welcoming voice at the other end of the phone. How pleasant people were to the rich, Bennett thought, and went downstairs to shower, the sound of *La Traviata* greeting him from speakers in the bedroom and the Olympic-sized bathroom.

Half an hour later, dressed in a lightweight gray flannel suit, a white shirt, and a loosely knotted polka-dot bow tie that he hoped would give his appearance a touch of insouciant prosperity, he took a glass of wine out on the terrace and looked at the floodlit palms and the glittering coastline of Monaco by night. Glamour, that elusive and indefinable sense of magic, was in the air. One of the best dinners in Europe was awaiting him. All he lacked was a playmate, someone to share in his new life as a subsidized boulevardier. Tomorrow he'd make a couple of calls and see if any of his old girlfriends had managed to avoid the Volvo, the cottage in the country, and the two children that had taken so many of them out of circulation.

He went inside to refill his glass, stopped at the sound of the phone, and looked at his watch. Eight o'clock.

"This is Shimo. Is everything in order?"

"Couldn't be better. I even managed to get a parking ticket."

"So there are no problems? Nobody's called?"

"No. Why? Is someone supposed to?"

There was a brief pause. "No, probably not. You have the number here?"

"Of course."

"Good."

Bennett looked at the phone, now buzzing in his hand, and shrugged. Our Mr. Shimo, he thought, is not one for a chat. Or else he's late for his karate practice.

———

Two hundred miles away, Shimo was reporting to Poe. "He's there. He says there are no problems and nobody's called."

Poe reached for the dish of black olives in front of him, chose one, and looked at it thoughtfully. "I don't imagine he'll call. You know how nervous he is about the phone. When is he due to deliver?"

"Saturday evening. I'll call Bennett nearer the time and tell him to stay in the apartment."

"Fine." Poe bit into the olive. "It's been a long time, Shimo, hasn't it?"

The Japanese almost smiled. "Worth the wait, Mr. Julian. Worth the wait."

———

Bennett was shown to his table in the great golden room, allowed himself to be persuaded to accept a glass of champagne, and reflected on the pleasures of dinner for one. He remembered the story told to him about an eligible man highly placed in London social circles, the target of every mother with a marriageable daughter. One particularly ambitious and persistent dowager, frustrated by his lack of immediate availability but determined to snare him, invited him to a dinner party three months ahead. With polite deliberation, he took out his pocket diary, turned to the date in question, and shook his head sadly. "What a pity," he said. "I'm dining alone that night."

It was a story that appealed to Bennett. There was a solitary side to his nature, probably inherited from his father, and he occasionally liked nothing better than to eat and drink slowly and well without the distraction of small talk, to observe and eavesdrop if the other diners were sufficiently interesting, or to read if they weren't.

Tonight's batch, he thought, as he looked around the room, wouldn't occupy his time for long: subdued, well-to-do, and barely clinging on to middle

age, for the most part, with one or two classic speci-
mens of the Riviera Girl—lithe, overjeweled, perma-
nently bronzed, laughing on cue at the conversation
of elderly escorts. By July, the boutiques of Monaco
would be crawling with similar girls, the yachts fes-
tooned with them, the nightclubs clattering with the
sounds of little *bijoux* picked up at Cartier or Bulgari,
the campaign medals of the Riviera Girl. Bennett
caught the eye of one of them—a beautiful Eurasian,
with skin of palest saffron, wearing dark-green silk,
matching emeralds, and an expression of polite boredom—and winked. Her gaze flicked up to a point two
feet above his head. He turned his attention to the
menu.

After a short, delightful, but indecisive study, Bennett gave up. There was too much, all of it sounding
wonderful, and he decided to enlist professional help,
never a bad idea in a serious restaurant. One barely
raised eyebrow was enough to bring the headwaiter.

"Monsieur Poe?"

"I'm going to put myself in your hands. What do
you suggest? Something light would be perfect."

The first part of the conference lasted five minutes.
Then the sommelier was called in, he and the head-
waiter frowning with heads together as they discussed
flavors and textures, vineyards and vintages. Bennett
leaned back and felt thoroughly pampered. Here were
two highly expert men, learned in every gastronomic
nuance, worrying about the precise combination of

tastes that would give him the greatest pleasure over the next two hours. He realized that the last time he'd eaten out had been in the café, with its paper napkins and fifty-franc menu. What a treat this would be for Anny and Léon. What a treat it would be for anyone. Being rich, even if only vicariously, was fun.

The two men bustled away, and a dapper waiter came to fuss over Bennett's cutlery and glassware, moving the small vase of fresh flowers a centimeter to the left, smoothing an imaginary wrinkle from the tablecloth. Bennett took out Poe's truffle notes and started to read.

The first page was headed by an unattributed quotation: "Man has invented vaccination, antibiotics, the computer; he races round the cosmos and sticks pennants on the moon—but up until now, he hasn't been able to make truffles grow." Below this, a simple chart showed France's truffle harvests, from a high point of more than a thousand tons in 1905 to sixty-nine tons in 1987. The projection for 1995–96 was lower still— a paltry twenty tons, against an estimated demand of sixty to eighty tons. Bennett took a thoughtful sip of champagne. No wonder the fashionable gourmet grocers in Paris could charge eight thousand francs a kilo. It was a seller's market. He was trying to work out what a ton would fetch, when the sommelier's deferential murmur made him look up. "The Chassagne-Montrachet '92." The capsule was cut and the cork was drawn with due respect, and Bennett's nose was treated to the scent of nectar. He put the notes aside as the waiter arrived with the first course.

Warm, fresh asparagus, green and violet, bathed in a delicate emulsion of olive oil and balsamic vinegar, a work of art on a plate, every last drop of juice to be mopped up with bread that reminded Bennett of the revelation of his first true French loaf, many years before. There is nothing quite like the taste of nostalgia, he thought. When the plate looked as though it had been cleaned by a cat's tongue, he sat back and returned to Poe's notes.

They indicated much more than a passing gastronomic fondness for truffles, and Bennett found himself becoming increasingly interested, and increasingly curious. Was Poe trying to grow them? Why had he underlined a particular passage? "A spore from a previous year's truffle, at the moment of putrefaction, is transported (by insect, animal, rain, or wind) into the soil. It germinates into an embryo fungus, whose vegetative part, or mycelium, consists of threadlike filaments called hyphae. These attach themselves to tree roots, whose sap nourishes the parasitical truffle in a symbiosis known as mycorrhiza." This was followed by notes on soil types, orientation, altitude, rainfall, tree species, and a regional breakdown of France's apparently dwindling truffle production.

The shortage had failed to affect Monaco, as Bennett found with his main course, a *colinot* just hours out of the Mediterranean, grilled on a wood fire, coated with melted butter and crushed truffles, and served with lightly fried basil. He couldn't remember having tasted anything so fine, and glanced with sympathy at the Riviera Girl two tables away, grazing on what looked like a plain salad. He wondered if she sucked her emeralds between courses for sustenance.

The unhurried ritual of clearing the table for the final course took place—plates removed, bread crumbs swept into a miniature silver coffin, the cloth smoothed, dessert cutlery placed—while Bennett sipped his wine and wished he could take what was left in the bottle home with him. Ordinary wines he swigged, but his rate of consumption dropped sharply when he was lucky enough to drink something exceptional. Somewhere here, he thought, was an argument in favor of the economies of buying nothing but great vintages. All it would take was three or four hundred thousand francs to start you off. With a last, lingering swallow, he put his glass to one side and watched as the waiter put the *gratin* of wild strawberries and pine nuts in front of him, in the manner of a supplicant making an offering to the gods. What was it going to be like to live like this every day? Addictive, Bennett decided, and set to with an eager spoon.

Over coffee and a *fine,* he came to the end of the notes. The last section was devoted to Poe's calculations, in which he had assumed an average retail market price of four thousand francs a kilo. In the margin,

Poe had written, *five tons minimum per year,* and had underscored it heavily. At the assumed price, which was on the conservative side, Bennett worked out that five tons of truffles would be worth twenty million francs, or four million dollars. A year. Bloody hell. Was he buying, or selling? Either way, the odd four-star dinner was a drop in the bucket, and Bennett signed his new name on the bill with a flourish, adding an impressively large tip. Nowhere does good news of this sort travel faster than in a restaurant, and Bennett's departure was personally attended by the head-waiter and the sommelier, both of whom expressed a deep and sincere desire to see him again very shortly.

And so you will, Bennett thought. He took a turn around the casino gardens, and went to his oversized bed a contented man.

6

THE tiles of the main terrace were still morning cool under Bennett's bare feet as he laid the table for breakfast: coffee, sunglasses, address book, and telephone. The sky was as blue as a postcard, with only a faint whisker of cloud hanging above Monaco's mountainous backdrop, the Tête de Chien. Heat was in the air already, and Bennett slipped out of the toweling robe to let the sun get to work on his winter skin. He had inherited his mother's Italian pigmentation, and within a week would darken to the color of chocolate, an annual transformation that he never ceased to enjoy. No matter how often the medical establishment shook its cautious head and warned of the horrors of a fried epidermis and premature aging, Bennett felt better when he had a tan, wrinkles or no wrinkles. He moved his chair so that he could sit in the direct path of the sun, and started leafing through his address book in search of companionship.

His history with women had followed a pattern familiar to many single men who prefer to stay single— a series of relationships brought to an end, sometimes amicably, sometimes not, by the increasingly insistent ticking of the biological clock. Entirely natural, Bennett had to admit, but even so, hints and midnight whispers about marriage, the joys of nesting, and baby Bennetts had the same effect on him as a bucket of cold water thrown over an ardent dog.

He realized, sometimes hoped, that one day this might change, but it would take a woman he had yet to meet. Until then, it would probably be the mixture as before, lust and affection. Not that there was too much wrong with that, while it lasted. He looked through the names in the address book, remembering, sometimes with difficulty, the circumstances of his various departures. Chantal had been tearful but brave. Karine had accused him of being a closet misogynist and had told him to grow up. Marie-Pierre had hurled a vase of flowers at his head. Or was that Rachel? Finding playmates for the summer wasn't going to be quite as easy as he had thought.

His finger stopped at the letter *S,* and he was reminded of a week he had spent in London on a job two years ago, a girl with hair like sunshine, dinner at the Caprice, tangled sheets, promises to call from Paris. Why hadn't he? Probably too busy dodging missiles from Marie-Pierre. He hesitated. Was late better than never? He decided it was, and called the office number she had given him

"Good morning. Redeeming Features."

"Hello. Could I speak to Susie Barber, please?"

Bennett sipped his coffee, half expecting to be told that she'd left. Two years in the film production business, where job hopping is almost as popular as lunch, is a long time. She might have had an offer to go and work in L.A. She might have a lover, a husband, a baby. She might not even remember him. His pessimistic train of thought was interrupted by a businesslike hello, followed by the sound of a cigarette being lit and inhaled. He remembered that she'd told him she could never make or take a phone call without smoking.

"Susie? It's Bennett. How are you?"

A silence. Exhale. "Surprised, if you must know."

"Look, I'm sorry. I know I said I'd call from Paris . . ."

"Did you?"

"Yes. Well, no. I mean, I didn't call. All hell broke loose when I got back, one of the directors got busted the night before a shoot, and I was up to my ears in crap . . ."

"Bennett?"

"Yes?"

"That was two years ago."

"I know, I know. What can I say? I was a slave to my job, Suze, a thoughtless brute, driven by ambition, days and nights at the desk, hollow-eyed from lack of sleep, no time for the finer things in life, like you— God, I was a mess. Not fit to be with."

"Are you finished? I've got a busy morning."

But she didn't hang up, and Bennett rushed on. "That's all changed now. I've reformed. Actually, I've retired." There was no response, but Bennett sensed curiosity at the other end of the line and took advantage of it. "In fact, I'm sort of working out what to do next. I'm in Monaco. You'd like Monaco, Suze—warm and sunny, terrace overlooking the sea, polite policemen, wonderful food, friendly natives. We could have a terrific time."

"We?"

"My treat, Suze. I'll pay for the ticket, bring you champagne in bed, rub your back with Ambre Solaire, run your bath, peel your grapes, take you on nature rambles in the casino gardens, anything you like. There's a lovable side to me, I promise. Thoughtful and kind. House-trained. You'll see."

"Creep."

"Great. When can you come?"

"I didn't say I would. How do you know I'm not with someone else?"

"Ah. I was rather hoping you might be saving yourself for me, prepared to bring comfort and joy to the heart of a lonely man. You'd be doing a good deed, Suze. And you'd get a tan. How's the weather in London? The usual? Gray and wet? It's seventy-five and sunny here. I'm having breakfast on the terrace."

"Piss off."

But he didn't, and after another five minutes of his cajolery, flattery, and protestations of devotion, she agreed to take the early flight to Nice on Saturday morning. Bennett put the phone down with a pleasurable sense of anticipation, made a mental note to buy flowers and stock up the fridge, and spent the rest of the day flat in the sun, a human lizard.

The week slipped by in a warm and well-fed blur. Bennett tried the other two restaurants Poe had suggested, and found them both excellent. He made a brief expedition across the border into Italy and did his shopping at the Ventimiglia market. He stopped at the Café de Paris every evening to have an aperitif and watch the passing parade. Daily, as the lubricant of money smoothed away the rough edges from his life, he felt more and more comfortable in his role as a rich layabout. He was discovering that while it takes years to accept adversity, a man becomes accustomed to good fortune almost overnight.

The only flaw in this week of solitary bliss was a call from Shimo, giving Bennett instructions to stay in the apartment on Saturday evening to receive a delivery for Poe. It was important, Shimo said, in his flat, intimidating monotone. He himself would be coming over to collect the item later that same night. Did Bennett understand?

Bennett understood. He had planned to take Susie to Louis XV, but after a moment's irritation, he persuaded himself that a simple dinner on the terrace, with its convenient proximity to the bedroom, might be a more personal way to celebrate her arrival in

Monaco. Smoked salmon, he thought, followed by something cold and delicious in aspic from the *traiteur* in town. Cheese, fruit, and then a dive between the sheets. What more could a girl want?

Saturday morning found him—tanned, scrupulously shaved, and tastefully cologned—driving the Mercedes, top down, along the Corniche to Nice airport. This was once, so an old Côte d'Azur hand had told him, a small, almost rural terminal, smelling of black tobacco and suntan oil, where on Sunday mornings elderly British expatriates, still in their slippers and ancient dressing gowns, could be seen shuffling up to the newsstand in search of a copy of the London *Times*. It was hard to believe now, Bennett thought, as he turned off into the tangled spaghetti of airport side roads, past pollution-proof palm trees, and up to the gleaming modern blockhouses that had been built during the reign of Mayor Médecin, who had ruled Nice during its boom years.

There was no need to check the arrivals board to identify the flight from London. The gray straggle of passengers coming out of the gate couldn't have been anything but British. There was a uniform pallor to the faces, and their owners, particularly the men, announced their positions on the class ladder by their clothes—bright new panama hats, shirts of a violent stripe, and double-breasted blazers with a surfeit of brass buttons for the gentry; wrinkled jeans, scuffed running shoes, and bags bulging with duty-free liquor for the less exalted. Bennett was studying a tall, knobbly man in shorts that displayed veal-white legs, black socks, and sandals, when he saw the burnished hair and wildly waving arm of Susie, dressed as though on her way to a smart lunch at the Ivy, in a clinging dark suit and high heels. Her sole concession to the holiday spirit was a pair of small and modish sunglasses, which clashed with Bennett's as they exchanged pecks of greeting.

Bennett stepped back, smiling. "You look fantastic," he said, and she did—the hair blonder than he remembered, the makeup luminous and subtle, the body displaying the results of ruthless exercise, an altogether more sophisticated version of the giggling, pretty girl he had met two years before.

She took off her sunglasses and looked at him, her head cocked to one side. "And you're disgustingly brown. But it's quite nice to see you after what I had to sit next to coming over."

"It wasn't the one in shorts, was it?" Bennett took her arm, and they walked over to the baggage claim area, Susie's heels clicking on the floor.

She nodded. "He asked me if I liked hiking. Can you believe it? I mean, do I look like a hiker?"

"You look like a dream come true to me, Suze."

"Wanker. There—that's mine, the black one." She pointed to a squat mass the size of a steamer trunk, and Bennett wrestled it off the carousel, marveling at the sartorial requirements of the modern woman.

"You've got some heavy swimsuits, Suze."

"Funny you should say that. I need to get some. They're always better in France. And a hat. The sun's very bad for your hair."

Bennett, risking rupture, heaved the suitcase onto a trolley. "Can you survive lunch without a hat? I thought we might go into Nice to eat. There's a good little place in the flower market."

Susie approved of the Mercedes and liked the simple fish restaurant in the Cours Saleya. It was one of her protein days, she told Bennett, so clams and a grilled *daurade* would suit her very well. She was into health, she said, lighting another cigarette and draining a glass of Muscadet, very strict about not mixing protein and carbs in the same meal. Bennett sat back and enjoyed her as she ate, drank, smoked, and chattered about her life over the past two years.

Work had gone well, and she had been promoted from production assistant to Producer—with a capital *P,* she emphasized—complete with all the trimmings: expense account, phone in the handbag, extensive wardrobe of black clothes, and membership in one of London's most fashionable gyms, where she and others like her strove to achieve the sculptured perfection of bust and buttock while comparing notes on the shortcomings of the men in their lives. And here, Susie said, the news was disappointing. She allowed Bennett to pour her another glass of wine and pat her hand in sympathy.

"What's the problem, Suze? Are all the good ones married?"

"Worse," she said, and wrinkled her nose. "Divorced, and sorry for themselves. I can't tell you the number of times I've had to sit through dinner and listen to horror stories about ex-wives. And then they have the nerve to try to jump on you afterwards. Animals."

"Outrageous," said Bennett, admiring the sheen of a silken thigh as Susie leaned back and crossed her legs. "Never mind. The age of chivalry isn't quite dead. Finish your wine, and we'll go and buy you the most fetching hat in Nice."

Susie looked at him over her glass. "I never asked," she said. "You didn't get married, did you?"

"Me?"

"Silly question." She grinned. "No one would have you."

———

They strolled arm in arm through the sunny streets behind the Promenade des Anglais, where the boutiques lie in wait for those lulled into extravagance by a good lunch. Bennett's tolerance of shopping was normally limited to a brisk and decisive half hour, but today he made an exception, following Susie in and out and back again to Saint Laurent and Armani and Cacharel, acting as the guardian of her handbag when she disappeared into minuscule curtained alcoves, and as fashion critic and interpreter each time she emerged to face the shameless flattery of the salesgirls.

"Mais c'est génial," one of them declared in rapture as Susie emerged in a microscopic shift that seemed to have been made from three gauze handkerchiefs. *"Moi, j'adore ça. C'est très, très cool."*

Susie turned to Bennett. "What do you think?"

Bennett blinked. "Where's the rest of it?"

"I knew you'd like it."

Two hours later, weighed down by their trophies, and with Susie feeling, as she said, shopped out for the day, they drove slowly through the traffic fighting to leave Nice, the slanting sun of early evening warm on their shoulders, a whisper of breeze coming off the Mediterranean. Bennett's suggestion of dinner on the terrace had been welcomed. Susie said she didn't want to go public in Monaco anyway, not with all those bronzed bimbos, until she'd got some color. As the car rolled sedately up the hill to the Place du Casino, he thought how well things were turning out. So often, old flames were best left to simmer in the memory. This one was going to be different.

Bennett let Susie into the apartment and staggered in after her with the bags.

"Well," he said, "will this do? A poor, modest place, but at least it's home." He slid open the terrace door. "Not a bad view, is it?"

Susie looked to the west, where the sun was beginning its spectacular dip into the sea. "Brilliant," she said. She turned and smiled at him. "You *have* done well. Is this all yours?"

"Sort of. Well, for the next six months, at least. It's a long story. I'll tell you over dinner."

They went downstairs, and Susie immediately fell in love with the enormous bathroom, fingering the thick pile of monogrammed towels and the cut-glass bottles of bath essence from Grasse, inspecting three different views of herself in the mirrored walls, exclaiming with delight as Bennett pointed out the speakers set in each corner of the room.

"Heaven," she said. "I think I'm going to have a musical bath while you do something manly and useful in the kitchen."

Bennett had been hoping to do something manly in the bathroom, but he put thoughts of a hygienic romp aside for the moment, telling himself there would be plenty of time later. He would be the perfect host, patient and considerate. "I'll take care of the music," he said, "and champagne will be served in five minutes. How about that?"

She blew him a kiss and bent over to turn on the bathwater. With a last appreciative glance at her shapely and indisputably well-exercised rear view, Bennett went upstairs, put a Brahms symphony on the stereo, and was on his way to the refrigerator and the champagne when he heard the buzzer sound at the front door.

Through the peephole, Bennett saw a man's dark face above a rumpled shirt collar and a crooked tie, his eyes flicking from side to side. Bennett opened the door. Before he could say anything, the man thrust an attaché case at him. *"C'est pour Monsieur Poe, d'accord?"* He turned, and stabbed at the elevator button, anxious to be away. Bennett stood in the doorway with the case. He could smell the man's sweat. Delivering packages for Julian Poe seemed to be a nerve-racking occupation.

Bennett shrugged and closed the door. He looked at the case, a slim rectangle of ribbed aluminum with a small combination lock set under the carrying handle. Probably Poe's pocket money for the weekend. Bennett tried the clasps and wasn't surprised to find them locked. It was none of his business, anyway. He put the case on the hall table, so he could give it to Shimo without inviting him in, and went back to the kitchen, where the sink had somehow filled up with dirty glasses. Next week, he thought, he must do something about a housekeeper. Rich men don't do dishes.

———

The two Italians in the travel-stained Fiat were becoming increasingly frustrated and irritable. There were no spaces near the apartment building, and every time they tried to double-park they were moved on by the same snotty Monaco cop, which forced them to keep circling the block. That's why they'd missed him. It was only luck that they'd been passing the building when he came out, and saw him walking fast toward the underground parking garage on the far side of the Place du Casino.

The driver slammed on his brakes. "*Merda!* That's him."

The passenger, the younger and larger man of the two, with bulky shoulders that started at ear level, opened his door. "I'll pick him up. No problem."

The driver shook his head. "Forget it. What's the point? He's dropped it off."

"*Merda.*"

"We'll have to go and get it from the apartment."

"*Merda.*"

———

Bennett had surpassed himself. He had found a small silver tray, and a bud vase, which now held a single rose taken from the bouquet he had bought as a predinner surprise for Susie. He placed a glass of champagne next to the vase, made his way carefully down to the bathroom, and tapped on the door.

"Room service."

There was a delighted squeal from the cloud of warm, scented steam that rose from the bath. Susie, in foam up to her shoulders, extended a hand to take the champagne. "Brilliant," she said. "You are sweet. This is wonderful."

"We aim to please, madam." Bennett placed the vase on the marble slab at the end of the bath and looked down at her. "You seem to have mislaid the soap. May I be of assistance?"

"Bennett, actually there *is* something you could do for me." She raised her eyebrows. "That is, if you're still feeling lovable."

"Try me."

"I forgot to get any cigarettes at Heathrow, and I wondered if you'd be an absolute angel and pop out and get me some. I promise I'll be partly dressed by the time you come back." She sucked in her cheeks and batted her eyelashes energetically. "I might even find you a tip."

Bennett smiled, scooped up a handful of foam, and dropped it on her head. "I'll be back."

The Place du Casino was clogged with the weekend crowds as Bennett strolled across to the Café de Paris, which seemed to have been taken over for the evening by a convention of businessmen, each wearing a prominent name tag in his lapel. The terrace was a sea of suits, and the small kiosk that sold postcards, guidebooks, and cigarettes was three deep in customers waiting for the girl behind the counter to finish talking on the phone. Bennett decided to wait at the bar.

He stood next to a solitary conventioneer, identified by his label as "Hi! I'm Rick Hoffman," and ordered a Scotch. He paid with a hundred-franc note, and

Hoffman shook his head. "Can you believe this place?" he said to Bennett. "They just stiffed me six bucks for a beer. Plus they expect a tip. Plus they look down their noses and treat you like you're some kind of retard." He shook his head again, then looked at Bennett more closely. "You're not with International Digits, are you?"

Bennett thanked his lucky stars. "Afraid not," he said. "I'm a local."

Hoffman brightened up. "You are? Tell me something." He leaned closer. "Where's the action?"

"The casino's just across the street."

"Nah. You know, *action.* Babes."

"Ask the doorman at your hotel." Bennett felt obliged to add a warning. "But it won't be cheap."

Hoffman nodded, then leaned closer still. "These French chicks. Do they . . ." He stopped to take a swig of his beer.

Bennett prepared himself for what he was sure would be an intimate question about some cherished sexual fantasy. "Do they what?"

"Take American Express? I've got a gold card."

Bennett's expression became serious as he whispered in Hoffman's ear. "Those girls can do things with an American Express card you wouldn't believe." He finished his Scotch. "I've got to go. Good luck."

He bought a carton of cigarettes at the kiosk and went back across the *place,* hoping that Hoffman's search for sexual bliss on a credit card would end well, and thinking pleasurably of his own evening. It was good to have a girl around again. If the week went well, perhaps Susie could come out for another visit later in the summer. He'd show her Cannes and Saint-Tropez. As the elevator took him up to the apartment, he was thinking where he could take her tomorrow for a serious French Sunday lunch. Life was good.

Brahms had been replaced on the stereo by the new Alain Souchon CD that Susie had bought in Nice, and she came swaying out of the sitting room, champagne in hand, to welcome Bennett.

"Buona sera, signore." She giggled and spun around. "Well, do you still like it?"

If anything, the scraps of gauze she was wearing looked even more transparent and vestigial than they had in the boutique, and Bennett had to swallow hard before commenting. "I'm so glad you decided on something sensible, Suze. I'm sure your mother would approve."

She pouted. "That's so *English*. You should have seen those nice Italians—kissing their fingers, rolling their eyes, shouting *'Bellissima'* all over the place. It did a girl's heart good, I can tell you."

Bennett frowned. "When was this? What Italians?"

"Now don't get all prickly, or I'll start to think you're jealous. There was a knock at the door, and I thought you'd forgotten your key, and there they were.

They just came to pick up that little case in the hall, and they were *very* sweet. They could teach Englishmen a thing or two. I mean, can you imagine old Henry from Chelsea saying *Ciao, bella* without sounding like a complete pronk?"

"Wait a minute, Suze. Shimo was supposed to be picking up that case. He never said anything about two randy Italians."

"There you go again. Charming, I'd say, not randy. Charming. Who's Shimo, anyway?"

Bennett felt a knot of foreboding tighten in his stomach. "Someone I think I'd better call."

But Shimo wasn't there. He was on his way to Monaco. Would monsieur like the remote number? Bennett put down the phone. "Oh, shit."

"What's the matter?"

"I have a nasty feeling something's just gone wrong."

7

"BENNETT, you look as though you're going to throw up. What's the matter? What's going on?" Susie had reloaded her glass, and she came to stand next to him as he stared out across the terrace into the Mediterranean night.

"I'm not sure yet, Suze, but I don't think it's good news." He sighed. "Come and sit down. It's probably time for an explanation."

Susie's eyes widened as Bennett came to the instructions about the attaché case. "Oh my God," she said. "I should never have let those men take it, should I?"

"How were you to know? I'd probably have given it to them if I'd been here. I'd have assumed that Shimo had sent them."

They looked at each other in silence, Susie puzzled, Bennett feeling a growing sense of gloom and job anxiety. His budding career as a millionaire was almost certainly over if this bloody case turned into a problem. Shimo's words came back to him. *It is important. I will come over myself to pick it up. Do you understand?* Nothing could be simpler than that, and he'd blown it. He got up, and was heading toward the whisky, when the buzzer sounded.

Shimo was accompanied by a broad slab of a man who might have had "Bodyguard" printed on the front of the black suit that appeared to be regulation dress for Poe's employees. Bennett led them into the sitting room, and they perched on the couch like two hostile crows while he fumbled his way through an apologetic explanation.

Shimo lit a cigarette, and there was a low, hissing sound as he inhaled. He turned to look at Susie. "So," he said, "the two men were Italian. Are you sure? Definitely not French?"

"Well, they spoke Italian. I mean, that's often a clue, isn't it?"

Shimo studied her impassively. Bennett nudged her. "No jokes, Suze. I don't think this is the moment."

Shimo leaned forward, tapping his cigarette on the rim of a crystal ashtray. "Describe these two men."

"Oh, both dark-haired, dark clothes, very polite. Let's see—oh yes, one of them was sort of, well, lumpy. You know, he looked as if he was going to burst out of his suit." She glanced at Shimo's silent colleague. "Rather like him, actually. Meaty, if you know what I mean."

Shimo nodded. "And the other one?"

"Thinner, older, a little mustache." Susie's brow furrowed with concentration. "There was one other thing. He had a bit of a limp. But he was a sweetie, very nice."

"A limp?" Shimo nodded again. "I know about him. You were lucky he was feeling friendly. He often isn't." He turned to the bodyguard. "That was Vallone. One of Tuzzi's men." He got up, went over to a desk in the corner, picked up the phone, and turned his back to the room. Susie and Bennett exchanged bewildered glances. The bodyguard stretched, yawned, and tried to muffle a belch.

Shimo finished his brief, inaudible conversation and came back to the couch, where he stood looking down at Bennett. "You will come with us. Your friend can stay here and entertain herself."

Despite his apprehension, Bennett felt his hackles go up. "Absolutely not," he said. "She's only just arrived, and we've made plans for this evening." He attempted a winning smile. "Haven't seen each other for ages, lots to catch up on, I know you'll understand." There was no response from Shimo. "Look, I'm sorry about the case, and of course I'll do anything I can to help, but tonight's out of the question. Let's have a chat tomorrow."

Shimo dropped the butt of his cigarette in the ashtray. "Mr. Bennett, we're leaving now. You can either come willingly, or Gérard here will assist you, which would be painful. It makes no difference to me."

Bennett looked at Gérard, who smiled amiably, clasped his thick hands in front of him, and cracked his knuckles. The sound made Bennett think of broken bones. He turned to Susie and shook his head. "I'm sorry about this, Suze. Will you be OK? I'll be back as soon as I can."

"When?"

Bennett stood up, and looked at Shimo. "Well?"

"I couldn't say."

Susie put her glass down on the table and reached for her cigarettes. "That's brilliant," she said. "Welcome to bloody Monaco."

———

The drive to Nice airport was, for the most part, silent. Shimo sat in the back and ignored Bennett's questions until he gave up. Gérard confined his remarks to occasional muttered streams of profanity directed at any car that wouldn't get out of his way fast enough. Bennett assumed they were going back to see Poe, and felt the hollow chill of a criminal on his way to be sentenced. What lousy luck. Fate, cudgel in hand, had slugged him just when everything was looking rosy. It was with a sense of foreboding that he climbed into the helicopter and buckled up for the flight to Poe's estate and, he felt sure, summary dismissal.

Or maybe worse, he thought, as they headed northwest, away from the brightly lit coastal strip and over the black emptiness of the backcountry. Poe was clearly a powerful man, and some of his employees—

certainly the two who were flying with him—were the most sinister executives Bennett had met since he'd had to deal with film union officials and their leg-breakers in Paris.

The helicopter tilted abruptly, and he instinctively grabbed the back of the pilot's seat. Shimo smiled. "Nervous flier, Mr. Bennett?"

Bennett wiped his palms on his trousers. "I should watch out if I were you. I get terribly airsick. Buckets of it, all over the place."

Shimo grimaced, and moved as far away as he could. For Bennett, it was the only pleasing moment of the trip.

———

They hovered above the floodlit landing pad, cypresses bowing in the downdraft as the helicopter eased its way to the ground and settled as delicately as a bird on its egg. Ducking through the turbulent air beneath the rotor blades, Shimo and Bennett made their way through the garden toward the back of the house and across the terrace. The plate-glass window slid aside. Poe was standing in front of the fireplace, remote control in one hand, an unlit cigar in the other.

Bennett heard the window close behind him, nodded at Poe, and followed the pointing cigar to a chair. Shimo sat off to one side, alert and watchful.

"Well, Mr. Bennett, this is a bugger's muddle, isn't it?" Poe fussed over the lighting of his cigar with a long wooden spill, puffing deliberately until he was satisfied with the uniform dark-red glow of the tip. "I'm not pleased. You haven't exactly distinguished yourself."

Bennett took a deep breath. "Look, I'm sorry, I really am, but as I said earlier—"

Poe held up one hand. "Spare me the excuses. Shimo told me what you told him. What I want to know is this: Are you completely sure that you weren't seen by the men who took the case?" He peered intently at Bennett, eyes narrowed behind the gray-blue smoke.

"Positive. They'd been gone at least ten minutes by the time I got back."

"Positive. That is some small consolation, I suppose." Poe sat down and crossed his legs, the light reflecting from the mirror-polished toe cap of his shoe. "Well, now. If that's the case, you will no doubt be relieved to hear that your employment will continue for the time being, but under slightly different circumstances. Does that please you?"

"I think so. Well, yes, of course. That would be great."

"Excellent." For the first time since Bennett had arrived, Poe smiled. "I find people perform so much better when their hearts are in their work. It's almost as powerful a motivating force as money. Although, in the end, there's nothing like fear." He smiled again, and drew on his cigar. "But I'm forgetting my manners. Do help yourself to a drink, and then we have one or two things to go over."

Bennett half filled a large tumbler with Scotch. It could have been worse, he thought. At least he hadn't been thrown out of the helicopter, and Poe didn't seem dangerously angry. It was too early for relief, perhaps, but he felt something close to it—a moment of whisky-induced hope—as the first swallow went down. He leaned forward, and Poe began to speak.

"I think I might have mentioned to you that one of my minor interests is the truffle, not simply because of its taste but also because of the mystique that surrounds it—the secrecy, the unpredictability of the market, the outrageous prices, the trickery and dishonesty." Poe spoke the words with gusto, as though they tasted good. "And, above all, the fact that truffles have resisted all efforts so far to grow to man's bidding. They cannot be cultivated with any guarantee of success. Believe me, the French have been trying for years—and not just the farmers, but the government, too."

Poe paused while Shimo got him a drink, and Bennett remembered the notes he had read in Monaco. The man was certainly interested in truffles, but it was hard to imagine him as Farmer Poe, with dirty fingernails and mud all over his shiny shoes, scratching a living from the earth. He smiled at the thought.

"Something amuses you, Mr. Bennett?"

"Oh, it's just that I can't see you wandering through

the woods with a pig and a stick—you know, truf-
fling."

Poe raised his eyebrows. "What a hideous thought.
Now, I suggest you contain your hilarity for a few
minutes and listen carefully." He gazed up at the ceiling, and his voice took on a measured, professorial
tone. "Some years ago, the work of a rather extraordinary man came to my attention. A boffin, an agricultural researcher of great vision and ability—but, as
exceptionally clever men tend to be, somewhat arrogant, and not what our sporting friends would call a
team player. Eventually, he fell out with the high-
and-mighties of the French Ministry of Agriculture,
and when I met him he was unemployed, broke, and
resentful. He felt that his research had been ignored
by jealous men of lesser intellect. Not uncommon, as
I'm sure you know."

Poe blew a smoke ring, and watched the gray halo
shiver and curl in the air. "It was then my interest in
truffles changed from that of the gourmet to that of the
businessman. Because, Mr. Bennett, our little boffin
claimed that he was close to developing a formula, a
serum, that would guarantee the consistent growth of
Tuber melanosporum—given the right trees and climate and soil conditions, obviously, but they're not
difficult to find. There are hundreds of thousands of
hectares in France that are suitable."

Bennett, feeling like a backward student, held up
his hand. "What did you call it—*Tuber* . . . ?"

"*Melanosporum.* The black truffle. It's also known, quite inaccurately, as the Perigord truffle. Here in Provence, it's called the *rabasse*. It grows at random—up till now, at any rate—on the roots of hazelnut or oak trees. It's said to be heterotrophic."

"Really?" said Bennett, nodding vigorously in incomprehension.

"Closer to the animal than the vegetable. Fascinating, isn't it?"

"Absolutely." Bennett doubted that his Scotch would last as long as the lecture, and wondered what all this could possibly have to do with his revised terms of employment. But Poe seemed to have mellowed in his role of instructor, and Bennett sensed that trying to rush him might be a mistake.

"I won't burden you with too many details, but to appreciate the genius of my boffin, you should know that the birth of a truffle is a very haphazard process. A question of spores."

"Ah," said Bennett, "spores."

"From a rotting truffle. During the period of putrefaction, a spore can be transported—by insects, birds, wind, whatever—from one spot to another. If it should find a hospitable tree, such as the pubescent oak, it will attach itself and feed off the root. And if conditions are right, it will grow."

"Remarkable," said Bennett.

"Indeed. But not predictable. As any farmer will tell you, Mother Nature makes an unreliable partner." Poe examined the long, wrinkled cylinder of ash that had grown on the end of his cigar, and flicked it into the fireplace. "And that has been the problem. People have tried, God knows. There was the Somycel plan, the Signoret plan, the INRA plan—all schemes to make truffles grow to order. None of them worked. But where the French government has failed, Mr. Bennett, my boffin succeeded—with some considerable assistance from me, I might add. I set him up. Bought a patch of land in the Drôme, built him a laboratory, gave him time—years of time—gave him money. Also, I gave him what he really wanted. Recognition." Poe nodded. "I believed in him. And he didn't fail me."

What a charitable soul you are, thought Bennett. And I bet you want nothing in return. "Well, congratulations. It was quite a gamble, wasn't it?"

"And it paid off. Two years ago, the oaks on my land in the Drôme were treated with serum injected into the roots. The first season, we had a success rate of seventy percent. The second season was over ninety percent. Imagine, Mr. Bennett, being able to produce tons—year in, year out—of a commodity that sells for anything between three and eight thousand francs a kilo. We're talking about very substantial amounts of money. Millions." Poe tapped the side of his nose, echoing the gesture of the sly French peasant. "And of course, because of the nature of the business, a great deal of that would be in cash."

There was a moment of silence while Poe sipped his whisky. He put his glass down and leaned forward. "And now for the bad news." His voice changed, as though it had been sharpened. The edge was audible, and Bennett felt a strong desire to be somewhere else.

"The case," said Poe, "the little case that was so generously handed over by your friend, contains everything—vials of the serum, the formula for manufacturing more, field notes, production records, application instructions, everything. Whoever has that case can control the truffle market. Now do you understand its importance?"

Bennett's mouth felt suddenly dry. "Yes, but surely your man—you know, the boffin—I mean, he could make some more serum, couldn't he?"

"I'm afraid he's no longer with us. Apparently, the brakes failed on his car. A great loss to agriculture." Poe seemed unmoved by this tragedy.

Bennett finished his whisky in one long, nervous gulp. "Can I ask you a question?"

Poe nodded.

"If the case was so important, why was it delivered to Monaco? Why not here?"

"It's impossible to develop a long-term project like this in total secrecy. Rumor, speculation, bar talk, village gossip—one way or another, word gets out. We have obviously been as discreet as possible, but I know that in the past few months several interested parties have had their people out all over Provence, looking for the laboratory." Poe held up a hand, counting off on his fingers. "The Corsicans, the Japanese, a syndicate based in California, and, of course, the Italians. Some are conventional businessmen, and some aren't. Or perhaps I should say that their business practices aren't conventional."

Bennett couldn't help but wonder if tampering with car brakes was one of them. "What do you mean?"

"Oh, bribery, physical persuasion—primitive stuff, really, but it's been known to be effective on a certain type of person."

Me for one, Bennett thought. "So that's why you wanted me in Monaco, was it? In case things turned nasty. Thanks a lot."

Poe shook his head. "Give me more credit than that, Mr. Bennett. You were a convenience, not a target. You see, the Italians know where I am. Maybe the others do, too. In any case, this property is being watched. And so I thought it prudent to have the case delivered to Monaco." He looked at Bennett under raised eyebrows. "It seems I was wrong."

Bennett smiled, and shrugged. "Well, don't let it get you down. We can all make mistakes."

"And they all have to be paid for. Which brings me back to you." Poe held his empty glass toward Bennett. "Another drink?"

There was silence while Bennett refilled the glasses

and settled back in his chair. Poe examined the ceiling thoughtfully. When he resumed speaking, it was no longer the professor imparting knowledge: it was the general briefing his troops.

"We know who has the case. A man called Enzo Tuzzi. Not one of nature's gentlemen, but effective enough in his own crude fashion. He and I have had one or two disagreements in the past, which have ended badly for him, and possession of the case—*my* case—will give him great satisfaction. He has this juvenile urge for revenge."

"You're a businessman. Isn't there any way of—well, I don't know—coming to some kind of arrangement?"

"An *arrangement*?" Poe looked as though someone had spat in his whisky. His mouth set, and Bennett could see the twitch of muscles in his jaw. "My property has been stolen, my investment is at risk, and you talk to me about an *arrangement*? With that organ-grinder's monkey?"

"Sorry," said Bennett. "Just a thought. Trying to be helpful."

Poe took a deep breath, and his composure returned. "And you *will* be helpful, Mr. Bennett, believe me. Now, one of Tuzzi's many failings is that he can never resist quick money. It is my belief that he will want to sell the formula, and he'll probably try to get the other groups to bid against each other. Whatever he decides to do, he will have to put the word out, and one of my people will hear about it. I expect to know within the next few days. He's not a patient man. He won't want to wait."

Bennett jumped as he heard the scratch of a striking match behind him. He'd forgotten Shimo was sitting in the shadows, watching. Creepy bastard.

"What will happen is this." Poe stood up, the glow of the reading lamp from below giving his face the appearance of a grim, shadow-etched mask. "Once I find out where and when the sale is to take place, I shall send my representative to the bidding . . ."

"Damn good idea," said Bennett. "Except that if he knows you're bidding . . ."

"He won't. He's never met you. His people never saw you."

"*Me?* You want *me* to bid?"

"Not exactly, Mr. Bennett, no. I've already paid quite enough for the formula. I have no intention of paying again. I want you to find the case, and bring it back to me."

"Steal it?"

"Recover it. You won't find me ungenerous. There will be a bonus, which is rather more than you deserve under the circumstances. And then you can go back to Monaco and play with your little girls."

Bennett felt his stomach fighting a losing battle with the whisky and forced himself to swallow. "But I couldn't do that. These people are crooks—they're dangerous, you said so yourself. I'm not James bloody Bond." He shook his head decisively. "No. I'm sorry, but no. I couldn't do it."

"I'm not asking you. I'm telling you."

"Supposing I refuse?"

"That would be most unwise." Poe looked at his watch. "Sleep on it, Mr. Bennett, and think about possible alternatives. They aren't attractive. Shimo will show you to your room."

Bennett followed the Japanese to the end of a long corridor and into a large, comfortably furnished bedroom. The bedcover had been turned down, the curtains drawn. Fresh flowers, mineral water, and a selection of biographies and best-sellers, in English and French, was on the bedside tables. Through an open door, Bennett could see the marble floor of a bathroom. He felt trapped and angry and suddenly tired, and craved a hot bath. He remembered Susie, covered in foam in Monaco. He turned to Shimo. "I'd like to make a call. To my friend."

"Tomorrow."

"Tomorrow." Bennett shook his head wearily. "Do the regulations say I can have a bath?"

Shimo looked at him as though he hadn't heard. "Don't attempt to get out through the window. The alarm will go off, and it would upset Mr. Poe's Dobermans."

Bennett nodded. Meeting an upset Doberman in the dark: the end of a perfect day.

Shimo closed the door behind him, and Bennett heard the key turn in the lock. He started to undress. What a cock-up. What an almighty, god-awful, frightful cock-up.

8

BENNETT settled uneasily into his confinement. Meals were brought to him in his room. He was forbidden to leave the house, except for a brief stroll each night after dark, in the company of the dog handler and the Dobermans. They slithered soundlessly through the trees, a shoal of four-legged sharks, their eyes blood red in the beam of the flashlight. Only once did Bennett attempt to pat one of them; he had the sense to stop halfway when he saw the lips curl back and the ears go flat. The handler watched with amusement and seemed disappointed when Bennett withdrew his hand.

The helicopter was flying in and out three or four times a day, the edge of the landing pad just visible from Bennett's bedroom. One of the early-morning departures was Chou-Chou, escorted by Poe and two men carrying large quantities of Vuitton luggage. There was a fond leave-taking, Poe waiting and waving until the helicopter had lifted off. Bennett wondered where he was sending her, and why. To stock up on this year's jewelry in Paris? Or to keep out of harm's way in case of trouble on the property? The population of men in black suits had increased. Unless he was locked in his room, Bennett was constantly under someone's eye. There was tension in the air, and the Domaine des Rochers was beginning to feel like a fortress.

A beautiful fortress, Bennett had to admit, made even lovelier by the weather, which he had plenty of time to appreciate from his bedroom. Summer had come early, but the sun hadn't yet baked the country-side brown. The forested patches on the hills looked as though they had been freshly painted a vivid, shining green, and the clarity of light added a sharp edge of focus to the contours of the land. It was heaven on earth, Bennett thought, which made his situation even more depressing.

He had called Monaco several times, under Shimo's cold, attentive stare, to speak to Susie. All he heard was his own voice on the answering machine, promising to call back. He told himself she had got tired of waiting and returned to London, probably incandescent with fury. So much for a romantic week in the sun. So much for his new, improved life.

———

The maid knocked on his door, delivering his only set of clothes, laundered and pressed daily, one of the small comforts of being held prisoner by a fastidious millionaire. He took off his bathrobe and dressed, preparing himself for another restless day of trying to read, watching the weather go by, and fretting about the future. He picked up Robb's biography of Balzac and hoped that he could escape for the day to the nineteenth century.

Barely a page had gone by when Bennett heard the key turn in the lock. He looked up to see one of the black suits standing in the doorway. A jerk of the head. *"Venez."*

Bennett followed him along the corridor, through the kitchen, and down a flight of worn stone steps that led to the cellar, which ran the length of the house. Bennett stopped on the last step, taking in a sight that would have given a teetotaler nightmares. Floor-to-ceiling brick compartments had been built along each wall, and each whitewashed compartment bristled with bottles. The various wines had been organized by origin and identified by varnished wooden signs, the black, hand-painted letters on white backgrounds looking formal and Dickensian. Meursault, Krug, Romanée-Conti, Petrus, Figeac, Lafite-Rothschild, Yquem—the great names were well represented, and, Bennett had no doubt, the great years as well.

"A comforting sight, Mr. Bennett, don't you think? One of the best private cellars in France, so they tell me." Poe was sitting at a small table, his leatherbound cellar book open in front of him, reading glasses perched on the end of his nose. He took them off and stood up. "But I didn't drag you down here to look at bottles. Come with me. I'd like you to see something equally impressive, in its own way." He was relaxed and affable; suspiciously affable. Bennett had the feeling he was about to have an unpleasant experience.

Poe opened a door at the far end of the cellar. As they went through, Bennett had to narrow his eyes against the glare of hard light that bounced off the walls of an austere white space.

"This is Shimo's pride and joy," said Poe. "His personal dojo. He spends hours in here. I've asked him to give us a short demonstration, something to divert you from the tedium of captivity. I thought you'd find it fascinating to see what the human body can do."

The room was a rectangle, perhaps forty feet by twenty, with mirrored walls and a floor of polished pine. Apart from a narrow slatted bench beside the door, the only fixture was what looked like a diving board standing on its end, its base embedded in the floor, the top twelve inches of its surface covered with a binding of straw.

"That's a striking post," Poe said. "The Japanese name escapes me for the moment, but Shimo says there's nothing like it for conditioning the knuckles. There are days when he gets quite carried away. I've known him to hit it a thousand times without stopping. Ah, here's the man himself."

Shimo came through from the cellar without acknowledging them. He was barefoot, dressed in a white canvas training suit, a black belt tied around his waist. He was carrying a short bamboo pole, two inches thick, which he placed by the bench before going to the center of the room.

Poe's voice, still genial, was little more than a whisper. "Take a look at the belt. See where it's worn through to the white threads? That's from years of use. He's been a black belt since he was a young man. Now he's sixth dan. Quite exceptionally gifted, so my Japanese friends tell me."

Bennett whispered back. "What's the bamboo for?"

"One of Shimo's party tricks. You'll see."

Shimo began warming up, his feet spread to shoulder width, his movements continuous and fluid, arms crossing and recrossing his body, his face blank with concentration. He could have been a dancer, Bennett thought, graceful and poised.

And then the tempo changed. Smooth, peaceful movements gave way to blurs of controlled violence as Shimo moved into a pattern of punching, kicking, and blocking, his body staying perfectly balanced, the destructive force behind his feet and fists apparent even from a distance. Bennett changed his mind. That was no dancer. That was a weapon on legs.

Shimo continued the sequence of disciplined mayhem, moving gradually toward the bench where the two spectators were sitting. A final spin and a head-high kick placed him, crouched and still, in front of

Bennett. He looked into Bennett's eyes, a deep, guttural roar came from his throat, and his arm shot out like a piston.

It was the sudden blast of noise, as much as anything, that made Bennett's head jerk backward. When he looked down, he saw that Shimo's fist had stopped with the swollen, calcified knuckles touching his shirtfront a fraction of an inch from his heart.

"Lucky he's such a good judge of distance," said Poe, as Shimo straightened and moved back. "Another few inches, and that would have killed you. The sound effects are interesting, too, don't you think? It's what they call the spirit shout. The idea is to unify the mind and body and shock the enemy while the blow is being delivered." Poe smiled at Bennett. "Makes boxing under Queensberry rules look rather tame, doesn't it?"

Bennett let out his breath and swallowed. "Does he ever do this seriously—I mean, fighting someone?"

"There aren't too many men in the world at his level. Most of them are in Tokyo, which is a long way to go for a scrap." Poe nodded toward the center of the room. "Watch this."

Shimo had taken up his position in front of the striking post, staring at it as though he intended to turn it into firewood. He started to punch, straight-armed blows coming from the shoulder, vicious and precise. The post bent under each impact, sprang back, bent again.

"That's called a focused punch," Poe said. "One shudders to think what it might do to the human head."

A hundred, two hundred punches, with no apparent signs of diminished power—and then the final punch, delivered with another explosive roar, half grunt, half shout. The striking post quivered. Shimo stepped back, turned, and came over to the bench. His eyes never left Bennett as he picked up the bamboo pole and held it at arm's length, in front of Bennett's face. His body tensed. Hypnotized, Bennett watched the hand holding the bamboo, saw the tremor of concentrated effort as the fingers tightened, saw the bulge of muscle by the base of the thumb, saw, with disbelief, the thumb split and penetrate the wood.

Shimo's arm dropped to his side. He handed the bamboo to Bennett, inclined his head to Poe, and left the dojo.

Poe took the bamboo and ran his fingers over the split made by Shimo's thumb. "Don't know how he does it. Of course, this is merely a strengthening exercise. In a combat situation, the thumb would be used to rupture the windpipe, or take out an eye. Not a man to trifle with, our Shimo." He passed the bamboo back, and smiled. "You might like to keep this as a souvenir."

Back in his room, Bennett stared out at the landscape and tried to forget what he'd just seen. It had been the "alternative" that Poe had mentioned, a brutal and graphic reminder of what he could expect if he was foolish enough not to volunteer his services. Bennett fingered his throat and thought of Shimo's steel thumb. How much longer before he could get out of here?

————

Shimo came for him late the following afternoon. Bennett had mixed feelings as he followed the Japanese, welcoming the prospect of activity but apprehensive about what it might be. They climbed broad stone steps to a part of the building Bennett had seen only from outside, the tower that grew out of one corner of the house. Shimo knocked, then opened a heavy steel door, and they entered an office from the twenty-first century.

Poe was sitting behind his desk, a thick oblong of polished teak supported by a single chromed-steel column. The wall facing him was entirely covered by the flickering, silent images appearing on a dozen screens. Behind him, a line of smaller screens, for the moment blank, and a matching pair of fax machines. The gray mass of a computer occupied the whole of an alcove to one side. There was a level, barely audible hum coming from the assembled equipment, the sound of electronic breathing. It was a cold, efficient room. No books, no pictures, no softness anywhere.

Shimo nodded at Bennett to sit on one of the low leather-and-chrome chairs in front of the desk, and they waited while Poe finished making notes on a pad, took off his glasses, and, rather to Bennett's surprise, smiled and nodded.

"Well, Mr. Bennett, you'll be pleased to hear that your period in durance vile is very nearly over. I hope it hasn't been too uncomfortable. I'm sorry we haven't been able to let you out of the house during daylight, but as I told you, there are watchers in the hills out there, and it wouldn't do at all if your face were seen. Most unhealthy." He smiled again, the picture of a benevolent host concerned with his guest's welfare. "I must say, it's gratifying when one's competitors behave predictably. Puts me in rather a good humor, as you've probably noticed." He leaned back, and smoothed the dark-blue silk of his shirtfront with a tanned and manicured hand.

"As I thought he would, our Italian friend Tuzzi has succumbed to greed, which is his habit, and he is planning an auction. The bidders are to meet in Cannes, where they will be taken on board Tuzzi's boat." The corners of Poe's mouth turned down in distaste. "The *Ragazza di Napoli,* if you can believe that. Neapolitan Girl seems an inappropriate name for one of the largest and ugliest gin palaces in the Mediterranean, but that's Italians for you. Sentimental to the core. Anyway, the auction will be conducted at sea, sailing west. Tuzzi has an estate on Ibiza, and he goes there every summer to play the squire and chase little Spanish girls. Repulsive creature."

Bennett hardly heard Poe's comments about

Tuzzi's summer plans; his mind was still taking in the horror of being cooped up on a boat with a bunch of brigands. And he was supposed to outwit them, steal the case, and return to dry land in one piece. The whole thing was a nightmare.

"You're looking glum, Mr. Bennett. What's the matter? Poor sailor?"

Bennett clutched at the excuse. "The worst. I've been seasick in port. Even the deep end of a swimming pool—"

Poe cut him short. "Take some pills. As I was saying, the boat will be sailing west. Once the auction is over, all the bidders will be put ashore at one of the ports along the French coast, but I have every confidence that you'll have made the switch by then. If not, you'll have to stick close to the buyer."

"Switch?" Bennett wondered if he'd missed something vital. "What switch?"

Poe chuckled, enjoying the game he was playing. "Surely you don't think I'd send you on this important errand unprepared?" He swiveled around in his chair and bent down. When he straightened up, he was holding the identical twin of the case Bennett had last seen in Monaco. Poe placed it on the desk. "This will fit easily into an overnight bag." He snapped open the lid. "Obviously," he said, "the contents are counterfeit. The vials are filled with doctored water, and the paperwork is bogus, but it all looks authentic enough,

I think. Particularly if nobody is expecting a substitution. Here, take a look."

Bennett leaned over to inspect the contents of the case. The top section was taken up by rows of vials set into a bed of foam rubber, each vial labeled in a spidery French hand, corked, and wax-sealed. The rest of the case contained dossiers. Bennett flicked through them: pages of formulae, computer printouts, notes on soil conditions and irrigation, temperature charts—more than enough to deceive anyone who didn't have a degree in agricultural science. He felt a sense of reluctant admiration at Poe's thoroughness. "It would fool me," he said.

"No doubt," said Poe. He closed the lid and turned the tumblers on the lock. "It's set at the same combination as the original. You like women, Mr. Bennett, so it should be easy enough to remember: thirty-six twenty-four thirty-six." Poe then picked up a small, dark-blue box and pushed it to the edge of the desk. "Your cover."

Bennett opened the box and saw the engraved copperplate of a traditional business card, announcing that the Honorable L. Bennett was president of Consolidated European Investments S.A., with an office in Zurich.

"As you see, I've promoted you to Honorable. Italians love titles, and Tuzzi's a frightful snob—probably comes from being such a vulgarian himself. He'll be impressed. In fact, we've already contacted his people, sent them your card with a covering letter. They're delighted that the aristocratic representative of a Swiss investment syndicate is coming to join the auction. Any calls or faxes to the numbers on the card will be rerouted via Zurich to us here. Isn't technology a blessing?"

Bennett took a card from the box and ran his thumbnail over the surface, feeling the raised letters of the copperplate.

Poe laughed. "I can assure you they're the very best quality. We wouldn't want our noble bidder to be embarrassed by shoddy stationery."

Bennett stared at the card with a mounting sense of awful inevitability. He seemed to have no choice but to go through with it. He looked up at Poe, who was watching with a patient, slightly amused expression, and made one last attempt to get himself off the hook that was biting into him more deeply every minute. "Look, it'll never work. I'm just not the man for the job. I can't deal with a gang of thugs all by myself. . . ."

"Come, come, Mr. Bennett. Where's your spirit of adventure? In any case, you won't be by yourself. All the time you're on land, at least two of my men will be keeping a discreet eye on you. We shall be tracking the progress of the boat. And when you run away to sea, you'll have an assistant—a most able assistant—to come on board with you. It's all been arranged."

Bennett glanced at Shimo.

"No, Mr. Bennett, not Shimo. I won't spoil the surprise for you. All you have to do is meet the Delta flight coming into Nice tomorrow morning from New York. Carry this for identification." Poe slid a copy of the London *Financial Times* across his desk, the distinctive pink paper pale against the dark wood. "You'll be approached. All clear?"

Bennett bowed to the inevitable, and nodded. "There's just one point. You know, looking on the bright side—you mentioned a bonus."

Poe looked at him speculatively. "I do believe you're entering into the spirit of things at last. Shall we say ten thousand dollars?"

Bennett hesitated, then decided not to push his luck. "Fine."

"Excellent. You'll be leaving tonight, as soon as it's dark. Call me tomorrow from Monaco, when you get back from the airport, and we'll go over your sailing arrangements. And Mr. Bennett?" Poe put his hands flat on the desk and stood up. "Don't even think of attempting anything foolish. I would take it very badly, after all the inconvenience you've caused me."

———

It was close to midnight by the time a pensive, hungry Bennett let himself into the apartment, to be welcomed by a note left on the hall table:

Dear Bennett:

Guess what? I'm smitten! I met this rather divine Frenchman the day after you left, and one thing has led to another. It's brilliant! And it's all thanks to you. I'm sure you managed to charm your way out of the little problem—you always do.

Must dash. Jean-Paul's taking me up to Paris. He has an apartment on the Île Saint-Louis. Isn't that romantic?

Big kiss,
Susie

Bennett was too drained to feel any worse than he already felt. He went into the kitchen, found a stale baguette, and opened the fridge. Next to a forgotten pot of Susie's face cream was a leathery slice of Brie. He chewed without tasting, set his alarm, and went to an unmade, empty, and faintly perfumed bed.

9

BENNETT was up at dawn. He stood on the terrace, drinking coffee and feeling sorry for himself as he watched the first layers of light trickle across the surface of the sea. A street-cleaning truck grumbled up the hill below him, spraying and scrubbing the sidewalks so that they would be suitably pristine for the privileged feet of Monaco's residents. For them, it would be another fine, carefree day, a day of sunshine, with perhaps a gentle stroll to the bank to visit their money before lunch—the kind of day he should have been looking forward to. Then he considered reality: a trip to the airport to pick up some gorilla, followed by danger, a good chance of failure, and an unknown but certainly nasty retribution. His coffee suddenly tasted bitter. He tossed the dregs into a tub of geraniums, and went inside to dress for his ordeal.

He drove along the coast, the morning air cool and still fume-free, the sun coming up fast over his shoulder, and parked behind the terminal with ten minutes to spare before the New York flight was scheduled to arrive. But it was early, and by the time he reached the gate the first passengers were coming through, gritty-eyed, rumpled, and yawning after spending a night above the Atlantic. Bennett held the *Financial Times* like a pink banner in front of his chest and made guesses about the man he was going to meet. Poe's business colleagues were becoming murkier by the day, and Bennett assumed, because of the Italian involvement, that Poe had found a recruit from one of the New York families. A Sicilian equivalent of Shimo, no doubt, handy with knife, gun, and garrote. He scanned the passengers, looking for someone with a blue-black chin and matching suit.

After five minutes, he had seen nobody who resembled the caricature, and he was hoping against hope that the immigration authorities had come to his aid and arrested his prospective partner, when a tap on the shoulder made him start.

"You're Bennett, right?"

He turned to see a girl—a tall, dark girl, her eyebrows raised as she waited for his reply. "Well? Are you?"

Bennett nodded, and found his voice. "Yes. Yes, I am."

"I'm Anna Hersh. Where's your suit? You don't look like one of the usual goons."

"Good God. Are you . . . ?"

The girl smiled, amused by his surprise. "What did you expect? Uncle Vinnie from the Bronx? Didn't Poe tell you?"

"No. He just said to turn up with the newspaper."

The smile faded. "He loves his little games." She shook her head. "God, he hasn't changed."

Bennett was still in mild shock. He was looking—staring—at beauty instead of the anticipated beast. Her hair was closer to black than brown, shiny and cut as short as a man's. The whites of her eyes were startling and accentuated the deep brown of the pupils. A long, fine-boned nose, olive skin, a strong mouth, a succulent lower lip. Dressed in jeans, a white T-shirt and an old leather jacket, she stood almost as tall as Bennett.

"Well," she said. "Finished?"

"I'm sorry. You're right—I was expecting Uncle Vinnie from the Bronx." Bennett pulled himself together and became brisk. "Now then. Let's go and get your luggage."

The girl nodded at the canvas overnight bag on the ground. "That's it. I'm not planning a long trip."

They drove away from the airport and found a gap in the breakneck cavalcade of amateur Grand Prix drivers heading toward Nice. Bennett's empty stomach rumbled along with the engine, reminding him that his last full meal had been lunch in his padded cell the previous day. He glanced at Anna. "Look, I'm starving. Do you mind if we stop for breakfast?"

"Fine with me. I haven't had French coffee for years." She tilted her head back to take the sun on her face, and Bennett wondered why she appeared to be so relaxed. Maybe she knew something he didn't know. In any case, it was contagious, and he felt his morning gloom begin to lift. Putting aside the possible horrors the future might hold, he concentrated on the much more immediate dangers posed by his fellow drivers. Unlike the sedate Monegasques, the motorists of Nice seemed to take personal exception to the Mercedes, flashing their headlights and sounding their horns as they did their best to squeeze their small cars past, weaving from lane to lane like demented steel insects. Bennett had long ago come to the conclusion that most French drivers needed three hands: one to hold a cigarette, one to use for abusive gestures aimed at other road users, and the third to navigate. It was with some relief that he turned off the Promenade des Anglais to join the crawl of traffic inching through the narrow streets of the old town.

They found a table outside one of the market bars and ordered. Anna took off her jacket, stretched in the sun, and lounged in her chair, one slim arm hooked over the back. "So tell me," she said. "You're not one of Poe's regular bozos. How did you get involved with him?"

Bennett went through the whole story, from the ad in the paper to the abducted attaché case and the note from Susie, while Anna sipped her *café crème* and worked her way through the ham-filled baguette that Bennett had ordered for himself.

"And that's about it," he said, beckoning the waiter.

"I'm not left with much of a choice—that is, if Poe's serious about coming after me if I do a runner."

Anna nodded. "He's serious. He doesn't like losing. And he has friends, believe me. Five, ten thousand dollars, and they'd bury their own mothers." She looked at Bennett's empty plate and grinned. "I can recommend the sandwiches."

He ordered another from the waiter, and more coffee. "You don't seem too worried at the thought of working for a homicidal boss. Or are you a bozo?" He tilted his head and looked her up and down. "Damned good disguise, if you are—no black suit, no obvious weapons, no cauliflower ears." He frowned. "Slight criminal tendencies when it comes to other people's breakfasts, but otherwise I'd take you for a genteel, well-brought-up young lady. A librarian on holiday, something like that. The kind of girl you could trust with your dog."

Anna took a long, thoughtful look at him as the waiter came with fresh coffee, and a sandwich that Bennett grasped with both hands. "I'd forgotten how complimentary the British could be." She unwrapped a sugar lump and dipped it in her coffee, watching it turn brown. Bennett noticed that there were no rings on her fingers, no polish on the short, well-kept nails. She let the sugar sink slowly through the froth of milk. "I guess it's my turn, isn't it?"

"Well, it always helps to know a little about the person you're working with—background, qualifications, next of kin, religious affiliation, blood group, leisure interests . . ."

"OK, OK." She looked up. "Did you know you're wearing some of your sandwich?"

Bennett wiped crumbs from the corner of his mouth and leaned forward to listen.

"You know New York?" He nodded. "Well, I come from Riverside Drive. Papa was a professor at Columbia, my mother worried about life and made chicken soup, I grew up a nice Jewish girl. I guess they hoped I'd fall for a dentist and settle down, but I wanted to travel. So I dropped out of college in my freshman year and went to Paris. Lucked into a modeling job my first week there, started wearing nothing but black and smoking Gitanes, all the usual things. And then I met this guy. He was French, and he was a photographer, which is about as bad a combination as you can get. An ego the size of a house." She stirred her coffee and took a sip.

"On top of that, he had a coke habit. Like a vacuum cleaner. In the end, most of what we both made was going up his nose, and I was finding out that a model is a piece of meat. You leave your brain at home, and nobody notices, as long as you're smart enough to change your clothes fast. Well, one way and another, it was definitely time to leave Paris. Then I thought, Number one, I'm Jewish, and Number two, I'm on the right side of the Atlantic. I should see Israel, send Papa a postcard from Eilat, visit my roots. We're big on roots in the States. And that's how I ended up in the army."

Bennett looked puzzled. "You were drafted?"

"Believe it or not, I enlisted. I was twenty years old, and I'd never been anywhere like Israel. There was a fantastic spirit in those days—us against the rest: Saddam, Arab hard-liners—and I felt I should be part of it. What was I going back to in New York? College seemed kind of tame. So I joined up, and I did OK. I made sergeant. Sergeant Hersh."

Bennett found it difficult to imagine the slouching, graceful figure opposite him marching up and down in the drab camouflage of an Israeli uniform. "What was it like?"

"It was exciting at first—border patrols, antiterrorist stuff. Then it became routine. I guess everything does, even if it's dangerous. After a while, it was pretty much like police work. But I learned a lot." She smiled. "I bet I'm the only woman in Nice who can drive a tank."

Bennett looked around at the other tables, where an assortment of carefully groomed ladies had gathered for coffee before launching an assault on the shops. "Not a tank driver to be seen," he said. "That's the Saint Laurent cavalry, armed to the teeth with credit cards. Anyway, go on. You decided not to be Israel's first female general."

Anna shook her head. "Not me. Three years was enough. The last few months, things got ugly in the occupied territories, and I couldn't take it. I used to wake up wondering how many more people I was going to see slugged or shot or blown up. And I'm an American. It wasn't even my country." She shrugged. "So I didn't reenlist. I had some money saved, and I thought I'd go home the slow way, through Europe." She lifted her coffee cup and looked at Bennett without seeing him, her eyes back in the past.

He waited in silence until she was ready to go on.

She focused again. "I wanted to see Venice. My parents went there on their honeymoon, and they were always talking about going back. I had this idea to get them to come out and meet me. And that's when I met Poe. It was a pickup, at one of those cafés in Saint Mark's Square."

"Don't tell me. He offered you a ride in his gondola."

"Almost that bad. Well, you've met him. He's quite an operator, and after being with guys whose idea of a date is a beer and a wrestling match, he was different. So was his idea of a date. The best hotels, private plane, clothes, flowers, the whole bit. I was completely snowed. I guess I wasn't as sophisticated as I thought." She made a face and shrugged.

Bennett tried to imagine the contrast between army life and the luxurious cocoon offered by Poe. "It made a change from driving tanks, didn't it? And he's an attractive man, if you happen to like rich old Etonians."

Anna went on without commenting. "He had an

apartment in Geneva at the time, and we lived there—I lived there, anyway. He was always off somewhere, doing his deals."

"What kind of deals?"

"Currency, real estate—those were the ones he talked about. There were some he didn't. Arms, maybe. For a straight businessman, he had a lot of friends who were generals. But he mostly kept me out of all that. I spent my time in Geneva learning French and waiting for him to come back. And then, after a couple of years, one day he didn't come back. Sent one of his guys with a bunch of roses and a note saying it was all over."

"Any reason?"

"Oh, it all came out later—he has this thing about young girls. You get to be twenty-five, twenty-six, and you're over the hill. He trades you in. I hear he's with some French chick now. Did you get to meet her?"

Bennett nodded. "Chou-Chou. Definitely not a tank driver. You must have been rather upset."

"Jesus, you Brits." She mimicked him. "Rather upset? I wanted to strangle the son of a bitch. Sending a *note,* for Christ's sake. I felt like an expired magazine subscription."

"I don't understand," Bennett said. "If you feel like that, why are you working for him?"

She sighed, and hid her eyes with sunglasses. "Fifty thousand dollars, that's why. My papa died last year, and my mother's sick. I've been doing some modeling, and I have a job at a gallery in SoHo, but the doctors are getting through it faster than I can make it. So Poe calls out of the blue last week, offers me fifty in cash for a few days' work. He said my army training might come in handy, whatever that means. Anyway, I need the money, so here I am. This is not a labor of love, believe me. It's business." She drank the last of her coffee and stood up. "Let's get to it."

Bennett scrambled to his feet. "Yes, Sarge, right away. I'll go and commandeer transport. Shall we synchronize watches?"

Anna slipped into her jacket. "God," she said, "Brits. Are you born with that sense of humor, or is it something you catch?"

They drove back to Monaco, Anna dozing and Bennett's mood much improved. A pretty face never failed to cheer him up, and if Poe was paying this girl so well to be his partner, she must have abilities that were goingto be useful. She didn't seem too fond of Englishmen, admittedly, but after being ditched like that, it was hardly surprising. He took a sharp right-hand bend on the Corniche, Anna's sleepy head slipped sideways to rest on his shoulder, and he spent the remainder of the drive in a pleasant daydream: They wouldn't stop in Monaco; they'd go on to Italy, find a small hotel on the coast, and he'd change her mind about Englishmen. Yes, he thought, and then they'd come downstairs one morning and find bloody Shimo chopping the place to bits with his bare hands.

Anna woke as the car pulled up at the entry gate of the garage, she jerked away from his shoulder, rubbing her eyes.

"Home sweet home," said Bennett. "But I expect you know it, don't you?"

"Poe talked about it, but I've never been here."

Bennett pressed the elevator button for the top floor. "It's about as cozy as a hotel lobby, but the terrace makes up for it. And it's very handy for the casino, if you should feel like a flutter."

"You go flutter. I'll take a shower."

Bennett looked at his watch. "Hang on a minute. We'd better tell Poe you've arrived. I think he wants to talk to you."

Anna rolled her eyes upward. "I can hardly wait."

Poe was still in his brisk mood of the day before, the director of operations briefing his man in the field. He gave Bennett the number of Tuzzi's assistant in Cannes, who would arrange transport out to the yacht, and spent several minutes fussing over details before asking to speak to Anna. She took the phone Bennett passed her as though it were contaminated.

She spoke in frigid monosyllables, clearly irritated at what Poe was saying. Eventually, she shrugged. "OK," she said. "It's your money." Scowling at the phone as she put it down, she glared at

Bennett. "Jesus."

"What's the matter?"

"I'm supposed to be your executive secretary. Little Miss Hersh. What a joke."

"Oh, I don't know," Bennett said. "Sounds like rather a good idea to me. How's your shorthand?"

"Not as good as my unarmed combat, so save the sense of humor for someone else, OK?" She stood up and went across to get her bag. "Where's the bathroom?"

Bennett pointed her downstairs, then looked over the notes he'd made while speaking to Poe and called the number in Cannes. The girl who answered greeted him like a favored client. She hoped his flight from Zurich had been pleasant, offered suggestions about where he might like to dine that night, and asked him to be at Port Canto, the Cannes harbor, the following evening at five. A boat would take him out to the *Ragazza di Napoli.* Mr. Tuzzi was planning a gala dinner on board, which Mr. Bennett and his assistant (a word she spoke with the faintest hint of a raised eyebrow) would undoubtedly find memorable and most enjoyable. After assuring him of her personal attention at all times should he need it, she wished Bennett *bon voyage.*

There. It was done. He was committed. He had his fake case, his fake business cards, and his reluctant executive secretary. Detailed plans were impossible until they'd had a chance to find their way around the yacht and assess the security arrangements. There was nothing to do but wait.

"Bennett? Is there a beer in this place?"

Anna had come upstairs, barefoot and wet-haired from the shower, dressed in fresh jeans and T-shirt, and Bennett was reminded of her lack of luggage. An admirable way to travel, he'd thought at the time, but one small bag doesn't hold a wardrobe. He went through to the kitchen and brought back two bottles of Kronenbourg. "Now, Anna, you mustn't take this personally, but do you think you've brought enough clothes?"

She drank straight from the bottle, a good long pull, before answering. "Sure."

"Well, what I really mean is, have you brought anything except jeans and T-shirts? Frocks? Skirts? Anything like that?"

"Frocks? You mean dresses?" She shook her head. "I left them in New York, along with the ball gowns and the cocktail hats and the floor-length chinchilla. You want a fashion show, I'll wear a different T-shirt tomorrow."

She wasn't making it easy for him. Deliberately, he felt sure. "The thing is," said Bennett, "I'm supposed to be an investment counselor, and you're supposed to be my . . . well, my secretary."

"Thanks for reminding me."

"Don't be so touchy. This is business, remember? Just think for a moment. Would a high-powered investment counselor from Zurich—which is hardly known as the leisure-wear capital of Europe—have a secretary in jeans and a T-shirt? It's not likely, is it?"

Anna chewed her bottom lip and sighed. "No," she said, "I guess not."

"So we'll have to get you kitted out. Regulation dress, uniform, whatever you want to call it. It means going back to Nice, but I know just the place."

Anna raised her eyebrows. "Really? So you've given up Savile Row?"

"Jesus," said Bennett. "Yanks."

———

Late afternoon found them in the boutique where Susie—it seemed so long ago now—had stretched her credit card to shreds. The salesgirl had clearly not forgotten Bennett, and while Anna was in the changing room, she sidled up and gave him a look like a poke in the ribs. *"Félicitations, monsieur. Toujours les jolies nanas, eh?"*

"A business colleague." He cleared his throat. "We're working together." The girl smiled, and went to the racks to make sure she hadn't overlooked anything suitably expensive.

Anna, emerging in a tailored silk suit, was a revelation. She moved differently wearing what Bennett thought of as real clothes, and he saw the model reappear as she turned and posed—hips thrust out, one knee pushed forward—and cocked her head to examine herself critically in the full-length mirror, oblivious to the twitters of approval from the salesgirl. "Not a bad fit," she said to Bennett. "Is the skirt long enough for Zurich, or do they go for ankle length over there?"

Bennett took his time studying her legs. What a waste it was for the girl to wear jeans. "Just above the knee," he said. "Smart, but very businesslike. In fact, a credit to the secretarial profession. Particularly the bare feet. But you need a couple of skirts and things. And for shoes, we can go to Clergerie. It's just down the street."

Anna looked over her shoulder on her way back to the changing cubicle. "How come you know all these places?"

"Remember I told you about Susie? She shops for England."

Two hours and half a dozen stops later, Bennett pronounced himself satisfied that Anna was properly equipped. For him, it had been an unexpected pleasure to see the transformation from tough girl to elegant woman. Even for Anna, who declared loudly and often that she hated shopping, it had been good to feel a man's obvious interest and—despite Bennett's facetious way of expressing it—admiration. Unlike Poe, whose flattery had always been delivered word perfect, as though he had memorized lines from the roué's phrase book, Bennett's compliments had an unrehearsed, engaging warmth about them, as there was about him generally. At least, whenever he allowed it to show through.

They sat in the clot of early evening traffic leaving Nice, the sea air lightly tainted with the scent of diesel, the hysterical clatter of passing motor scooters making conversation almost impossible in the open-top car. Bennett longed for calm, a cold glass of wine, and, he realized, something to eat. With a decisive stamp on the accelerator, he cut sharply in front of a truck heading back to Italy, waved an airy acknowledgment of the furious driver's klaxon blast, and turned off toward the sea and Villefranche. The noise level subsided immediately.

"Thought you might be peckish, as we missed out on lunch," he said to Anna, who had been within inches of the truck's snout. "Do you fancy a bit of fish? Hungry work, shopping."

"Just being alive is fine," she said.

"Sorry about that, but it was a sudden inspiration. There are some nice little places on the port, and you can't ask an army to march on an empty stomach, or so Wellington used to say."

"Napoleon. It was Napoleon who said that."

"So it was. Well, that's the French for you. Always thinking about their rations."

———

With a grateful swoop, the Mercedes nosed into one of Villefranche's precious parking spots. Bennett and Anna walked down to the row of restaurants on the quay. It was early for dinner, and the waiters were still at work on the outdoor tables, clipping on the paper covers, dealing out cutlery and glasses like cards, having one last cigarette before the torrent of customers, in varying stages of sunburn, descended on the port.

After browsing through the remarkably similar menus on display—Bennett had a theory that there was a single giant kitchen serving all the restaurants—they chose a table with a view of the setting sun. Bennett picked up the wine list with a sigh of satisfaction, then looked up at Anna.

"You do drink wine, don't you?"

"Why not?"

"Well, military background, Jewish . . ."

"Do you mean kosher?"

"That's the word."

"I ate a ham sandwich, didn't I?"

Bennett looked up to see the smile. "How could I forget? Snatching the crust from a workingman's mouth. You ought to be ashamed of yourself."

"Although," Anna said as Bennett went back to the list, "there's a lot about the Jewish faith that makes sense."

"Oh, I'm sure. Do you like white or pink?"

"Circumcision, for a start."

"Fine. Great. We'll have pink."

For half an hour or so, they forgot who they were supposed to be, and talked like any other couple thrown together by chance and finding the experience interesting, even pleasurable. Anna's knowledge of

France was limited to Paris, and she asked Bennett to tell her about the south. He spoke of Saint-Martin and Avignon and Aix, of the people and the seasons, always lightly but with an affectionate enthusiasm that came through the banter. More than once, Anna felt her guard begin to slip—a guard that had been put up after her experience with Poe and hadn't been seriously challenged since. And more than once, Bennett had to stop himself from staring at her quite so obviously, as the setting sun painted light on her skin and picked up the shine of her eyes.

Their waiter brought them back to real life. *"Monsieur Bennett? Téléphone."*

Puzzled and irritated, Bennett followed the waiter into the restaurant and picked up the phone. "Yes?"

"You must excuse me for disturbing your intimate little dinner." Poe's voice didn't sound in the least apologetic. "Is everything arranged with Tuzzi's people?"

"Yes. We're getting on the boat tomorrow evening."

"Splendid. I'm so glad that you and Miss Hersh are having such fun. Quite the shoppers, aren't you?"

"How did you know we were here?"

"I told you we'd keep a friendly eye on you. Let's hope that the next time we speak, you'll have good news. *Bon appétit.*"

Bennett paused on his way back to the table and looked along the quay, now becoming noisier and

more crowded. Somewhere in this apparently innocent swirl of people were Poe's human Dobermans.
They were looking at him now. They would be watching him have dinner. They'd follow him back to
Monaco. He wondered if they'd bugged the apartment.

Anna saw the tightness of Bennett's mouth as he sat
down. "Let me guess," she said. "That was our
beloved leader, letting us know he's on our case. Am
I right?"

Bennett nodded and poured some more wine.
"They must have been tailing us all day. Not a pleasant feeling, is it?"

"I told you. He's not a pleasant guy."

They ate without speaking for a few minutes, glancing around from time to time at the neighboring tables,
now all occupied. Surrounding their silence were
snatches of cheerful conversation in a variety of languages, the sound of laughter, the clink of glasses
raised in holiday toasts. Another jolly evening on the
Riviera. Bennett's appetite deserted him, and he
pushed his plate away.

"Well," he said, "have you got any ideas about tomorrow?"

Anna leaned over and speared a forkful of the
pommes frites that Bennett had left. "Depends where
Tuzzi keeps the case. The bidders will want to see it,
and there may be a chance to do the switch, but I
wouldn't bet on it." She chewed, swallowed, and

shrugged. "I think we'd have better luck after the auction. Follow the buyer, and jump him once we get off the boat."

Bennett began to understand why Poe had recruited Anna. "Have you had much experience at that sort of thing? Jumping people?"

She looked at him with a half-smile. "More than you, I guess."

"That's settled, then. I'll hold your coat."

The mood was gone. Bennett paid the bill, and, leaving the quay, they walked up the steep street that led to where they had parked. As they came up to a *bar-tabac,* Bennett went in to buy a newspaper and a cigar. Anna looked at the knot of tourists in front of the counter, agonizing over their choice of postcards. "I'll meet you at the car, OK?"

Emerging from the shop, he paused under a street-lamp to read the headline of the day. Preelection politics, accusations and promises. He tucked the paper under his arm and turned the corner into the tiny square where he'd left the Mercedes. Anna was standing by the car, talking to a man. One of Poe's goons, he thought, delivering yet another message of goodwill. He quickened his step.

It was over before he had time to shout. He saw the man raise his arm, the blur of Anna's hand slapping his face, the backward jerk of his head, and then the violent forward jerk as Anna pulled his head against the bar of the forearm that she'd jammed against his throat. The man's legs buckled, and he went down like a dropped sack.

Bennett found his voice. "Anna! Are you all right?"

She looked up from the carcass on the ground and took a breath. "I'm fine. Look at this." Pointing to the driver's window of the car, she pulled out a long strip of steel that had been inserted between the edge of the door and the glass. "Little creep. Another thirty seconds, and he'd have been in."

Bennett bent over the body. "What the hell did you do to him?"

"Basic chokehold. He'll be out for two or three minutes." She yawned and walked around to the passenger side of the car. "Let's go. It's been a long day."

Bennett drove slowly, Anna drowsing beside him. For the second time in a few days, he'd been witness to violence. Shimo had been terrifying, but there had been a ritualized detachment about his demonstration, and the only casualty had been a length of bamboo. Anna had put a man down, could easily have killed him had she wanted to, and apparently with no more emotion than the Japanese had shown. It was another unpleasant reminder that he was caught up in what might be a rough game.

They got back to Monaco as the first stars were appearing over the casino to welcome the disconsolate early gamblers coming out, luck and money exhausted, dreams of caviar and Krug replaced by more affordable thoughts of beer and sandwiches. Long, sleek cars dropped off their passengers at the Hôtel de Paris, and the lobby was alive with the sound of air kisses and the soft click of colliding necklaces as the girls and their temporary uncles gathered for dinner. Nothing would have been nicer, thought Bennett, than to take Anna in for a glass of champagne and forget about tomorrow. He looked at her, curled in a jet-lagged sleep next to him, and shook her gently by the shoulder.

"We're here."

He followed her into the apartment and downstairs to the bedroom, where he dropped the shopping bags next to the bed. "Thanks," said Anna, and slid the window open to catch the night breeze. "Where's your room?"

"Well, this was it, actually."

"Tough luck, buster." She dropped onto the bed with a sigh. "Enjoy the couch."

"You don't mind if I take a quick shower?"

"Be my guest."

By the time he came out of the bathroom, she was sprawled across the bed, one arm curled around a pillow, her face younger and softer in sleep. Bennett considered doing her the kindness of taking off her boots, but thought better of it. She'd probably think he was trying to steal them, execute the basic response kick, and send him through the window. With one last look at her face, he turned off the light and went upstairs to his chaste and uncomfortable couch.

He poured himself a whisky and sat in the darkness, thinking of how his life had changed so abruptly, how far away Saint-Martin seemed, how close he now was to dangerous people. Shutting his eyes, he saw again the sudden pull of Anna's hand on the back of the man's head, the slump of the unconscious body. He drained the glass, shook his head, and reached for the bottle.

10

BENNETT woke to the sound of France Musique on the radio and the smell of brewing coffee. For one semiconscious moment he thought he was back in Saint-Martin, with Georgette in the kitchen and a pleasant, uncomplicated, danger-free day ahead of him. Then he became aware of the stiffness from a cramped night's sleep, opened his eyes, and raised his head cautiously from the makeshift pillow of his rolled-up trousers. His neck ached. Someone seemed to have embedded a screwdriver in his skull while he had slept and was turning it every time he moved. He looked down to see shoes, socks, shirt, empty whisky bottle, and overturned glass on the floor beside him. He groaned, pushed himself off the couch, and felt his way into the kitchen.

"You look like shit," Anna said brightly. "Coffee?"

Nodding, Bennett watched with eyes half closed against the light as she filled a cup and passed it to him. She looked fresh and rested, and smelled of mimosa from one of Poe's expensive soaps. Bennett looked down at his rumpled shorts and scratched his unshaven jaw. He felt like shit, too.

"I'm going to get some croissants," said Anna. "Why don't you take a shower?"

He nodded cautiously. "Yes, Sergeant. Ablutions. Fall in for breakfast at 0800 hours." He shuffled off toward the bathroom, clutching his coffee with both hands. She watched him go, caught herself staring at his tanned back and the way it tapered into narrow hips.

Half an hour later, fortified by aspirin and protected from the glare of the morning by sunglasses, he joined Anna on the terrace. He had nicked himself shaving, and was dabbing at his chin. He saw her looking at it. "Wounded in action," he said. "You'll have to take over. I'm going on sick leave."

"My hero." She passed him a croissant. "I've been thinking," she said. "Say we don't switch the cases on the boat. That means we have to follow the buyer."

Bennett bit into the buttery pastry and felt it float in his mouth. The aspirin was starting to work. Maybe he would survive the day.

"Big problem," Anna said. "How are we going to follow him? The car will be back in Cannes."

Bennett forced himself to engage his mind, which was only just beginning to master the problems of physical coordination required to deal with breakfast. As Anna said, the car would be in Cannes, and they would be leaving the boat at some unspecified port along the coast. Would the buyer arrange someone to meet him? Almost certainly, probably to take him to the nearest airport. How do you jump someone if you're on foot and he's in a car? Or do you take a cab and follow him? And then what? Bennett felt a fresh stab of discomfort in his skull, but somewhere, fighting through the dregs of his hangover, was a solution struggling to emerge.

"Bennett? You still there?"

He held out his cup for more coffee, and with it came inspiration. Poe's men would be tracking the boat. Poe's men would be waiting wherever it stopped. Poe's men would have a car, and a small arsenal of weapons. Poe's men could do the dirty work. It was simple. All they had to do was identify the buyer to the goons, and leave it to them. Immensely cheered by the thought, Bennett beamed at Anna and brandished the remains of his croissant energetically, like a conductor urging his orchestra to swoop into the finale. "Reinforcements," he said. "That's the thing. Bring in the troops."

Anna listened while he explained. "No," she said, "I don't go for it. If we let Poe's guys get the case back, I won't get paid." She looked at him unblinking, her face set. "I'm counting on that fifty grand. So are the doctors."

Bennett persisted, becoming increasingly excited at

the thought of a neat and painless resolution. "Let me talk to Poe. Look, it's only a fallback, if we can't make the switch. Better than losing the case altogether, isn't it?"

Anna said nothing. She was beginning to make plans of her own for the case, and they didn't include any assistance from Poe. But telling Bennett about them now would be an unnecessary complication. And so, after a lengthy and mostly genuine show of reluctance, she agreed that he should make the call.

Ten minutes later, with a grin of triumph, he came back from talking to Poe. "It's all set," he said. "The goons will meet us off the boat. They'll be dressed as French cops. If we haven't made the switch, we give them the fake case. They'll stop the buyer on the road, pretend to be looking for drugs or counterfeit Camembert or something, and search his car. They'll distract him, take the real case, and plant the fake one." Bennett paused and shook his head. "He's a devious old bugger, Poe. He *wants* the buyer to find out he's bought a fake—which won't take him long once he gets it to a laboratory—and then go after Tuzzi. Do you know what he said? 'That should take his mind off chasing girls around Ibiza.' "

"He's a great one to talk."

Bennett's hangover was giving way to giddy euphoria. He was off the hook. All they had to do was play their parts for a day or two, lose convincingly at the auction, and pass the case and the problem over to Poe's private police force. His tender head had miraculously recovered. A small celebration was in order.

He beamed at Anna. "Now, Miss Hersh, I know it's against company policy for executives and their secretaries to fraternize socially, but under the circumstances I think the rules can be bent a little, don't you?"

His face was a study in happiness. Anna couldn't help smiling back. "What exactly do you have in mind? An office party?"

"Lunch, Miss Hersh. Lunch." He looked at her over the top of his sunglasses. "Will you do me a favor? Wear a skirt? Proper shoes? We'll go to Chez Bacon, and the chef will come out and kiss the hem of your garment, astounded by such a ravishing customer. Promise. And it's great fish."

They took turns in the bedroom, changing and packing for the boat. Bennett's mood was infectious, and Anna found, to her surprise, that she was dressing to please him, in a short, sleeveless shift of pale-beige linen and high heels, an extra dab of Coco at the base of her throat. She remembered a line from an old perfume advertisement: *Wear it where you'd like to be kissed.* She looked at herself in the bathroom mirror. Did she want Bennett to kiss her? She'd think about it.

He was waiting for her upstairs, blazered and flan-
neled, an Old Etonian tie purloined from Poe's closet
at the collar of his best blue shirt. Once he'd done up
his fly, Anna thought, you could take him anywhere.
She nodded approvingly. "Not bad. You clean up
pretty well."

Bennett bowed. "You're not so bad yourself, for a
retired NCO." He watched the interesting movements
going on under her dress as she walked to the hall and
bent to put down her bag. This would soon be over,
he thought, and then he might be able to persuade her
to stay on. What would she think of Saint-Martin?
What would Georgette think of her? "Got everything?" he asked. "Don't forget there's supposed to be
a smart dinner tonight on the boat. I hope you've
brought your campaign medals."

She opened the front door and looked back at him.
"Zip up your fly. That's an order."

———

For as long as Bennett could remember, the Restaurant de Bacon on Cap d'Antibes had been something
of a shrine for people who were more interested in the
fish on their plates than in who might be sitting at the
next table. Never breathlessly fashionable, and largely
ignored by would-be celebrities, it was what the
French would call *sérieux*—exquisite food, telepathic
service, a long, shaded terrace overlooking the sea,

and memorable bills. Bennett loved the light, the atmosphere of quiet, concentrated enjoyment, and, on
this particular day, the thought that Poe's watchdogs
would be sitting somewhere not far away in a hot car,
eating sandwiches and sweating.

He ordered two glasses of champagne, and pro-
posed a toast. "To my favorite sergeant."

Anna inclined her head. "How many others do you
know?"

He pretended to think. "Not many. And they all
have to shave. It was supposed to be a compliment."

They looked at each other, a long, smiling silence,
until their waiter arrived with a diplomatic cough and
the menus. "Can I recommend something?" Bennett
said. "They have bibs here—you know, for those of
us who might be a little untidy. Be a shame to spoil
that dress."

"I'll try not to drool, but OK. I'll have a bib."

"Sensible girl. Anything to go with it?"

The unhurried ceremony of the meal began with a
white Bandol and wafer-thin ravioli, no bigger than
postage stamps. Bennett found it hard to imagine his
sleek, well-dressed companion stiffing a car thief. She
looked as though she belonged in places like this.
With someone like Poe. "Tell me," he said, "what are
you going to do when this is all over?"

Anna looked out at the sea and then at Bennett, the
skin of his face dark against the white of his bib.
"Back to New York, I guess. Pay off the doctors, see

my mother, maybe tell her about this guy I met in France."

"What would you say?"

Anna pretended to think. "Let's see. Not a dentist. Not a lawyer. Not Jewish. Not employed."

Bennett mopped his plate with a scrap of bread. "Oh. You mean quite a catch. Every girl's dream."

"What would you tell your mother?"

"Well," said Bennett, "I'd have to find her first. She went AWOL when I was seven. I'm an unofficial orphan." He told her about his roving parents, and she might have felt sorry for him if he had showed any trace of self-pity, and if she hadn't been laughing. She'd forgotten how attractive a sense of humor was in a man, how easy it made him to be with.

Bennett paused, and they watched a display of dexterity that would have done credit to a surgeon as the waiter filleted their fish with nothing but a deft spoon and fork. For a while, they concentrated on their food, glancing at each other occasionally, Bennett solicitous with the wine, Anna finding herself more and more relaxed.

They finished eating and leaned back. Anna watched Bennett looking down at his bib. "I have this cleaning lady in Saint-Martin," he said. "She loves telling me the English can't eat without spraying their food all over the place. Now she's got me believing it."

"Do you always believe what women tell you?"

"Absolutely. I've been putty in a woman's hands ever since I had a crush on the head matron at boarding school." He smiled. "I remember one day we were all making our beds in the dormitory, and matron was inspecting them. 'Bennett,' she said, 'if you don't start making your bed properly, you and I are going to fall out.' Then she realized what she'd said, and blushed. I was mad about her for a whole term."

"How old were you?"

"Thirteen. Then she broke my heart and ran away with the music teacher. Never got over it. To this day, I pine. Shall we have some wild strawberries? They're wonderful with *crème fraîche.*"

The strawberries came and were wonderful. Bennett ordered a Havana with the coffee. They talked on, both avoiding the immediate future, content to float on the pleasures of the moment. The meal had stretched over two and a half hours, and seemed to have passed in minutes. It took another discreet cough from the waiter to bring them back to earth.

Bennett covered the bill with five-hundred-franc notes and looked around the restaurant, now almost empty. In the soft light of the diffused afternoon sun, Anna seemed to glow, her bare arms silken and brown, her face faintly flushed by wine, light dancing in her eyes. Bennett leaned toward her. "We could always stay for dinner."

"That's what I like about you—all play and no work." She reached over and brushed cigar ash from his lapel. "But it would be nice to come back."

———

When they arrived in Cannes, Tuzzi's taxi service was waiting for them at the port—two bulky men in white, with *Ragazza di Napoli* on the T-shirts that were strained across broad expanses of chest. Anna, Bennett, and their bags were settled in the back of a gleaming Riva. With a watery burble from the exhaust and some theatrical flourishes on the wheel that were not strictly necessary, they slipped through the other boats and headed for what looked like a small apartment building half a mile offshore.

The *Ragazza* was, in fact, as close to Bennett's kind of floating accommodation as any boat could be. It was monumentally ugly, but reassuringly big. Antennae, radar, and satellite dishes grew from the cabin roof on the top deck, giving it the appearance of an urban skyline. Canopies of white canvas shaded the acreage of deck fore and aft, and as they climbed the stern gangway, they were greeted by the sight of an oval swimming pool. It was an island rather than a boat, insulated as far as possible against any intrusion from the surrounding sea.

A steward in starched dress whites showed them to adjoining cabins. Signor Tuzzi would be pleased to welcome them on the forward deck when they were ready. Did they require any assistance unpacking? Thinking of the fake case wrapped in a sweater, Bennett waved the steward away with a hundred-franc note before closing the door and taking stock of his cabin and the small bathroom. He noted with approval the presence of a real bed and the absence of any nautical horrors like pump-action lavatories. He could have been in a hotel room. The only hint of life at sea was a porthole, now open to catch the breeze. He stuck his head through and looked at the immense sweep of the hull, curving away forward.

"Anna? Are you OK? Found your sea legs?"

An arm appeared through her porthole, and a beckoning finger invited him next door. As Bennett came into the cabin, Anna put a hand over his mouth before he had a chance to speak, then went into her bathroom, returning with a lipstick and a sheet of Kleenex. He looked over her shoulder as she scribbled: *Cabins may be bugged.*

Bennett looked around furtively and nodded. "Ah, there you are, Miss Hersh," he said in what he hoped was a suitably businesslike voice. "Well, you've got to hand it to the Italians. Very comfortable quarters. If you're ready, I think we should go and meet our host."

Anna winked, and gave him a signal with her upraised thumb. "Yes, Mr. Bennett. Will you be wanting me to take notes?"

"No, I don't think so. If you need your book, I can always send you back."

She smiled sweetly at him and signaled again, this time with an upraised finger.

The group of men seated around a low table rose to greet Anna and Bennett as they reached the deck; one of them came forward, his arms spread wide. "Ah, Signor Bennett. Welcome to the *Ragazza*. I am Tuzzi." His face, the color and cracked sheen of old leather, split into a smile, the whiteness of his teeth accentuated by a thick black mustache. Above it, he had a hooked, slightly crooked nose and disconcertingly pale eyes, somewhere between gray and green. What remained of his black hair was pulled back from the gleaming tanned dome of his skull and fastened in a ponytail. The more abundant hair on his chest frothed at the open neck of his white polo shirt. He pumped Bennett's hand vigorously and then, with a dramatic intake of breath, closed his eyes and shook his head, as if to clear it. "Forgive me," he said. "I am dead and in heaven. Who is this?"

"My secretary, Miss Hersh," said Bennett.

"*Signorina.*" Tuzzi bent over Anna's proffered hand and caressed it lightly with his mustache. "*Non è vero.* A secretary? A princess."

Anna smiled at him and struggled for repossession of her hand. "Pleased to meet you, Mr. Tuzzi."

"Enzo. For you, Enzo." He clapped a hand to his forehead. "But I forget my polites. Permit me."

He took them through the introductions. There was an elderly, wizened Corsican, Monsieur Polluce from Calvi; the small, neat, and courteous Mr. Kasuga from Tokyo; a dark, middle-aged man in yachting clothes and gold jewelry, Anthony Penato from California—"a good Californian," Tuzzi said. "He smoke, he drink, not like those goddamn health fruits." And, finally, an Englishman with a sharp, intelligent face, an absentminded air, and steel-gray hair: Lord Glebe, Tuzzi's business adviser. "And we mustn't forget my little chap, Genghis," Glebe said to Bennett, indicating a caramel-colored Pekingese lying on a large dish under the table. "Or perhaps, as I'm a peer of the realm, we should call him the Honorable Genghis. My little joke. Hmm?"

"Ah," said Bennett, "the god of frolic." He crouched down obligingly to make himself known to Genghis. The dog opened one eye, studied Bennett, and emitted a disdainful snuffle. "Why is he on a plate?"

"Because it's cool, old boy," said Lord Glebe. "Eighteenth-century Willow pattern. Goes with him everywhere. Your Pekingese suffers from heat, particularly round the vitals."

As the bowing and shaking of hands concluded, a burly young man came up to whisper in Tuzzi's ear. *"Sì, sì. Andiamo."* Tuzzi turned to the others. "Now we make a small cruising before dinner. *Signorina?* For you I am arranging a perfect sunset, but first you must allow me to show you my little boat. Come. We take a conductor's tour."

To Bennett's surprise, Anna seemed thrilled by the invitation, smiling prettily and taking Tuzzi's furry arm. "I've always been fascinated by boats, Enzo. Is it true there's a golden rivet somewhere in the engine room?" As they strolled aft, the deck gave a barely perceptible shudder, there was a muted hum from the turbines, and the *Ragazza* got under way.

Lord Glebe motioned the others to sit down. "Now that we're all here, gentlemen, perhaps I could go over some details with you. No doubt Mr. Tuzzi will have some comments also." He peered at them over the top of his half-glasses. "Unfortunately, while he takes a brave aim at colloquial English, he frequently misfires, as you may have noticed, and I wouldn't want there to be any little misunderstandings."

He lit a small cheroot before continuing. "The auction will be held tomorrow morning, once you've all had a chance to examine the contents of the case. They don't make much sense to me, I must say, but I presume you chaps know what you're looking at. What?"

Bennett found himself nodding wisely with the others.

"Excellent. Now, if you'll forgive my bringing it up, I must touch on the subject of payment. We shall be putting into Marseille tomorrow as soon as business is completed. I've alerted my bank there to be on parade to receive a transfer of funds from whoever of you is the eventual purchaser. I assume that each of you has made arrangements with your banking people, and of course you can get in touch with them at any time from the boat. Chap up there"—he waved his cheroot in the direction of the bridge—"has all the communications technology. Not like sailing in my young day, but there we are. All clear so far?" Another owlish look from Glebe was met by more nods.

"Very good. Now then. Once we've parked at Marseille, the purchaser and I will toddle over to my bank, verify that the transfer has been made, the case will change hands, and Bob's your uncle."

Glebe noticed puzzled frowns from Polluce, Kasuga, and Penato. "Ah," he said, "forgive me. Figure of speech. It means that everything is done. There is no actual Bob, you see." He smiled. "Marvelously confusing language, English. No wonder they use it so much in the EEC. Well? Any questions?"

Kasuga held up a finger. "We are definitely coming ashore at Marseille?" Glebe nodded. "So. I must contact my colleagues."

"Of course, old boy. I expect you'll all want to have a chat to your people. You'll find young Benito, or whatever he's called, very helpful. Knows which buttons to push. So you can all feel free to call your secretaries, bodyguards, and dear ones at any time." He smiled at Bennett. "You, of course, Mr. Bennett, won't need to call, as you have your secretary with you—damned handsome gel, too. Officer's comforts, eh?"

"Well, nothing like that. But she is very efficient."

Glebe's voice dropped. "I should keep an eye on her and our chum Enzo, if I were you. A prince in many ways, but he's the closest thing I've ever seen to a stoat in rut. A fondler, if you take my meaning. Don't know where he gets the energy from." He leaned closer to Bennett. "Tell me something. I think I know most of the financial outfits in Europe, but Consolidated doesn't ring a bell. Been established long, have you?"

Bennett hadn't thought about inventing a corporate history to go with his business cards, and for a moment he was caught with his cover down. He stalled by asking for a cheroot, and took his time lighting it. "Just between you and me, Lord Glebe, it's a front."

"Ah," said Glebe, "thought as much. Acting for Brunei, or someone like that, I suppose."

"Saudis, actually. But I'd prefer not to go into the details."

"Quite. Well, money's money, wherever it comes from." He looked at his watch, then turned to the others. "I hope you'll excuse me, gentlemen. We're going to take a turn around the deck. Cocktails at seven, dinner at eight." He bent down to the sleeping Pekingese.

"Woof, woof, old boy. Woof, woof." Genghis rose sleepily from his dish, and the two of them sauntered off, trailing clouds of cheroot smoke.

———

Tuzzi unlocked the double doors leading to his cabin and threw them open with a flourish. "And this," he said, "is my poor little corner." Anna took in the vast, canopied bed, the mirrored ceiling, the fireplace framed by two giant elephant tusks, the curtains of heavy, dark-red silk, the gilt-encrusted furniture, and, on a desk below the main porthole, looking very much out of place in surroundings that would have suited an expensive bordello, the aluminum attaché case.

She stopped to look at a life-size nude statue clutching a breast in one hand and a lamp in the other. "What a charming room, Enzo."

He sighed, a gusty, melancholy sigh. "But so lonely. I have a little *pisolino* in the afternoon, I come to bed at night. Always I sleep with my pillows, with my memories. Is tragic." He looked at Anna as though he were going to burst into tears, and took her hand. "No, life is not a bowl of cherry."

She patted his arm, and glanced at her watch with an exaggerated start of surprise. "My, Enzo, look at the time. I'd better go and change for dinner."

"*Sì, sì.* I take you." His fingers slid to the small of her back, and were continuing downward as she moved to go through the door. He left her outside her cabin with another protracted bout of hand-kissing, and she sat on the bed feeling as though she'd been stroked from one end of the boat to the other.

She heard a tap on the door. Jesus, she thought, he's coming back for more. "Enzo, I'm going to take a shower."

"Anna, it's me. Bennett. Can you come out? We need to talk."

They found an empty stretch of deck and leaned on the rail, watching the long, flat stripe of the wake stretching out behind the boat. Bennett spoke first, reporting what he'd heard about the auction arrangements, delighted at the thought of getting back on dry land and leaving the rest to Poe. "So how about you? Did Tuzzi behave himself? I saw him pawing the ground."

"That's not all he pawed. I swear he's got two pairs of hands. But I saw the case. It's in his cabin."

Bennett's eyebrows shot up. "You were in his cabin? Anna, you didn't . . . I mean . . ."

"Sure I did. It's on his desk, next to his Venus de Milo paperweight."

"And it can bloody well stay there. Listen, it's simple. All we have to do is go through the motions tonight and lose at the auction tomorrow. And that's it. No heroics. You resigned from the army, remember? And you certainly don't need to play hide-and-seek with that overweight Lothario. Glebe told me about him. Lecherous bastard."

"Most of it's for show. He's just one of those Italian guys who don't wear underwear."

"What?" Bennett was stunned. "How do you know?"

"It's a type. Girls can tell." She smiled at the look on his face, a mixture of shock and disapproval. "Bennett, you're looking stern. It'll give you wrinkles. Stop worrying. Come on—we'd better get changed. Don't wait for me."

———

The entire afterdeck of the *Ragazza* was dressed for dinner, with a necklace of tiny lights strung along the edges of the canvas canopy. A round table set with silver, crystal, a centerpiece of fresh flowers, and tall glass hurricane lamps occupied the middle of the deck. To one side, a steward arranged ice buckets and champagne on a small bar. They had dropped anchor at an angle to the setting sun, and a path of red-gold light lapped against the hull of the boat. As Bennett came up to join the others, he found Tuzzi, draped in a pale-blue caftan, holding forth.

". . . and so I tell him. My friend, I say, if you think you can do this to Tuzzi, you are putting your head in a moose. *Capisce?*"

Lord Glebe was offering a murmured interpretation to the bewildered audience when Tuzzi saw Bennett standing by the bar and walked over to join him. "Ah, Mr. Bennett. You have a drink? *Bene.*" He put an arm around Bennett's shoulder and led him farther away from the others. "I ask a personal question, yes? Man to man."

Bennett buried his nose in his champagne glass to escape the force of Tuzzi's overwhelming eau de cologne. "Of course. What is it?"

"The *bellissima* Miss Hersh. Are you very close?"

"Well, you know. Good working relationship. She's a first-class secretary, speaks a couple of languages, reliable girl."

"No, no, I mean *close*." Tuzzi hunched his shoulders and made a pumping gesture with his free hand, his eyebrows performing a semaphore of inquiry. The implication was clear.

"Ah," said Bennett, "you mean bonking."

"*Sì, sì.*" Tuzzi nodded vigorously. "Bonking."

Bennett smoothed his Old Etonian tie. "Good heavens, no. Strict rules in Consolidated against that sort of thing. Bad for morale. Takes your mind off your portfolio, and we can't have that."

Tuzzi grinned, and nodded again. "*Bene, bene.* This makes me happy." He patted Bennett on the shoulder. "You see, in Sicily, to like the woman of another man is *pericoloso*. Most dangerous. You are skating on thin eggs."

"Yes, I've heard Sicily's a tricky place." Bennett took a sip of champagne and tried to suppress a feeling of outrage at the thought of this hairy libertine mauling Anna. Outrage and, he had to admit—the idea of mauling her himself crossing his mind—a stab of jealousy. Thank God they'd be off the boat tomorrow. He'd better warn Anna to lock her cabin door.

"Ah," said Tuzzi, with a final pat on Bennett's shoulder, "here is coming Miss Hersh now. *Ai, ai, ai.*" He shook his hand as though he'd singed his fingers. "What magnificence!"

Bennett looked at Anna in dismay. She was wearing a skirt that seemed several inches shorter than Bennett remembered it being when they'd bought it in Nice, and a small halter top that left her stomach bare. Tuzzi, in a transport of concupiscence as he went across to greet her, used the pretext of kissing her hand to conduct a close and thorough investigation of the bosom that was so generously displayed. This is going to lead to trouble, Bennett thought. He took a glass of champagne across to Anna, and waited until Tuzzi was out of earshot.

"You're mad," he whispered. "He'll break the bloody door down to get at you."

She smiled, as though she'd just received a compliment. "You like the outfit? It's business, Bennett. Remember?"

Before Bennett could reply, Tuzzi called them to the table, placing Anna between himself and Lord Glebe. As they all sat down, a steward bearing Genghis on his plate knelt to place the dog carefully under his master's chair. Glebe looked down, and tapped the steward on the shoulder. "Just a little of the foie gras, Piero," he said, "and one of those bread sticks, broken up. And some flat water. That dreadful fizzy stuff gives him wind."

Penato, the Californian, turned to Bennett, shaking his head. "Now I've seen everything. Are all Brits like this with their dogs?"

Bennett had been watching Anna, who was graciously allowing Tuzzi to arrange a napkin on her lap. "What? Sorry—yes, dogs. They're usually much better treated than our wives."

With Anna's napkin arranged to his satisfaction, Tuzzi tapped the side of his wineglass with a fork and looked around the table. "My dear friends, no business tonight. Tonight is gala, in honor of our most beautiful guest. After dinner, we have a movie in my little screening room, and the *Ragazza* is now on anchor for the night, so we can eat and sleep comfortably. *Buon appetito!*"

Bennett attempted to engage his neighbors, Polluce and Kasuga, in conversation, but had very limited success. The two men were drinking more water than wine, and seemed content to maintain a watchful silence. After the first course, Bennett gave up to concentrate on the *loup de mer* that had been placed in front of him, and to glance from time to time at Anna with increasing misgivings. She was flirting— flirting, in Bennett's opinion, quite outrageously— with both Tuzzi and Lord Glebe, who were trying to outdo each other in their elaborate attentions.

"And now, my dear, a special treat." Glebe bent over his fish while he performed some delicate surgery on its head with his knife and fork. "Ah, there we are." He presented his fork to Anna. "Have a cheek. An excellent beast, the sea bass, and his cheeks are delicious."

The men around the table fell silent and watched as Anna leaned over, pushing her shoulders up and forward to emphasize the already generous valley between her breasts. She opened her mouth, passed the tip of her tongue over her lips, and, with her wide eyes fixed on Lord Glebe, very slowly and deliberately sucked the tiny piece of white flesh from the fork. A performance, Bennett thought, that left absolutely nothing to the imagination. "Mmm," Anna said, "that's *so good.*"

The table let out a collective breath. Glebe beamed, and regained control of his trembling fork as Anna dabbed her lips with her napkin. Tuzzi, not to be outdone in the matter of fish cheeks, insisted on helping her excavate the head of her own fish. Bennett glared at her. She smiled back. From the other side of the table, Penato called across to Tuzzi.

"Hey, Enzo. Enough with the fish. What's the movie tonight?"

"Momento." Tuzzi completed the operation and patted Anna's arm. "Tonight is coming Fellini."

"Dear God," said Lord Glebe. "Again?"

"My friend," said Tuzzi, "Fellini was the maestro.

You have sour gripes because he wasn't English."

Anna put down her knife and fork, and batted her eyelashes at Tuzzi. "I *adore* Fellini. I think he's my favorite."

Bennett was finding it difficult to watch Anna, but impossible not to. Tuzzi was mentally turning down the sheets every time he looked at her. The evening was going to end in tears, he was convinced of it, unless he could talk some sense into her during the movie.

But when dinner ended, and they moved with their brandy and cigars into the screening room, Tuzzi again insisted on supervising the seating arrangements, reserving two armchairs at the back for himself and Anna. The lights dimmed, the opening titles of *Amarcord* appeared on the screen, and Bennett sank into a deep sulk, which lasted throughout the film. Next to him, Lord Glebe fell asleep with Genghis at his feet, their snores providing a profundo accompaniment to the sound track.

As the lights came up, Bennett nudged his neighbor awake. "What? What? Oh, it's finished. Thank the Lord for that. I can't take him after dinner. Best on an empty stomach, Fellini."

Bennett stood, stretched, and turned. It was as he had unwillingly forced himself to expect. The two chairs at the back were unoccupied.

11

"DEAR ME," said Lord Glebe when he noticed the two empty seats. "We seem to have lost our host." He looked around the screening room with an air of mild irritation. "Ah well. I suppose I'd better do the honors. If you gentlemen feel like a nightcap, help yourselves at the bar on the afterdeck. Or I'm sure young Piero will make you a cup of cocoa if you ask him nicely." He stooped to pick up Genghis's plate. "I'm off to the land of Nod. Busy day tomorrow."

Bennett went below. Without any real hope of an answer, he stopped to knock at Anna's door, listened to silence for a moment or two. He let himself in and sat scowling on her bed, feeling a sour, confused mixture of disappointment and jealousy. It wasn't a night for sleep. Restless and angry, he returned to the deserted main deck.

The boat was completely silent now, at anchor, steady under his feet except for the gentle rise and fall of a lazy swell. The floodlit surface of the swimming pool barely moved, a slight tilt one way, a slight tilt the other. The air was soft and salty, warm and still;

the stars were sharp. Bennett swore under his breath and stared at the shore. He could see a small port in the distance, the shallow curve of the harbor defined by lights, a mass of hills, blacker than the blackness of the sky, rising behind the huddle of houses. A beautiful, miserable night.

A whisper of sound, no louder than a scuff against the deck, made him turn his head. Something was there, in one of the deep pools of shadow between the bulkhead lights. Probably Glebe's dog, making his evening rounds. Curious, Bennett walked toward it, then froze in shock as a figure stepped into the light.

Anna was naked except for a brief triangle of white at her hips, the aluminum attaché case clutched to her chest. Her eyes bright with relief, she jerked her head toward the stern and led the startled Bennett in silence along the length of the boat until they reached the gangway that led down into the sea. Anna put her mouth to Bennett's ear. "You go first. You'll have to swim on your back and pull me. I'll hold the case out of the water."

"What happened? Are you OK?"

"Jesus, Bennett. Get going."

He eased himself into the sea, blazer billowing and Old Etonian tie floating bravely in front of him, and took hold of Anna under her upraised arms. With the case held clear of the surface, they kicked away from the boat and began to swim backward to the shore.

After ten laborious minutes they rested, treading

water. There was no sign of life on the *Ragazza,* no alarm bells, no hurrying figures on deck.

"What *happened*? Where's Tuzzi?"

"He's out of it, but I don't know for how long. Come on. Let's go."

They continued trying to kick in unison, slow and awkward, Bennett's sodden clothes weighing more and more heavily, Anna's arms aching with the effort of holding up the case, their eyes constantly on the *Ragazza.* A long and exhausting hour passed.

At last, Bennett's shoulder bumped against the sharp prow of a moored sailing boat. He turned his head and saw the welcome closeness of the harbor lights. Five minutes later, they were standing chest-deep in viscous, oily water. Another fifty yards, and they were crouched on the stone steps leading from the beach up to the quay, the light spilling down across Anna's shoulders and a bosom that was still heaving from the effort of the swim.

"Bennett, cut it out."

"What?"

"You're leering. Let me have your shirt."

Bennett stripped off his blazer and gave Anna his shirt, doing his best to ignore the way the sodden fabric clung to her body. He was starting to feel light-headed with fatigue. But they'd done it. They'd escaped. Poe's men were bound to be somewhere in the port, keeping an eye on the boat. Find them, give them the case, and then home for a hot bath. He touched Anna's cheek. "Well done, Sergeant. The medal's in the post. Let's go and find Poe's men, and get rid of that damned case."

Anna shook her head. "We need to talk about it, but not here. Not now. This is the first place Tuzzi will come looking. We've got to get out." She looked over his shoulder toward the boat, her face intent. "Bennett. Please."

Bennett struggled back into his waterlogged blazer. "Well, it's a bloody long walk to anywhere from here."

"We'll steal a car."

"Fine. Yes, of course. We'll steal a car. Any particular color?"

"It's only a couple of wires, and you can start the engine. I know how to do it." The strain left her face as she grinned. "Trust me."

Hearing the two most ominous words in the English language, Bennett sighed and looked cautiously over the top of the wall. At one end of the port was a small hotel and a row of shuttered shops. Next to them, three restaurants, side by side. More shops, some houses, and the road leading out of the village. But cars? Why weren't there any cars? Bennett had a moment of panic, and then he recognized something familiar about the trio of restaurants. He'd been to one of them, years ago. He realized that this was Cassis, and in Cassis cars were forbidden on the quay. He remembered having to park above the village.

"I can't see anyone," Bennett said, "but we'd better not risk the street. Stay close to the wall."

They made their way along the shingle to the far, unlit end of the harbor. Nothing moved. Nothing broke the silence except the occasional scratch and creak of rigging from the moored sailboats, and the sound of pebbles under their feet. Bennett hoisted himself over the wall and pulled Anna after him, and they followed the road out of the village.

———

In the cramped, hot room in the hotel at the end of the port, Gérard rubbed his eyes and looked at his watch. Thank God for that. His shift was over. He got up from the chair by the window and shook his partner awake. "It's all yours until dawn. Have fun." Gérard stretched out on the bed, sticky and uncomfortable in his ill-fitting police uniform. His partner lit a cigarette to discourage the mosquitoes and looked dutifully at the distant lights of the *Ragazza,* bracing himself to stay awake through four hours of boredom. Still, it was good money. The *patron* paid well.

———

Anna and Bennett walked slowly through the parking area, searching for a car without an alarm system, trying door handles, looking for an unlocked trunk, hoping not to have to smash a window. Bennett stopped by a dusty Peugeot 205 convertible and saw that it had no alarm stickers, no red light winking on the dashboard. He called softly across to Anna. "Could you start this?"

Anna came over to the car. "Sure. You get it open, I'll get it going."

Bennett went back to the entrance of the parking area, where two large garbage containers had been placed for the use of civic-minded motorists, and fished among the remnants of beach picnics until he found a beer bottle. It broke easily against the wall, and Bennett returned to the car with a jagged glass knife, which he used to hack a slit in the canvas top. He reached through it and unlocked the door. "You're in."

"You're learning," said Anna. She knelt, and began fumbling under the dashboard. The shirt had ridden up to her waist, and Bennett found himself mesmerized by the sight of wet, transparent cotton stretched over a bottom that dreams were made of. This isn't the moment, he told himself. Concentrate on the job.

The little car coughed, the engine turned over. Bennett switched on the lights and checked the fuel gauge; half full. "We're OK," he said. "That's plenty to get us to Monaco."

"Bennett, *think*. Monaco's bad news. They may be watching the apartment. They may be *in* the apartment. We need to talk."

"We can talk on the way. They won't be watching the apartment. They think we're still on the boat."

"No. Somewhere else. Not Monaco."

"Anna, look at us. We're filthy, we're soaking wet, you're dressed in a shirt and a pair of knickers, we're in a stolen car, and it must be two in the morning. What do you want to do? Check into the Hôtel du Cap? Do we look like respectable tourists?"

"There must be somewhere we can go."

"Oh God. All right." Bennett slammed the car in gear and headed for the autoroute. "We'll go to Saint-Martin."

"Bennett?"

"Now what?"

"You're mad at me, aren't you?"

"Bloody furious. It's done. We've got the case. You'll get your money. Why complicate everything? What more do you want?"

"I'll tell you when we get there." Anna settled back in the passenger seat, the attaché case between her knees. "Shall I tell you what happened?"

"No." He kept his eyes on the empty road, his foot hard on the accelerator. "Yes. Spare me the sordid details."

"There weren't any. We watched the movie for a few minutes, and then he said he had something he wanted to show me."

"Let me guess."

"It was the moon. . . ."

"What moon? There wasn't a moon. . . ."

"OK, so it was the stars. Anyway, we left the screening room, checked out the stars, and then he asked if I'd like a glass of champagne somewhere comfortable."

"I can't imagine where that might have been. God, I've heard some pretty feeble lines in my time . . ."

"You think I haven't? So, big surprise, he takes me to his cabin—champagne on ice, lights down low, music, the full routine—but I couldn't see the case anywhere. I asked him about it, told him I wanted to see what all these high-powered business guys were so excited about. Ah, he said, it's in my private safe. We can look at it later. Then he said: How about a little coke?"

"The perfect host. I hope you sneezed."

"I never touch it. But he had a snootful, and made a grab at me, and we chased around the bed for a couple of minutes. Then he stopped, and he had a kind of sneaky look on his face, and he said, OK, I make a deal: I open the safe, you take off the skirt. I open the case, you take off the top."

Bennett sighed. "And they say romance is dead. Then what? Don't tell me. He wanted to take you home to meet his mother."

"He opened the safe. He opened the case—I wanted to make sure the stuff was still in there—and then I gave him the West Bank handshake." She was silent for a moment. "I kicked him in the balls and knocked him cold with one of the bedside lamps. Then I gagged him and tied him to the bed with lamp wire. And then I kind of lost it and came looking for you."

Bennett slowed down at the entrance to the autoroute, felt in his pocket for some damp change. He said nothing, imagining the scene in Tuzzi's cabin, more pleased than he cared to admit that it hadn't ended in bed. But it hadn't ended. Efforts at retribution would surely follow as soon as the Italian and his vital organs had recovered. "Well," he said as the car pulled away, "that's one place we won't be invited back. How hard did you hit him?"

"Oh, you know. Hard."

"Good." They headed north to pick up the A7. Two hours, and they'd be in Saint-Martin.

Anna looked at the set of his face in the glow of the dashboard light. He'd forgotten to joke. He'd been jealous. That was nice, she thought, as she closed her eyes.

———

Tuzzi ached. His head, his testicles, and, most of all, his pride had been severely bruised. Once he'd regained consciousness, it had taken him a supremely painful half hour to tug one hand free of its binding, raise the alarm, and order a search of the *Ragazza*. Now, with his head bandaged and an ice pack melting between his legs, he was sitting with a pajama-clad

Lord Glebe, the case found in Bennett's cabin open on the table in front of them.

Glebe frowned and shook his head. "Should have known he was a wrong 'un. Chap doesn't put 'Honorable' on his business cards unless he's a jumped-up tradesman."

Tuzzi looked puzzled. "Is a title, no?"

"Of a sort. Basically, it means that you're waiting for daddy to fall off the perch."

"Eh?"

"Die, old boy. Then the title passes on." Glebe shook his head again and studied the case. "Well," he said, "it's a ringer, but it's a damned good one."

"It has to be Poe." Tuzzi began to cross his legs, winced, and changed his mind. "That *stronzo*. Only he could know. I will take out his heart. I will make him wish he never left the tomb of his mother."

"Womb, old boy." Glebe scratched his head. "Of course, the others wouldn't know it's not the real case. Eh?"

Tuzzi stared at him, the bandage around his head giving him the air of a damaged pirate. "Maybe not. Except the papers are different."

"But you only know that because you've seen the real papers."

"*Sì.*"

"Well, then," said Glebe, "my view is that the auction should proceed as planned. Of course, it won't take the buyer long to realize he's been sold a pup. He'll come back to us. We'll be suitably shocked and horrified, put the blame on Poe, and join forces to go after him. Meanwhile, we'll send the lads out to look for Bennett and the girl, and the cash from the sale will be on the money market, earning interest until we give it back. Every little helps. What?"

Tuzzi pursed his lips and rocked slowly back and forth. Then he smiled and nodded and, very gently, tapped his cheek just below his eye with an index finger. "*Bene.* You're thinking like a Sicilian, my friend."

"Really?" said Glebe. "Oh dear. I must have been away from England too long."

———

Bennett ran his hand along the top of the stone lintel until his fingers found Georgette's key. As he opened the front door and turned on the lights, he was aware of the familiar scent of lavender, furniture polish, and linseed oil. The small living room was, as usual, spotless.

Anna looked around and gave a low whistle. "Are you sure you're not married?"

"Oh, I'm just a housewife at heart." Bennett went to the kitchen, in search of coffee. "Actually, it's Georgette. She's what they call a treasure." He poked his head around the kitchen door. "You'll find the shower upstairs. I'll see if I can dig out something for you to wear."

While the coffee was brewing, Bennett turned out his pockets. He spread his sodden banknotes carefully across the bottom of a frying pan and put them on the hob to dry. His passport, he realized, was still on the boat. So was Anna's. If they had any thoughts of leaving Europe, they'd better think again.

The money began to steam. He turned down the gas, went to see if Georgette had considered any of his clothes worth keeping, and laid what there was on the bed. As he passed the bathroom door, he called to Anna to help herself.

It felt good to have her in the house. For a moment, he thought of getting Poe on the phone and telling him to collect the case. Then life would return to normal. He could show Anna the Lubéron, sit in cafés, eat in restaurants without being watched, pick up where they'd left off at lunch on Cap d'Antibes. But of course, Tuzzi was going to be looking for them.

He peeled off his blazer and hung it over a chair in front of the stove. Despite the warmth of the night, he felt chilled and in need of a hot shower. Why did women take so long in bathrooms? What did they do? He found a bottle of *marc* and laced his coffee, holding the cup in both hands as he stared at the banknotes, now beginning to show signs of crispness in the frying pan.

"What's this? Breakfast?" Anna was standing in the kitchen doorway, dressed in a T-shirt and a pair of boxer shorts, barefoot, wet-haired, scrubbed, and smiling. An enchanting waif. Bennett felt his heart give a soft but definite lurch.

"How do you like yours done?" he said. "Keep an eye on it while I take a shower. It's all we've got."

———

"Now then, Sergeant," he said ten minutes later. "Time for a chat." He led her into the sitting room and sat her down. "We have one stolen car, a few thousand francs in cash, my credit cards, and some deeply pissed off Italians who are going to come looking for us any moment now, presuming Tuzzi wakes up. Also, we have no passports. And just to make things interesting, we shall have Poe on our backs once he finds out what's happened—which will be in a few hours, when the boat gets to Marseille and we're not on it. Yes?"

Anna nodded, wide-eyed and solemn. "Yes."

Bennett began to pace across the living room. "But," he said, "we have the case. And the case entitles you to fifty thousand dollars in cash, with a small but welcome reward for yours truly." He stopped pacing to look at her. "Yes?"

"Yes."

"Fine. So as soon as it's light, we wire up our little stolen car, drive over to Poe, give him the case, take the money, and run. Yes?"

Anna shook her head. "No."

Bennett sighed. "I had a nasty feeling you were going to say that." He fetched the bottle of *marc* and poured some into his empty coffee cup. "You've been ducking the question ever since we got off that bloody boat. Now, I like to think I'm a reasonable man." He felt the bite as the *marc* hit the back of his throat. "But since my personal safety and well-being are involved here—or, as you might say, since my ass is on the line as much as yours—I think I have a right to know exactly what you have in that devious little mind of yours."

"Let me have some of that." Anna held out her cup, took a swallow, and shuddered. "Jesus. OK, Bennett, here's what I think." She put down her cup and took a deep breath. "Poe's a crook, right? A rich crook. He's also a mean son of a bitch who screwed up my life for a couple of years. Someday I'll tell you about it. It was bad, believe me. He's a lousy human being."

"And you want revenge. Well, this isn't—"

"Part of it's revenge, sure. I'm human. But I need money for my mother. Fifty grand doesn't go far in America if you get sick. I want more for the case. I want a lot more, and he's got it."

"How much are you talking about?"

Anna held up an index finger. "A million. The case would have fetched at least that in the auction."

"A million? Why not two? Why not five?" Bennett

sank onto the couch, shaking his head. "This is ridiculous. You're going to ask a certified crook and his army of thugs to pop round, hand over a million dollars, and let us go. Why should they?"

"Because they want the case back."

"They can take the bloody case anytime they like."

"They have to find it first." Anna's mouth set in a stubborn line. "Bennett, listen to me. A million is nothing to Poe. It's one lousy deal with his friends in Iraq, or Africa. He'll pay."

Bennett looked at her determined, unsmiling face. The bloody woman was serious. It was a cockeyed scheme, and he'd be insane to get involved in it. They were already in enough trouble with Tuzzi, but at least Tuzzi didn't know where they were. Poe would know where to come looking, and Poe would not be pleased. No, the whole idiotic idea was out of the question. If Anna wanted to go off and play dangerous games with dangerous men, she could damn well get on with it. But not with him, not in a million years.

As if reacting to a signal concluding a meeting, they both stood up. Anna came over to Bennett and took his face between her hands. Her eyes, dark, enormous, liquid in the half-light, were inches from his.

"Bennett. Help me."

He couldn't look away. He felt himself drowning. But a part of him was detached, off to one side, watching with amusement as his resolve faltered, weakened, and collapsed. He realized he'd been holding his breath, his shoulders tense. "Oh, shit," he said, and then again, *"Shit."* And Anna's face lit up.

12

AS the darkness of the sky over Saint-Martin softened to gray, and then to pink, Anna and Bennett considered their immediate problems. They needed a legitimate car. They needed a safe hiding place. They needed a plan. And they had a few hours, no more, of breathing space.

Bennett surprised himself. The combination of *marc,* adrenaline, and Anna's gratitude was turning him from the unwilling fugitive into a figure he'd never expected to become, the man with a mission. He wanted to outwit Poe and Tuzzi. He wanted to collect the million dollars. He wanted to win. He paced back and forth across the living room, thinking out loud.

"Now, a car. We've got a car. It happens to be in Monaco, but I'm pretty sure nobody will be watching the apartment. Why should they? Poe won't know anything's wrong until the boat gets to Marseille. Tuzzi has no reason to connect us to Monaco. We can duck in, pick up my car, and get out. Next question: Where do we go?"

"We can't stay here?"

Bennett shook his head. "It's too close to Poe. Anyway, Shimo knows the house. And besides, we couldn't hide in this village. Everybody would know by lunchtime. Maybe we can find a hotel out in the hills somewhere, but I'm not too keen on hotels, not with Poe's fake policemen wandering around checking the registers. No, I think I know somewhere better." Bennett stopped his pacing and frowned at the case that was next to Anna on the couch. "I don't want to be lugging that around, though. Too risky. We'll leave it with Georgette. It'll be safe with her. Give her something else to polish." He looked out the window. It was light enough to make out the shapes of rough stones in the wall of the house on the other side of the alley. Full dawn was a few minutes away.

"Bennett?" Anna was smiling. She sensed the change in him, from an amiable but uninvolved companion to a true partner in crime. "You're kind of enjoying this, aren't you?"

"Absolutely," he said. "I can't think of anything I'd rather do than be chased around the countryside by bad-tempered men with guns." He picked up the case and switched off the lights. "Let's get going."

Walking quickly through streets that still had the cold stone smell of night, they turned into the cul-de-sac where Georgette lived. Bennett heard the echo of the doorbell inside the house, and then the creak of a shutter being opened. A suspicious face under a turquoise hair net looked down at him from an upstairs window.

"Eh, alors," said Georgette. "The Englishman returns. What's the matter? Lost your key?"

Bennett put a finger to his lips and nodded toward the front door. Georgette sighed loudly, closed the shutter, and came down to let them in.

"This is Anna," Bennett said, "a friend."

Georgette took in the T-shirt, the boxer shorts, and the bare feet, and pursed her lips.

"Now, Georgette, listen. I want you to look after this case for us. Hide it. Tell nobody—it's very important you tell nobody. We'll be back to pick it up soon. There's no time to explain now. Will you do that?"

Georgette looked down her nose at the case, flicked a finger at it. "And in the little valise there, what is so precious?"

"Documents. Business papers. Nothing illegal, I promise—it's just that we don't want to be carrying them around." Bennett tried his most ingratiating smile. "Trust me."

"The whole thing stinks." Georgette nodded with satisfaction, as though she had solved a particularly difficult problem. "Yes, it is without doubt a *magouille*. Are you in trouble?"

Bennett looked at Anna. "Well . . ."

"As I thought," said Georgette. She held out a hand. "Give it to me. I will put it in the *cave,* under the gravel. Something else to worry about, as if I didn't have enough."

"You're a sweetheart." Bennett gave her the case and kissed her. She watched them leave from the doorway, one hand on her hip, the other clutching the case, her suspicious expression at odds with the garish brightness of her hair net.

They hurried through the village, now beginning to show signs of life: cats sidling home after a night out, shutters opening, a warm breath of fragrant air drifting from the bakery, the sound of a radio and some virtuoso coughing in the café, the distant clatter of an ancient tractor being persuaded to start, the church clock whirring and clanging six times. Bennett was glad they had parked the car in a dark corner of the village square, half hidden by the squat concrete box that housed Saint-Martin's public *toilettes*.

As Anna crouched to connect the wires, he crossed his fingers and looked around the square. It wouldn't be long before the elderly ladies whose self-appointed task it was to monitor the comings and goings of everything that moved would be taking up their positions—the more blatant in chairs outside their front doors, the more discreet behind yellowing scraps of lace curtain. The sight of a young woman in gentleman's underwear tinkering with a car would provide material for an entire morning of speculation. Bennett thought of going back to borrow a skirt from Georgette. No. There wasn't time.

The engine spluttered to life, and Bennett breathed again. They coasted down the hill, crossed the N100, and headed east, keeping to the back roads in the hope that the gendarmes of Provence would be fully occupied with their summer work of distributing speeding tickets to the poor and needy on the autoroute.

———

On board the *Ragazza,* now moving slowly toward Marseille, Lord Glebe was preparing to conduct the auction. Tuzzi's bandaged head and tentative walk had been explained as the result of an unfortunate fall after too much champagne. Bennett, so the others were told, was experiencing problems with his backers, and was in his cabin on an extended conference call. However, as Lord Glebe said, plans must be adhered to, they were all busy men here, time was money, and there was no reason why the auction couldn't begin as soon as the merchandise had been inspected.

With the air of a magician fully equipped with white rabbits, Glebe opened the case and presented a view of the contents to the three bidders. "Naturally," he said, "you'll want your specialist chaps to vet everything later, but I'm sure you'll find it's all in order—book of rules, jungle juice, gardening tips, and so forth. But to be serious for a moment"—he adopted the expression of concerned sincerity that he had practiced in the course of many soporific debates in the House of Lords—"I should remind you once again that the purchaser of this case will be able to control the black-truffle market."

Tuzzi crossed himself vigorously. "On the head of my mother," he said.

"Indeed, Enzo, indeed. And God bless the dear lady. Now, whoever controls the black-truffle market can realistically expect an annual income in the millions. I'm sure you've all done your sums, and I'm sure your bids will reflect the potential return—a damned sight better than Lloyd's, even in the old days. Any questions?"

The three bidders studied the row of vials and the dossiers of paperwork with no more than a polite show of interest. They were moneymen, here to buy. Technicians would take care of the details of analysis and verification, and Tuzzi wasn't a difficult man to find if any problems should crop up. There were no questions.

"Splendid," said Glebe. "Multiples of one hundred thousand dollars please, gentlemen. Now, who'll start me off with a nice round million, just to get us warmed up?"

Kasuga lifted a finger. Penato nodded, then Polluce. Kasuga again, and then a pause.

"I have one million three," said Glebe, "which is an insignificant price to pay for a fortune. Come along, gentlemen. I think we can do better than this. Mr. Tuzzi has put a reserve on the case, and I'm afraid the bids are nowhere close so far." He put a hand up to his ear. "Do I hear something more realistic? Two million? What?"

"OK," said Penato.

Another raised finger from Kasuga.

Polluce looked at the expressionless faces of the other two bidders. How high would they go? They were businessmen, looking merely for profit. But he, Polluce, had another, higher purpose: to screw the French. His colleagues in Calvi had given him a mandate to get the formula, whatever the cost. He nodded at Glebe. "I bid for Corsica," he said, and raised three fingers. "Three million."

Glebe beamed. "Well played, Corsica." He rubbed his hands. "That's more like it."

———

Gérard and his partner sat in the unmarked black Citroën outside the Club Nautique, at the entrance to the Vieux Port, smoking and cursing the heat, the tedium, and the chafing of their creased uniforms. Earlier that morning, Shimo had called from the helicopter to tell them that the *Ragazza* was heading for Marseille, but the old tub was taking her time about it, the temperature inside the car was over a hundred, and Gérard was thirsty and uncomfortable.

"Putain," he said. "I could murder a beer."

His partner took off his sunglasses to mop the sweat from his face, and squinted out to sea. A pastis would go down well, he thought, in the bar of the Club Nautique, followed by a decent meal. An enforced diet of sandwiches and pizza over the past few days was playing hell with his digestion. Much more of this, and he'd develop a *crise de transit intestinal;* he could feel it coming. He took the binoculars from the dashboard and trained them on a girl in abbreviated white shorts who was waving at an incoming sailboat. *Merde,* look at the legs on her, right up to her armpits.

Gérard saw the *Ragazza* first, as she came slowly into view and dropped anchor halfway between the mainland and the Île d'If. Before he'd taken the binoculars from his partner, a motor launch had pulled away from the quay and was heading for the big boat. Thank God something was finally happening. He watched the launch come up to the *Ragazza,* where a group of figures waited on the stern. He picked up the car phone and punched in Poe's number.

"They're here. A launch is just picking them up."

Shimo's voice came through the blur of static. "How many? Can you identify them?"

"Wait." Gérard watched the launch turn slowly away from the *Ragazza* before picking up speed. A figure on the stern of the big boat, who seemed to be wearing a turban or a bandage on his head, was waving them off. Gérard adjusted the focus as he picked up the launch. "Four men in the back." The foreshortened images through the binoculars were becoming sharper and more detailed. "One with gray hair. A Japanese. An old man, thin. A younger one, dark hair."

"Is that the Englishman?"

Gérard studied Penato's broad, fleshy features, and compared them with the face he'd seen in Monaco. "No, not the Englishman."

"And the girl?"

"No girl."

The launch drew into the quay. Three men walked across from cars that were parked on the quay and waited at the top of the steps. Gérard continued his commentary. "The tall one with white hair has a case. He and the old thin *mec* are going to a Mercedes. The other two have Citroëns."

"Follow the case. The Mercedes. Keep in touch."

Shimo switched off the speakerphone and lit a cigarette. On the other side of the desk, Poe sat chewing his bottom lip and staring out the window, trying to sift through all the possibilities. Was the man with the white hair carrying the real case or the substitute? Had Bennett and Anna made the switch? Had they been found out? Were they still being held on the *Ragazza,* or had Tuzzi dumped them overboard?

———

The Peugeot limped into Monaco. Bennett coasted into the first spot he could find, and disconnected the engine. They'd been lucky, running on hope for the final half hour, with the fuel gauge showing minus empty.

As they walked up the hill to the Place du Casino, an ancient couple with an elaborately coiffed poodle stopped and stared, shaking their heads with disapproval.

"What's their problem?" said Anna.

"I think you may be contravening the Monaco dress code. I expect it's an indictable offense for a girl to be seen in public wearing a man's underpants. Keep going."

The apartment was exactly as they had left it—coffee cups and breakfast plates still in the sink, bed unmade, empty whisky bottle on the table. Anna threw some clothes in a bag, while Bennett spread out the Michelin map of the coast and the Vaucluse. Where was that place he'd stumbled on by accident last year? Somewhere high, somewhere near Banon.

"OK," said Anna, "I'm all set." She had changed into boots, jeans, and T-shirt, slicked back her hair with water, and she showed no signs of having passed a tense and sleepless night. Bennett folded the map and stood up. They'd head west. The place would come to him later.

The sound of the phone made them both freeze, an instinctive, guilty reaction, as though any movement would give them away to the caller. It rang four times, and then the machine cut in with Bennett's answering message. A beep. Shimo's voice, tinny and precise: "Mr. Poe would like to hear from you. Immediately."

Bennett looked at the clock. Twelve-thirty. The auction must be over. "That's it," he said. "They've found out something's wrong. Let's not stop to do the dishes."

They drove hard, reaching Aix in the midafternoon, hungry, thirsty, and happy to find a table in the cool back room of the Deux Garçons. Outside, on the Cours Mirabeau, an unhurried procession of tourists ambled along under the shade of the plane trees. The seated spectators, mainly university students recovering from their labors, laughed and flirted and tipped their small change onto the table to see if it would stretch to another cup of coffee, another Perrier *menthe,* another hour of café education. Aix had slipped into its summer rhythm, lazy and relaxed.

The beers came, and the *steak pommes frites,* and with the edge gone from their appetites, they tossed a coin to see who would order coffee, who would call Poe. Bennett lost.

He fed the pay phone, and heard Shimo's voice on the end of the line. Identifying himself, he asked for Poe.

"I've been waiting for you to call, Mr. Bennett," said Poe. "I hope you have good news?"

"Well, yes and no." Bennett took a deep breath. "We've got the case, but there's been a slight change in plan. It's going to cost you a little extra to get it back."

Silence from Poe.

"We thought a million dollars was about right, actually. In cash."

Poe laughed, a low, confident, insulting laugh. "You've had your joke, Mr. Bennett. Now, where are you? I'll send Shimo to pick you up."

"I'm serious. A million dollars."

"You're serious, are you, Mr. Bennett? That's foolish of you. That's very foolish. Stop playing games now. Where are you?"

"I'll call again in two days. Have the money ready, or the case gets a new owner." Bennett put the phone down. Smug bastard. He hoped his voice had sounded convincing.

Anna looked up from the map she'd spread on the table. "How was that?"

"I think it's the end of a beautiful friendship."

———

Poe was a man who set great store by self-control, but it was an effort to keep the anger out of his voice as he called the manager of his Monaco bank to arrange the withdrawal of a million dollars. If that shit Bennett thought he was going to live to spend it, he was in for an unpleasant shock. Sooner or later, he'd have to show himself, and then he'd disappear for good. It might be amusing to have him dropped from the helicopter onto the deck of Tuzzi's boat, and let the Italian clear up the mess he'd started. Yes, that would be a neat and symmetrical end. Feeling somewhat cheered by the thought, Poe then sent Shimo off to Saint-Martin. It was unlikely that Bennett would be stupid enough to hide in his own house, but one never knew with amateurs.

———

Bennett's Peugeot crossed the Durance at Pertuis and headed east toward Manosque. As he drove, Bennett told Anna the story of a winter evening the year before, when he'd been scouting for property in the high, sparsely populated country of Haute-Provence. Darkness had been setting in, and after making several wrong turns and bad guesses, he realized he was lost. In a final attempt before giving up, he'd taken a side road. It narrowed, and became a dirt track, but off in the distance he could see a light.

"So I drove toward it," he said, "and I came to this extraordinary place, surrounded by vines, absolutely in the middle of nowhere. If I can find it again, it'll be perfect for us. See if you can find l'Argimaud on the map, just above Banon. It's somewhere round there."

"How do you know we can stay?"

"I spent the night there, and the abbot and I hit it

off. He recognized a fellow believer. Said I could come back anytime."

"You and an abbot? Are you kidding? You don't seem like the religious type."

"Nor is he. But he runs this monastery. You know, cloisters, monks, habits. You'll like him. He's an old rogue, sees himself as a kind of Dom Perignon reincarnated, carrying on a long tradition."

Anna shook her head. "What's that?"

"Monks and booze. These boys take it pretty seriously. The Brotherhood of Bacchus, they call themselves. With a bit of luck, we might get there in time for cocktails at Evensong."

13

AFTER the crowded streets of Aix, Haute-Provence seemed to Anna like another planet, empty, harsh, and beautiful. This was unforgiving country, the soil thin and rocky, trees scarce and stunted from the winds that swept across from the Rhône valley. They drove past fields striped with lavender, the squat clumps huddled together in long, perfectly straight lines; past a herd of goats, their bells giving off a hollow clatter as they were chivied along by two rangy dogs; past faded signs advertising long-vanished aperitifs; past mile after mile of vines.

Traffic dwindled, then all but disappeared, except for tractors grinding home after a day in the vineyards. Figures in the fields straightened their backs and stopped work to watch the car go by, a slow, deliberate turn of the head, eyes slitted against the flat evening sun, an inspection that Anna found uncomfortable and faintly hostile. She tried waving at one of the figures, who stared back without acknowledgment.

"What's the matter with those guys?" she asked. "Haven't they ever seen a car before?"

Bennett shrugged. "That's the way they are in the country. Anything that moves across their patch is their business. It's lucky we're not in Poe's Mercedes. They'd have been talking about it in all the local bars tonight. When you live in a village round here, you can't scratch yourself without half a dozen people saying you've got fleas."

"You like that? Everybody's a stranger in Manhattan. I don't even know my next-door neighbor."

Bennett thought for a moment, about Georgette and Anny and Léon, the petty swindles of Monsieur Papin, the matrimonial ambitions of Madame Joux for her daughter, the café gossip, the endless curiosity. "Yes," he said, "I do like it. I feel as though I'm living with a slightly eccentric family."

Anna touched his arm lightly. "I've screwed that up for you, haven't I? I'm sorry."

Bennett shook his head. "Not at all. You've introduced me to a life of glamour and adventure, meeting fascinating people who probably want to kill me." He braked as the car approached a fork in the road. "I think we're getting close."

The surface changed abruptly from tarmac to rutted dirt as they followed a track up a gentle slope, through clumps of pine and scrub oak that were deformed, seeming to crouch, their backs bent by years of mistral. The car was heading directly into the sun, and their first view of the monastery was a low, silhouetted mass at the end of the track. Bennett pulled in and stopped by a group of dusty cypress trees. Above the tick of the cooling engine, he could hear the insistent, rustling chorus of a thousand invisible *cigales*.

The monastery had been built four hundred years before, in the form of the letter H. "Those are the cloisters over there," said Bennett. "The other side is the dormitory. The big building in the middle is for everything else—kitchen, dining hall, offices, tasting room, distillery, the abbot's apartments. Huge cellars underneath. It's quite a place, isn't it?"

Anna looked at the long, tiled roofline, devoid of crosses or spires. "Is there a chapel? Or do they just pray as they go?"

"Well," said Bennett, "it's not exactly an orthodox religious order. More like a little business, really."

"But they call themselves monks, right?"

Bennett grinned at her. "That's because they get what Father Gilbert calls celestial dispensation from the authorities. He'll tell you all about it."

They walked up a wide path of coarse, pale gravel. On either side, dense rows of lavender filled the area between the two wings of the monastery with a blurred haze of color. Ahead of them, a short flight of stone stairs, the center of each step worn to a shallow groove by the passage of centuries of feet, led up to an iron-studded door of blackened oak. Carved into the deep stone lintel was the credo of the monastery: *In Vino Felicitas.*

Bennett pulled at the handle that hung from a chain next to the door, and heard the double stroke of a bell, muffled by thick stone walls. "Have you ever met a monk before?"

Anna shook her head. "Are they anything like rabbis?"

"I doubt it. Not this lot."

With a squeal from the hinges, the door opened a few inches to reveal a brown face under a frill of white hair. It peered out cautiously, like the head of a tortoise emerging from its shell. "Are you lost, my dears?"

"Actually, no," said Bennett. "We've come to see Father Gilbert."

"Oh?" The face registered surprise, as though Bennett had revealed some secret knowledge. "Father Gilbert, whom God preserve, is tasting. He always tastes before the evening meal, sometimes for many hours. Such is his dedication. But I'm sure you've traveled far to see him." The monk opened the door wider and beckoned. "You must come in." They could now see that he was dressed in a plain, dark-brown robe of heavy cloth, belted around the middle, with a silver tasting cup hanging by a leather thong from his neck. His sandals slapped on the flagstones as he led them through a wide arch and into a long, classically proportioned room, the setting sun throwing bars of light through a row of high, slim windows. The monk stopped Anna and Bennett with an upraised hand.

A dozen brown-clad figures, looking like great hooded birds, were seated around a refectory table. Their heads, completely obscured by the cowls of their habits, were bent over large, bulbous glasses. Groups of unmarked bottles were arranged at intervals along the table. All was silent, except for the sound of air being drawn into a dozen pairs of nostrils.

Anna whispered to Bennett, who whispered to the monk. "What's going on?"

The monk leaned closer to them. "Father Gilbert is leading the brothers in deep inhalation."

"Why are they wearing their hoods?"

The monk put his cupped hands together, lifted them to his nose, and raised his eyes to heaven. "All the better to trap and concentrate the divine effluvium, my son, as it rises from the glass."

"The bouquet," said Bennett to Anna. "They're sniffing the bouquet."

"In pixie hoods? I don't believe it."

Murmurs then began around the table, a litany of comments as the monks reported on the findings of their noses. Bennett was able to pick up snatches, which he passed on to a bemused Anna. "Undertones of vanilla . . ." "Well balanced in fruit . . ." "A certain precocity, don't you think, brothers? Quite forward for a wine of its age . . ." "Spices, brambles, yes . . . un-sophisticated, but promising."

Father Gilbert, at the head of the table, picked up his glass. "Very well, brothers. Hats off, and let's taste the little rascal." He swept the cowl back from his head, and was about to drink when he noticed Anna, Bennett, and the monk.

"But wait. What have we here?" He stood up and put a finger to his chin as he looked at Bennett. "Do I recognize the thirsty traveler from last winter? The Englishman of many bottles? So it is. Come here, my son, come here. Let me welcome you."

Bennett was encircled by an aromatic embrace, in which wine fumes mingled with fertilizer and warm wool, and kissed vigorously on both cheeks. Gilbert's face—large, round, and baked to the color of vintage terra-cotta—was radiant (with pleasure, Bennett hoped, although the lunchtime liter of wine may have contributed to the good father's vibrant complexion). Anna was introduced, welcomed warmly, and taken with Bennett to meet the other monks sitting around the table.

The assembled brethren shared Father Gilbert's ruddiness, some even surpassing him in the high level of color around the nose and cheeks. As they nodded and beamed and raised their glasses, Father Gilbert described their monastic responsibilities. "Brother Luc here is our export sales manager—we do a very respectable fortified communion wine for third-world countries. Brother Yves looks after new-product development, mainly cordials and liqueurs, although he keeps trying to slip in a premium absinthe. Wicked fellow."

Anna looked at Brother Yves, a birdlike little man with a benign expression and a twinkling eye, the very antithesis of wickedness. "What's wrong with that?"

Father Gilbert did his best to look grave. "It's illegal, my child. Has been for many years. But I must admit it's *quite* delicious. If there's any left, we might have a drop after dinner. It settles the stomach and promotes the most delightful dreams."

The introductions continued. There were brothers in charge of everything from packaging and financial planning to marketing and public relations. There was, so Father Gilbert explained, a centuries-old link between monastic orders and the blessings of alcohol. He was merely carrying on the noble work, with the minor difference that he had dispensed entirely with spiritual requirements. This was an equal-opportunity monastery, open to all denominations. Or, to put it another way, a small corporation comfortably installed in a religious tax haven.

"You don't pay any tax?" Bennett asked. "None at all?"

"Good heavens, no. Not a centime." Father Gilbert frowned with distaste. "What a scandalous invention that is," he said. "We have nothing to do with it. Dom Perignon never paid tax. Why should we?"

"You don't make champagne, do you?" Anna said.

"No, my child, we don't. The conditions here aren't suitable. But what is champagne, after all? Nothing but grapes breaking wind, although our friends in Reims would doubtless disagree." And with that, he half filled two goblets with red wine and passed them to Anna and Bennett. "I hope you can join us for dinner. We have a *marcassin* that Brother Louis ran over with his tractor the other day." He smiled at them. "You see? The Lord provides."

"We'd love to," said Bennett. "As a matter of fact, it would be a great help to us if we could stay here for a couple of days. We've got a small problem."

Father Gilbert plucked a bottle of wine from the table and waddled ahead of them to a book-lined alcove off the main room. "Sit down, my dears, and share your troubles with me."

As the brothers set to work preparing dinner, Anna and Bennett went through the events that had led them to the monastery, Father Gilbert nodding over his wine, his mouth making an O of surprise at the account of their escape from the *Ragazza.* "How fascinating it all is," he said after they had finished. "And what exciting lives you young people lead. You're going to find it very dull here, I'm afraid. But tell me something." He waved plump fingers in the air, as if the question were of no great significance. "This formula, this magical serum—is it genuine, do you think? Does it work?"

"So I'm told," said Bennett. "Apparently, it's had a very high success rate—seventy, eighty percent."

Father Gilbert filled his glass thoughtfully. "It would be a most valuable addition to our work here at the monastery. The grape and the truffle, side by side. Who could imagine a more pleasing combination?" He looked at Bennett under raised eyebrows. "I suppose there's no chance of our coming to an arrangement? A partnership of some kind?"

"Well . . . ," said Bennett.

"Absolutely not," said Anna.

"You see, Father," said Bennett, "it's not officially ours. We're just sort of looking after it."

"Just a *pensée,*" said Father Gilbert. "Well, drink up."

———

The young wild boar, basted until it shone, had been spit-roasted in the kitchen fireplace and was now lying on a wooden platter in the center of the table, a large baked potato in its mouth. Father Gilbert carved, and served chunks of the dark, gamy flesh onto plates of battered pewter, the sleeves of his habit rolled up above his elbows, his face glowing in the candlelight. Glasses were filled, and the flat, round loaves of country bread were sliced thick. The only indications of the twentieth century were the two visitors, in their modern clothes. Everything else, everyone else, could have come from the Middle Ages.

The conversation was mainly of country matters—the prospects for this year's vintage, the vagaries of the weather, the threat of mildew on the vines, the productivity of the monastery vegetable garden. There were no arguments, no raised voices to disturb the air of contentment that hung over the table. Anna was intrigued. Where had they come from, these men who seemed happy to live in a medieval time warp?

"We are all fugitives from the world of business," said Father Gilbert. "I myself used to work for the Banque Nationale de Paris. Others have come from Elf Aquitaine, IBM, the Bourse, Aérospatiale. We hated corporate life. We loved wine. Fifteen years ago, we pooled our resources and bought the monastery, which had been empty since before the war, and we became monks." He winked at Anna. "Rather informal monks, as you can see."

She was looking puzzled. "Can I ask you a question? Didn't any of you have wives?"

Father Gilbert leaned back in his chair and considered the shadows cast by the candlelight on the vaulted ceiling. "That was another bond we discovered," he said. "The delights of female companionship are not for us. Remind me—how is that described in your country?"

"Gay?" said Anna.

"Ah, yes. A most inappropriate use of a charming word." He shook his head. "Gay. How ridiculous. I suppose, then, that one could say we are living in a state of perpetual gaiety. That will be a considerable comfort to us all, I'm sure." He laughed and raised his glass to Anna. "Here's to gay days, and many of them."

The cheese was served, and was ceremoniously unwrapped from its covering of vine leaves. But the combination of too much hospitality and too little sleep had caused Anna and Bennett to fall silent, and then to droop. Fending off Brother Yves and his homemade absinthe, they followed Father Gilbert to the visitors' cell in the dormitory wing. He left them with a fresh candle, and a cheerful warning that monastery life started shortly after dawn.

The cell was small and plain: a slit of a window, a table with a jug of water and a bowl, and two narrow bunks placed against opposite walls. Anna stretched out, moaning softly. "I think I may have had too much wine." She sat up and studied her feet. "Do me a favor?"

"A glass of absinthe?"

Anna flinched at the thought. "Pull my boots off. I'll never make it."

Bennett tugged unsuccessfully at one close-fitting boot. "I'm going to have to do this the old-fashioned way," he said. "Excuse the view."

He turned his back to her, straddled her legs, bent over, and eased off the first boot.

"Bennett?" Anna's voice was drowsy. "What you did today, what you're doing . . . I appreciate it."

"All part of the service." He struggled with the other boot.

A soft, sleepy giggle. "And you have a pretty nice butt, for an Englishman."

By the time he had lifted her feet onto the bunk, she was asleep. He reached down and stroked the hair from her forehead, and she smiled, rubbing her head against his hand like a cat, before turning on her side. He blew out the candle. In the warm darkness, he could hear the sound of her breathing. His last conscious thought was to remind himself to ask Father Gilbert if the monastery possessed such an amenity as a double bunk.

14

POLLUCE counted out the five-hundred-franc notes and watched the girl count them again, scarlet nails scratching against the paper, before folding them carefully and putting them in her bag. She had worked hard on him during the night. It had been a pleasant business transaction, at the end of a highly successful business day.

The girl let herself out of the suite, and Polluce picked up the phone to order breakfast. From his window, he could see the Vieux Port and the dark-blue sweep of the Mediterranean beyond. It would be hot again, perfect weather for lunch in the garden at Passédat before flying back to Corsica. Polluce had always liked Marseille.

He showered and shaved and dressed, taking pleasure in the featherweight pale-blue voile of his shirt and the discreet sheen of his linen suit. A man should dress appropriately for his age, he believed. Not like that buffoon Tuzzi, with his absurd caftans and shirts open to his hairy navel. He made a final adjustment to the show of his shirt cuffs, and went to answer the waiter's knock on the door.

Over breakfast, Polluce allowed himself to speculate on the opportunities for mischief and money that the formula would present to him and his colleagues in the Union Corse. Like their fathers and grandfathers before them, they had no great love for their neighbors on the French mainland. Good Corsicans, true Corsicans, wanted independence. If the French wouldn't grant it, then it would have to be taken.

Polluce, who seldom showed any emotion, smiled at the thought of manipulating the French truffle market and extracting millions from French pockets. No doubt the Union would see fit to contribute some of these profits to the Corsican nationalist movement and cause more trouble for the French, trouble funded by their own money. Polluce very nearly laughed, for the first time since his shrew of a mother-in-law had been overcome by too many glasses of Porto, fallen off a barstool in Bastia, and passed away, many years before.

He looked at his watch. In half an hour, he would have the results of the analysis he had ordered the previous afternoon. There was just time for a cigar. Normally, he would never permit himself such a luxury before lunch, but this was a special day, a day of celebration and indulgence. He took a Montecristo from a case of buffed leather and squeezed it gently: fat, almost juicy. Clipping off the end, he lit it carefully and drew in the first mouthful of heavy, fragrant smoke.

The ash was getting close to the chocolate-colored band with the simple white letters that Polluce found so plain and pleasing, and he was taking in a final mouth-filling puff, when his visitors arrived: Bruno, his young cousin and personal bodyguard, and Arrighi, the analytical chemist, a gaunt, long-faced man wearing somber clothes and a lugubrious air.

After the pleasantries, Arrighi put the case down, looked at Polluce, and shook his head slowly from side to side. "I regret to tell you that this"—he waved a contemptuous hand at the case—"is not what we were expecting it to be. The documents are meaningless. A collection of statistics that one could obtain for a hundred francs from the Société Agricole."

There was no change in Polluce's expression as he laid his cigar to rest. "And the serum?"

"Water, mixed with ordinary herbicide. All it would do is kill a few weeds." He spread his hands wide and raised his bony shoulders. "I am desolated."

Polluce stared out the window, his face tight with the effort of concealing his anger. That Italian clod and his tame aristocrat, they must have known. They had deceived him. Controlling the outrage that only a crook can feel when swindled by other crooks, he dismissed Arrighi and told Bruno to wait downstairs with the car.

He placed a call to Tuzzi's office in Cannes and was patched through to the *Ragazza*.

"Tuzzi? Polluce."

"Eh, my friend, how are you? Missing life at sea?" Tuzzi put his hand over the mouthpiece and told a deckhand to fetch Lord Glebe.

"I think you know why I'm calling."

Tuzzi did his best to sound puzzled. "Did you leave something on the boat?"

"No games, Tuzzi. I had the formula analyzed. It's *merde*. It's weedkiller."

There was an explosion of bogus surprise from Tuzzi. "This I cannot believe! *Non è possibile!* Wait— here is coming Glebe." Taking care to speak loud enough to be heard on the other end of the line, he launched into a torrent of explanation. "My friend Polluce, he says the formula is no good, there has been a trick. He has been bimboozled! He is in shock. I am in shock. What can we do? I swore on the head of my mother. My good name has been dragged in the pavement—"

"Gutter, old boy," said Glebe. "Here, let me speak to him."

Tuzzi passed over the phone and leaned forward attentively as Glebe began the story that they had agreed on the night before.

"Glebe here, Mr. Polluce. This is all most unfortunate, I must say. *Most* unfortunate. But it explains certain events that have occurred here on the *Ragazza*, events that have been puzzling us since last night. Do you remember the Englishman Bennett, and the girl?"

"Of course."

"When I returned from our little meeting in Marseille yesterday, they had disappeared—secretly, and in a hurry. Nobody saw them go, and they left everything in their cabins. We believe they must have swum ashore. Are you with me, Mr. Polluce?"

Polluce was going to have to report this to his Union colleagues. He began to take notes. "Continue."

"Now it makes sense, d'you see? They must have taken the contents of the case—the real formula—and replaced them with counterfeit material." Glebe's voice became indignant. "Mr. Polluce, we have all been deceived. All of us," he repeated solemnly. "They must be brought to justice. They must suffer consequences." Glebe frowned at Tuzzi, who was pumping a fist in the air and smiling broadly. Damned excitable Italians.

"They will suffer," said Polluce. "But we have to find them."

"I don't think they'll have gone too far. They were in such a hurry they left their passports behind. We found them in their cabins."

"They may be forgeries."

"Impossible," said Glebe. "One of them is British."

Polluce scrawled a name on his notepad. "Get them to me. I have associates in the police. With the passports, they will have something to work with."

"The police?" said Glebe. "Don't know about that,

old boy. Do you really think we ought to involve them?" Tuzzi was shaking his head violently, an expression of horror on his face.

"Monsieur Glebe, half the police in Cannes are Corsican, some true Corsicans among them. We have collaborated in the past."

Glebe looked at Tuzzi and nodded. "Splendid, splendid. That's settled, then. Marching shoulder-to-shoulder with the boys in blue. We'll put in to the nearest port immediately, and you shall have the passports by tonight. Where are you staying?"

Polluce gave the address and phone number of his hotel. "By tonight, yes?"

"An Englishman's word is his bond, my dear Polluce."

"Does that apply to Bennett?"

"Afraid he's a bounder. Probably got smacked by his nanny, or went to the wrong school."

"Merde." Polluce replaced the phone in disgust and went downstairs to his car. On a matter of this importance, it would be best to speak to the captain face-to-face. He told Bruno to turn up the air-conditioning and head for Cannes.

———

Tuzzi leaned over and pinched Lord Glebe on the cheek, a mark of approval that his lordship found thoroughly distasteful. "Bravo, my friend, bravo. What a performance! I think I call you Machiavelli."

Glebe wiped his cheek and lit a cheroot. "It did seem to go rather well, I must say. We'll leave it for twenty-four hours, and then call Polluce and tell him that we've found out Bennett's working for Poe. That should put the cat among the pigeons."

"Pigeons?"

"Never mind, Enzo, never mind. Figure of speech." Glebe blew a plume of smoke into the still air and smiled. "I dare say, in all the excitement, you've overlooked the most important thing."

"Eh?"

"Polluce forgot to ask for his money back."

Tuzzi smacked his forehead with the palm of his hand, then opened his arms wide. "Maestro! I kiss your feet!"

"Please don't," said Glebe. "The crew will start to talk."

15

POE looked up from his desk as he heard the chop of the helicopter coming in from Monaco, bringing with it a million dollars that he was determined Bennett and that ungrateful bitch would never spend. Normally, he was a man who was prepared to wait for his satisfactions, a man who subscribed to the view that revenge was a dish best eaten cold. But this was trying his patience. There had been years of humoring the dreary little scientist, with his constant demands for more time, more money, more praise. Then to have it all threatened by a clown like Tuzzi. And now to be double-crossed by two amateurs, with their pathetic games of hide-and-seek. Well, they had a surprise coming their way. The thought of it improved his mood, and he was whistling as he went downstairs to meet Shimo.

The Japanese unzipped the cheap nylon case, and Poe watched as he emptied the neat bundles of hundred-dollar bills onto the table. "I hope you'll be taking those back very shortly, Shimo. I'd hate to lose them. They have great sentimental value."

Shimo nodded. "This will bring them into the open, and then we have them. Has the Englishman called?"

"Not yet." Poe picked up the bag and examined the inside. "Where do you think we should put it?"

Shimo took from his pocket a small plastic box, half the size of a pack of cards. "We can sew it into the bottom lining, here in the corner, under the money. Range is not long, maybe five hundred meters, but anything more powerful would be too big to hide."

Poe smiled as he looked at the homing device in Shimo's hand. "Watch out, Bennett. You're being paged."

"Mr. Julian, something worries me." Shimo put down the homing device and lit a cigarette. "Suppose the Englishman is dealing with others, for more money. Suppose he is dealing with Tuzzi."

Poe had to admit that it was possible. In fact, it was exactly what he would do if he were Bennett: try his luck, see if he could make an extra few hundred thousand dollars from a couple of phone calls. "You're right, Shimo," he said. "Perhaps I'll have a word with Mr. Tuzzi. He might let something slip. God knows, he's stupid enough."

———

Tuzzi and Poe exchanged elaborately courteous greetings on the phone, as though they were old colleagues catching up after a prolonged separation. They were delighted to find each other in good health—Tuzzi avoiding any mention of the painful matter of his still tender testicles—and reassured each other about the continuing success of their businesses. Then Poe came to the point.

"Enzo," he said, "it appears that you and I have been the victims of a robbery. I think you know what I mean."

"The formula?"

"Exactly. It has been stolen from you once, and from me twice—although I'm prepared to overlook that and let bygones be bygones."

"*Bene, bene.* We are practical men, you and I. Civilized men."

Poe tried to keep the contempt out of his voice. "Indeed we are, Enzo. And above all, we are businessmen. So what I propose is that we join forces to find the Englishman and the girl, pool information, that sort of thing. What do you say?"

"My dear friend"—Poe recoiled at the phrase—"this is for me great honor, to work hand and glove with such a man as yourself." His voice became conspiratorial. "Tell me, do you hear anything from them? Has there been any contact?"

Poe looked at the piles of banknotes stacked in front of him. "Not a word. How about you? Anything to go on?"

Tuzzi thought about the passports, now on their way to Polluce in Marseille, and the imminent involvement of several Corsican police officers. He sighed loudly. *"Niente.* They disappear into the air, *pouf,* and leave us nothing. Now we must look for a pin in a haystack, no?"

"You have men out looking?"

"Of course. And you?"

"Of course. Well, we'll keep in touch, then, shall we?"

"My information is yours, my friend. On my mother's head."

Tuzzi was smiling broadly as he put down the phone. It had crossed his mind more than once that Bennett and the girl might have gone straight to Poe with the formula, which would have been a serious complication. But now all he had to do was find them first, and with Polluce and his friends in the police, the odds were promising. He gave orders for the *Ragazza* to turn back to Marseille. The girls on Ibiza could wait.

Poe hadn't expected too much from the conversation, and on principle distrusted anything Tuzzi said. But he was sure that if the Italian had held a trump card, he would have been unable to resist hinting at it, or trying to sell it. So it was a race to find Bennett and the girl, and they'd already made contact. Poe, too, estimated the odds as promising. He resigned himself to spending the rest of the day by the phone, waiting for news.

———

Anna and Bennett had slept late, and they found the monastery deserted by the time they came to the kitchen in search of coffee. The brothers were all at work in the vineyard, the distant chug of their tractors as steady and soporific as the buzz of bees in the lavender.

Anna waited for a pan of water to boil on the wood-burning stove, while Bennett hacked at the remains of a *boule* of unleavened bread. Their morning so far had been a mixture—slightly awkward for both of them—of intimacy and self-conscious, polite formality. They had taken turns in the large, open stone bathing area at the end of the dormitory, each staying discreetly in the cell as the other stood under the biting cold water. They had shared soap. They had shared a rough towel. A tension had developed between them that hadn't been there before, a nervous anticipation of what might or might not come next. A Frenchman or an Italian would have made a pass. Bennett made toast.

Anna looked at him as he frowned with concentration at the hunks of bread slowly browning on the cast-iron hob. His hair, still wet from the shower, was combed straight back from his tanned forehead, giving him the look of a sepia photograph from the 1920s.

She could imagine him in baggy whites, swinging a wooden tennis racket. He speared the bread with the point of a knife and flipped the slices over. "Tricky stuff, toast," he said, looking up at her. "It's all a question of timing."

"Isn't everything?"

Bennett looked at her for a moment without speaking, and realized he was smiling at her smiling at him. "Yes," he said. "I suppose it is."

The water in the pan bubbled, and Anna looked away. "Where do you think monks keep their coffee?"

They had breakfast on a stone bench in the shade of the cloisters and considered the next move. It was one thing to demand a million dollars; it was quite another to work out a safe way to collect it. Poe would have a man watching for the pickup, probably more than one. A public place, such as a railway station, would provide temporary security, but the minute they left, they'd be at risk. An isolated spot, with no witnesses, would be even more dangerous. As the morning wore on, and possibilities were examined and discarded, they began to feel that they had maneuvered themselves into a cage.

With a final mechanical shudder, a tractor came to a stop by the cypress trees. Brother Yves, who was on cooking duty, had returned early from the vineyard to prepare the midday meal. Bennett watched the monk hurry up the path to the entrance, mopping his head with a large spotted handkerchief. It must be damned hot in that habit, Bennett thought. And then it came to him.

He got to his feet and began to pace, head down, his hands clasped in front of him. "Anna," he said, "listen to this. It could work. We tell Poe to leave the money in a church—there are dozens around here, all shapes and sizes, most of them deserted except on Sundays."

Anna frowned. "I don't know," she said. "A church would be good, but they'd catch us coming out." She saw the expression on Bennett's face. "Wouldn't they?"

"That's just it. We won't go in. We'll get Father Gilbert to pick up the cash for us. They're expecting a man and a woman. They won't look twice at a monk going into a church."

Anna nodded slowly, then raised an imaginary hat. "Bennett, you crook, it's a pleasure doing business with you."

"We need a guidebook for church-spotters. Come on. We'll get one in Forcalquier."

———

With a guide to churches and historic monuments open on the table between them, they sat in a café behind the Place du Bourget and drank *rosé* and allowed themselves to feel hopeful. Bennett had selected three or four possible churches, which they would reconnoiter in the afternoon. They'd choose one, call Poe, and then deal with the task of persuading Father Gilbert to become an ecclesiastical bagman. And this, unfortunately for Bennett, was where Anna began to have misgivings.

"It's an awful lot of cash," she said. "And you hardly know the guy. Do you trust him?"

Bennett stared into his glass. He himself had said that Gilbert was an old scoundrel, a tax dodger, a businessman masquerading as a monk. He remembered trusting Brynford-Smith with the boat, and sighed. "Well, I'm not sure."

"That means you don't." Anna shook her head. "And neither do I. Not with a million bucks."

Deflation set in. Bennett finished his wine, and signaled the waiter for more. The café was beginning to fill up for lunch—shopgirls in their summer dresses, beefy, broad-faced men taking the obligatory two-hour break from their offices, a pair of off-duty *gendarmes*. The smell of garlic and steak and frying potatoes came from the kitchen, and a scrawny dog stopped in the doorway, his nose twitching hopefully before the waiter cursed him away.

Anna suddenly snorted with laughter, and covered her mouth with her hand.

"Now what?" said Bennett. "It was almost a great idea."

"It still is. Don't you see? All we need is the right monk, a reliable monk, the kind of monk you'd trust with a million dollars. And I happen to know just the guy." She leaned forward and put her hand on his shoulder. "Brother Bennett." She laughed again. "I love it."

———

Polluce and Captain Bonfils took an inside table at the back of the Poisson d'Argent, one of the half-dozen restaurants clustered around the Palais des Festivals, and ordered Ricard. Bonfils was known here, known to use the restaurant as a setting for confidential business discussions. The owner, who valued the patronage of the police in these dangerous times, would make sure that the tables next to them would remain empty. They could talk.

"Chin." Bonfils sipped his pastis, his eyes, from years of habit, never still, always watching the room. His progress from a uniformed *flic* on the Croisette to a captain in a suit had been rapid—helped, it had to be admitted, by Polluce and his friends in the Union. Strings had been pulled. Occasionally, such favors had to be repaid. This was normal. He looked at the dapper old man across the table and inclined his head respectfully. "You have come from Marseille in this heat. The matter is urgent, *non?*"

Polluce studied his manicure for a moment while he decided how much it was necessary to tell. "Urgent, and perhaps delicate. Something valuable has been stolen from my friends and me, something very valuable. It is essential that it's recovered." He traced a line with his finger down the sweating glass in front of him. "Luckily, we know who has it, a man and a woman, traveling together. By tonight you shall have their passports." He gave Bonfils a thin smile. "Useful clues, I would imagine."

"If they're genuine. Of course, Monsieur Polluce, you realize that with the EEC, it is not as good for us as it used to be—Italy, Spain, Belgium, they can drive straight through, no controls." Bonfils took a pack of Gitanes from his pocket and broke the filter off a cigarette before lighting it. "But the passports will be helpful, certainly. Are they French?"

"One British, one American."

Bonfils clicked his tongue against his teeth. He hated anything involving foreigners. One had to be so careful. He remembered the young *connard* who had been picked up as a vagabond last year and thrown in the can. It turned out that his uncle was the German ambassador, and the desk sergeant had been hauled over the coals and put back on the beat. "That's not good—unless they're French residents. You know? Registered. If they are, they'll be in the computers, and we can pull everything, from the date of birth to the color of their car."

"And of course, you'll have their photographs." Polluce leaned forward, tapping his finger on the table for emphasis. "They must be found. It would be most beneficial for your career, I can promise you."

16

BENNETT hadn't set foot in a church for years. Like many Englishmen of his background, he felt that any business he might have with the Almighty could be conducted with a minimum number of appearances at the head office. He paused inside the doorway to accustom himself to the unfamiliar surroundings.

Memories often return through the nose. As he inhaled the odor of sanctity, a blend of ancient dust, mildewed prayer books, and crumbling stone, Bennett was taken back instantly and vividly to his school days. He remembered Sunday mornings spent fidgeting on hard pews while the chaplain ranted from the pulpit, delivering impassioned warnings about the sins of the flesh that served only to inflame the curiosity of his youthful flock. Bennett's father, a man who preferred funerals to weddings—"Shorter service, and you don't have to send a present"—had provided a poor spiritual example on his infrequent visits to the school. These had ended one day after he informed the chaplain, over a glass of tepid sherry, that religion was responsible for more war, torture, death, and misery than anything else in recorded history. Bennett had then enjoyed a brief period of fame as the only boy whose father had ever been expelled from the school.

He shook his head to clear away the ghosts, and started to assess the church's suitability as a drop zone. He would be arriving and leaving on foot; they needed to find a church that was not too isolated from its environment, one that didn't require a long, exposed walk while clutching a million dollars. On the other hand, a busy church, filled with pious but sharp-eyed and curious worshipers, would be equally risky. This one certainly wasn't right. He called across to Anna, who was studying a stained-glass window depicting the mortification of a backcountry saint. "I don't think this is it, do you? It's too small. Maybe we should go for a cathedral."

For the rest of the afternoon, they shopped for churches, stopping at Banon and Simiane-la-Rotonde and Saint-Saturnin before turning up toward Mont Ventoux. While Bennett drove, Anna went from the guidebook to the map and back to the guidebook again, as she picked her way through dozens of chapels and abbeys, hospices and basilicas. Finally, she struck what she hoped was gold.

"Listen to this," she said. " 'Notre Dame de Poulesc, overlooking the main square of a bustling market town.' " She shook her head. "Why do market towns always have to be bustling? Can't they do anything else but bustle? Anyway, it sounds pretty good. Ready for the guided tour?" In a mock-professorial voice, she quoted from the book: " 'Saint Catherine was buried at Poulesc, and the rediscovery of her body in the late twelfth century prompted the construction of the church. This became such a popular place of pilgrimage that it had to be greatly enlarged in the sixteenth century. The south portal, though stripped of its sculptures during the Revolution, is the most notable survival of the Romanesque structure, and the nave is thought by many to be one of the most eloquent interpretations of the Gothic style in Provence.' " Anna looked up from the book. "I hope you're taking notes. It gets better.

" 'The nave has side chapels containing fine examples of seventeenth-century stained-glass work, and the relics of Saint Catherine are contained in the restored twelfth-century crypt.' " Anna closed the book. "So it's big, it's on the town square, and it has all these little alcoves along the side of the main building. Sounds good, doesn't it? And we're almost there. Stay on the D943, and we'll hit Poulesc in about five miles. This is the one, Bennett, trust me."

He smiled at her enthusiasm. "I did. Now look at the mess I'm in."

"You'll make a very cute monk, you know that? Except for one thing."

"If you think I'm getting a tonsure, forget it." Bennett glanced at Anna's puzzled expression. "A haircut with a hole in the middle."

"That's OK. You'll be wearing the hood. No, the problem is you're too skinny. Monks are fat, right? Jolly, like Friar Tuck and Father Gilbert." She looked at Bennett's lanky body for a moment and then slapped her hand on the dashboard, making him brake instinctively. "That's it. Here's what we'll do—we'll give you a stomach with a bunch of clothes. You unload those in the church and stick the money up there instead. You go in fat, you come out fat, nothing in your hands. How about that? Where would you be without me?"

Bennett's eyebrows went up at the thought. "Oh, I don't know—having a quiet, pleasant life in Monaco, driving a Mercedes, fighting off the girls, eating wonderful food, sleeping in a comfortable bed . . ."

She leaned across and kissed him on the cheek. He felt her breath warm and soft against his ear. "Asshole."

———

Poulesc sat placidly in the glow of early evening, a Provençal country town waiting for a postcard photographer. At one end of the square, a group of men in cloth caps and faded shirts cheated and argued and laughed over their *boules* game beneath the umbrella of shade cast by a row of plane trees. Anna and Bennett stopped to watch as the exchanges became more and more heated, the gestures more and more agitated.

"I thought this was a nice quiet game for nice quiet old men," Anna said. "Look at those guys. They sound like they're going to murder each other."

"I've never seen it get to that. But it's a savage game. Croquet's the same. Players do hideous things to their opponents." Bennett pointed to a man stepping up to the mark that had been scratched in the gravel. "See the one in the green shirt? I think he's going to bomb the other side."

Green Shirt bent into a crouch; the hand holding the *boule* swung back once, twice, then threw. The steel sphere rose in a steep, high arc, glinting silver in the sun, before landing with a clack among the other *boules,* knocking one of them away from its position next to the small wooden target ball. Jubilation on one side, consternation on the other. The men scuttled up the court to assess the situation, to take measurements, to dispute.

"How long does this go on?" asked Anna.

"Hours. Days. Until it gets dark, or their wives come and drag them away."

"It's easy to have a good time down here doing nothing, isn't it?"

"That's not doing nothing. That's living. It still goes on in the country."

"What do you mean?"

"They have this quaint idea that there's more to life than work and television." Bennett shrugged. "I'm not saying they don't have their problems—you can hear them moaning every day in the cafés about everything from the price of bread to the government's nuclear policy—but they know how to enjoy themselves. They play their *boules,* they hunt, they laugh a lot, they're addicted to conversation, they spend hours at the table." He smiled, his eyes still on the game. "Who else but the French would have an orgasm over a sack of truffles?"

Anna looked at the smile on his face as he watched the antics of the *boules* players, and she wondered what would happen between them when this enforced intimacy was over, when they could stop running. Would she go back to New York alone? Would he go back to his village? She didn't want to think about it. She tucked a hand under his arm. "I hate to say this, but we've got a church to check out."

Housewives crossed and recrossed the square, walking briskly between the butcher, the *épicerie,* and the baker as they made their selections for the evening meal. "See?" said Bennett. "They're bustling, just like it says in the book." Under the café awning, a young, dark waiter flirted with two blond girls with backpacks and German accents. Cars were parked everywhere, in the haphazard fashion of the Midi, cars half on the pavement, cars backed into impossibly small spaces, or cars simply left in the middle of the street, lights flashing, while their owners threw back a fast, belly-to-the-bar drink before going home. And on the west side, where it had been taking the last of the day's sun for hundreds of years, was the church.

It was deserted, cavernous, shadowy—the perpetual twilit gloom, almost like part of the architecture, that seems to settle on religious institutions after a few centuries. Anna and Bennett made their way down the long nave, flanked by rows of empty pews, then split up to explore the small, even darker chapels off to each side. There were discreet hiding places everywhere—black nooks, forgotten corners, crannies behind massive stone buttresses where the dust had lain undisturbed for months, maybe years. Bennett scribbled some notes in the margin of the guidebook and then walked toward the altar.

"*Psssst.*"

The hiss cut through the silence, an arrow of sound that made Bennett stop dead.

"Over here."

Off in a corner, at the very back of the church, he saw the shape of a narrow, dark opening, a flash of white from Anna's T-shirt. He made his way up the steps, behind the altar, and through a doorway barely the width of his shoulders.

"Bennett, this is *perfect.* Look."

They were in a tiny, square room, with a table and chair against one wall, a row of ramshackle wooden coat hooks nailed to the other; it was a primitive dressing room, where the priest could change into his Sunday vestments. And, on the outside wall, the cause of Anna's excitement: another door, which she had unbolted and left ajar. Bennett pushed it open. It gave onto an alley, running along the back of the church in either direction before connecting with streets that led into the square. It would allow him to enter the church unseen, and leave unseen. Yes, it was perfect.

They celebrated with a beer in the café, and on the way back to the monastery settled on a hiding place for the money. Tomorrow they would call Poe with instructions. They would pick up the million and head across the border to Italy. It would all go like clockwork.

———

Dinner with the monks was more than usually convivial, Father Gilbert having decided that the '92 vintage was ready for serious and prolonged examination. The bottles came and went, each one, by common consent, even more agreeable than the last, and by the time Anna and Bennett excused themselves from the table, they were buzzing pleasantly from a combination of alcohol and optimism. On their way out, Bennett picked up the spare habit lent by Father Gilbert—not without raised eyebrows and an arch invitation to join the brotherhood on a permanent basis, young blood being so hard to come by—and they walked down the lavender-scented path to their cell.

Anna sat on the edge of her bunk, her eyes bright in the candlelight. "OK, young man. Let's see what kind of a monk we can make of you."

"Now?"

"Sure."

Bennett held the habit up against himself, feeling its heaviness. "Go ahead," said Anna, "put it on. I need to see how much room we have to fill in the front."

He undressed down to his shorts and shrugged his way into the thick, suffocating wool. It was like being in a tent made for one. He gathered a handful of material, held it away from his stomach, and turned so that Anna could see him in profile. "This year," he said, "fitted cassocks are out. The fashion is for a looser, more casual look, topped off by a hint of intrigue around the head." He pulled the cowl forward until it covered most of his face. "How's that?"

Anna smiled at the baggy, shapeless figure, now totally unrecognizable as Bennett. "I was right," she said. "You are a cute monk. Now let's fatten you up."

She took jeans and T-shirts and a cotton sweater, and bundled them into a ball, which she stuffed, with some difficulty, down the neck of the habit. The ball settled at chest level. They looked at each other, two suddenly serious faces separated by Bennett's new and pronounced bosom.

"I think it needs a little adjustment, Miss Hersh." Bennett's voice was husky.

"I know." She knelt down, and looked up at him. "I'm going to have to ask you to lift your skirt."

He tensed as her hands slid up to his chest. He felt her breath against his stomach, the tip of her tongue on his skin. A soft giggle, muffled by the folds of cloth. "It's starting to get crowded down here."

He curled his fingers in the short hair on the nape of her neck and gently pulled her to her feet. Smiling, flushed, she slipped the cowl back from his head.

"Bennett? Will you take that damn thing off?"

17

CAPTAIN Bonfils, scenting promotion, had lost no time in ransacking the computers. Polluce would be pleased. He closed the glass door of his office, and used his private line.

"Nothing much comes up about the girl," Bonfils said. "Standard U.S. passport, entered the country four days ago through Nice, no criminal record. But we've had some luck with the Englishman." He broke the filter off a cigarette and lit it before reading from the notes he'd made. "Bennett, Luciano. British citizen, French resident with a valid *carte de séjour,* files taxes describing himself as *profession libérale,* current address Saint-Martin-le-Vieux in the Vaucluse, drives a white '93 Peugeot 205, registration number 29 SKN 84. Seems clean, no criminal record."

Polluce grunted. "He has now." It was ironic, he thought, that the highly developed French bureaucracy, so often his enemy—with its irritating, nosy insistence on knowing and recording every fragment of a man's personal and business life—had become a temporary ally. At least now he'd have something encouraging to tell his colleagues in Calvi. "It's a start, Bonfils. It's a useful start. Now what?"

"I'm doing the maximum, Monsieur Polluce. Details are being circulated already—photographs, everything. We have a good chance, as long as they haven't left the country. I'll call again as soon as anything comes up."

"*Bon.* You've done well. I won't forget."

Bonfils put down the phone with a sense of satisfaction, but it was short-lived. His office door opened, and Moreau, holding a sheaf of papers, came in and stood in front of his desk, sucking the pipe that never seemed to leave his mouth. Moreau was his chief, a foreigner from the Charente, a stickler with a reputation for tiresome incorruptibility. There was no love lost between the two men. Moreau was aware that Bonfils had influential friends helping him up the ladder, and that his rank didn't reflect his ability. This grated on Moreau, causing him to keep a close and critical eye on the Corsican. For his part, Bonfils hated Moreau's guts almost as much as he wanted his job.

Moreau tossed the papers onto the desk. "I'm sure you have an explanation for all this"—he nodded at the bundle of printouts—"but I find myself puzzled. It seems that the department has suddenly given priority to an alleged robbery, without knowing what has been stolen. Not helpful, is it? How are the men supposed to know what they're looking for? Sloppy work, Bonfils. Very sloppy."

Moreau, as usual, was doing his best to make Bonfils feel guilty, or incompetent. Now the bastard was staring at him as if he'd been caught with his hands in the till. Bonfils kept his voice flat. "We were tipped off about the couple. I'm waiting for a full description of the stolen goods."

Moreau's pipe made soft, wet sounds as he stared down at Bonfils. "So am I, Captain. So am I. See that it's on my desk this afternoon, without fail." He collected the papers and left, shaking his head as he went through the door.

Merde. Bonfils decapitated another cigarette. If Polluce hadn't told him, it was because Polluce didn't want him to know. Which probably meant drugs. Suddenly, it was turning into a lousy morning. He pulled out the number of Polluce's hotel, and picked up the phone.

———

A hundred miles away, Anna and Bennett were wedged together in a *cabine* in the Poulesc post office, giving each other moral support of a physical nature while they waited for the call to go through. Bennett removed his mouth from its lingering investigation of Anna's neck as Poe's voice came on the line.

The conversation was brief and cold and to the point. The money would be left in the church, following Bennett's instructions, by five o'clock that afternoon. Once it had been safely retrieved, Poe would be told where he could pick up the case. It was all over in three minutes.

For the second time that morning, they walked through the church, stopped by the hiding place, went out by the back door, checked the street where Anna would be waiting in the car. They left Poulesc and drove down to Simiane-la-Rotonde, to a little restaurant with a four-star view, for their first lunch as lovers. And, in the way of new lovers, made plans.

Italy was to be the first stop. They'd apply for replacement passports and lie low in style at the Villa d'Este. Once the passports had come through, they'd go to Switzerland, where they'd find a quiet little bank in which to deposit the money. And then . . . well, then they had the world.

Anna reached across the table and took Bennett's sunglasses off. "That's better. Now I can see your eyes. You know I have to go back to the States, don't you? For a while, anyway. Will you come?"

Leaving Saint-Martin, with a vengeful Julian Poe a few miles up the road, wouldn't be a problem. Leaving France would be harder. But being apart, Bennett realized, would be worse.

He pushed the carafe of wine aside and covered her hand with his. "Of course I'll come."

"Sure?"

"Just promise me one thing," he said. "Don't ever ask me to wear a baseball cap."

They ordered coffee and pulled their chairs over to the stone wall at the edge of the terrace. Below them, the land fell away steeply, and then dipped and rolled toward the mountains of the Lubéron, fuzzy in the haze of afternoon heat. The countryside was a painting, a muted wash of colors framed in blue. With Anna's head on his shoulder, Bennett looked into the distance and pictured the future, and he liked what he saw.

———

They stopped on the road outside Poulesc. Bennett disappeared into the bushes, and came out a monk—a rotund monk, with a substantial girth supported by a leather belt. They had decided that a paper stomach would be lighter and cooler than a bundle of clothes, and the bunched-up pages of half a dozen copies of *Le Provençal* prickled against his skin. He eased his way into the passenger seat. Tense and silent, they drove slowly into town, stopping a few streets away from the church.

Bennett took a deep, nervous breath. "Wish me luck." Anyone passing would have seen the unusual sight of a young woman kissing a man of the cloth firmly on the lips. With a final adjustment to his belt, Bennett pulled up his cowl and set off for the alley behind the church, hands clasped in front of him, head down, his paper belly rustling softly as he went.

The alley was in deep shadow as he turned into it,

and he had to blink to accustom his eyes to the change from the sun's glare. He reached the door to the church, looked quickly from left to right. Nobody. He turned the handle and pulled. Idiot. Doors open inward. He turned the handle and pushed. His stomach went into spasm. Someone had bolted the bloody thing since morning. He'd have to go in through the front.

Out in the main square, Gérard and his partner sat in the simmering heat of the car, the volume control of the receiver turned down, a low, steady signal coming from the homing device in the bag they had left in the church earlier. Gérard wished his partner would stop bitching about how hot he was. "You think it's bad for us," he said. "Imagine being that poor bastard, wrapped up in a blanket." They watched as the portly figure of a monk hurried up the steps and into the church. "It's enough to make anyone an atheist." He looked at the blank, uncomprehending face next to him and shook his head. "Doesn't matter. Don't wear yourself out thinking about it."

———

Bennett stood at the end of the nave. In front of the altar, an old woman rose from her knees and went to light a candle. He waited. She turned, came down toward him, and nodded respectfully. "Father," she said. Bennett had a moment of panic. What the hell was he supposed to say? He nodded back. "Bless you, my child, bless you." She smiled her thanks. Wonderful what a uniform could do, he thought.

He ducked into the second of the side chapels and reached into the space behind a blackened reliquary. His fingertips touched nylon, and he let out a long, grateful breath. His hands were nervous and clumsy as he unbuckled his belt and substituted a million dollars for yesterday's news, stuffing the bundles of newspaper out of sight, where the bag had been. Forcing himself not to run, he went up the nave and out through the back door. Less than two minutes later, he was in the car, wired with adrenaline. He took Anna's hand and placed it on the tightly packed bulge of his stomach. "How does it feel to be a millionaire?"

————

Gérard turned up the volume control on the receiver. The signal had faded. The case had been moved. He started the car, then winced as the whine of the signal suddenly increased. A white Peugeot came from a side street and drove across the square. As it drew away, the signal began to fade again. "*Putain!* There must be a back door." He pulled out and went after the Peugeot, keeping his distance.

————

Bennett unbuckled his belt, letting the bag fall through his legs onto the floor of the car. He unzipped it, and started whistling softly as he stared at the bundles of hundred-dollar bills, more cash than he'd ever seen in his life. Anna was grinning, driving fast along the twisting road that led up into the hills and the safety of the monastery, tapping her fingers on the wheel in time with Bennett's whistled version of "The Man Who Broke the Bank in Monte Carlo." "We did it," she said. "We goddamn well did it."

Bennett turned his head to look through the rear window. Nothing but the shimmer of heat rising over emptiness. He felt the adrenaline rush subside and exhilaration take over. "I happen to know," he said, his mouth close to Anna's ear, "that in the Villa d'Este, they have enormous beds with linen sheets."

"And room service?"

"*Endless* room service. Dinner in bed, tomorrow night. How does that sound? Better than a bunk?"

"Now he's complaining. You spoiled rich guys are all the same." She braked, and turned up the track that led to the monastery. "Personally, I thought we did OK in the bunk."

———

Bennett left Anna counting the money while he got out of his habit and stood under the primitive shower, letting the chill of the water wash away the strain of the last couple of hours. This time tomorrow, they'd be out of France, away from Poe and Tuzzi, out of trouble. He dried himself and dressed and padded back to the cell, the flagstones smooth and cool beneath his bare feet.

Anna was still arranging piles of banknotes on one of the bunks, systematically checking each bundle to make sure that Poe hadn't substituted cut paper. She looked up as Bennett came through the door. "So far, so good," she said. "Isn't that a pretty sight?" She rummaged in the bag for the last bundles, and then Bennett saw her smile change to a frown.

"What's the matter?" he said. "Did he forget to leave a tip?"

"There's something here, in the corner." She turned the bag inside out. "See? There." They looked at the small patch of tightly stretched lining, and Bennett poked at it with his finger, feeling its shape. "It's like a box."

Anna fetched a nail file from her toilet kit and unpicked the stitching until she could rip the lining away. Taking out a black plastic oblong, she held it up to the light, her face grave. "I've seen something like this before, in Israel. Some guys used to carry them on patrol."

"What is it?"

"It's a short-range homing device." She tossed it onto the bunk, on top of the money. "Jesus. It means Poe's goons have been tracking us. They know where we are. And they're not far away."

18

BENNETT was the first to break the silence, hoping to find a glimpse of silver in the cloud. "It could be worse. At least Poe doesn't know that we've found it. Also, he's not going to do anything until we tell him where we've hidden the case. Otherwise, they'd have picked us up on the road."

Anna looked unconvinced. "Maybe they're just waiting until it gets dark. Then they grab us, take us somewhere quiet, and . . ." She shivered. "He's a mean son of a bitch, believe me. He could make us tell him."

Bennett thought of Shimo's thumb puncturing the bamboo. He picked up the homing device and weighed it in his hand. "Supposing we smashed it?"

"If the signal stops, they'll come looking. They'll know we found it."

As the evening began its slow fade into night, with the cell and the mood of its occupants turning increasingly gloomy, they went over their options, and found little to encourage them. Unless they left on foot, there was only one way out of the monastery:

down the track to the road. And somewhere down there, Poe's men would be waiting.

"Look, we don't actually know that," said Bennett. "I mean, they might have missed us. What do you reckon the range of that thing is?"

"I'm not sure. Could be half a mile."

"OK. So to keep us within range, they'll have to be waiting on the road—if they followed us, and we're not certain they did. So that's what we need to know." He stood up and ruffled Anna's hair. "I'm going to go down and have a look. Pack the money in your bag. I'll be back in a few minutes."

"Bennett, be careful."

He put on his shoes, and what he hoped would pass for a confident smile. "I took a course in advanced stealth in the Boy Scouts. Won a prize for tiptoeing."

He stood by the side of the cloisters, listening to the night, letting his eyes adjust. Coming from the main building behind him, he could hear Father Gilbert's laughter, and the thud of an iron pot on the top of the stove. Ahead, the stony track was a pale smear between the inky smudges of bushes and trees. Better keep off the track. If Poe's men decided to close in, that's the way they'd come. He started to pick his way through the undergrowth in slow motion, placing one foot down, transferring his weight before moving the other, his arms stretched out in front of him, a wide-awake, apprehensive sleepwalker.

It took him ten minutes to reach a point where he

overlooked the road, with its odor of warm tar and rubber. Able to see nothing, hear nothing, he waited, hoping for a car to pass. Another ten minutes.

Finally, two yellow shafts in the sky, and the sound of an engine laboring up the hill. He knelt down, keeping his eyes on the approaching tunnel of light. And there it was, a split-second shining of glass as the oncoming headlights caught the windshield of the car that was backed off the road, half hidden between tall clumps of broom, no more than fifty yards away. He'd seen enough.

———

Anna heard his footsteps, and met him at the door of the cell with a hug of relief. "I was beginning to think you'd stood me up."

"Somebody's down there, parked off the road. Couldn't miss us if we tried to get out, even without headlights." He made a feeble attempt to be cheerful. "Feel like a walk?"

"Where to?"

"Italy." He sat on the bunk, fingering the homing device.

Anna leaned over and took it from him. "Couldn't we use this? You know, as a decoy."

Bennett stared at it, nodding slowly. "Sure. We'll give it to Father Gilbert and tell him to run like hell."

Anna's eyes opened wide, and she started to smile.

"Bennett," she said, pulling him to his feet, "sometimes you're smarter than you think. Come on."

———

Father Gilbert put down his glass. "Let me be sure I understand this, my dears," he said. "You want me to take this empty bag and drive in a tractor across the fields—"

"Parallel to the road," said Anna. "That's very important."

Father Gilbert frowned at her. "It may well be important, my child, but it's very rough country, and in the dark . . . well, our tractors are old and rather fragile. I'd hate to damage one. So easily done, you see, among the rocks." He paused to take more wine. "Savage, savage rocks. Why, only last year we lost something vital from a tractor's lower regions, and that was only a few meters from the vineyard. Just out of interest," he said, with a sly smile, "would this nocturnal mission that you're suggesting have anything to do with the affair of the truffles?"

"Well . . . yes," said Bennett. "In a way."

"So I dare say that a considerable sum of money is involved." The old monk gazed pensively into his wine. When he looked up, there was an acquisitive twinkle in his eye. "If you could see your way clear to helping the monastery . . ."

Bennett fielded the hint. "Absolutely." He looked

at Anna. "Be delighted to, wouldn't we? What do you have in mind, Father?"

"Two new tractors?"

"One," said Anna.

"A John Deere?"

"It's a deal."

A quarter of an hour later, with a wad of hundred-dollar bills safely under a flagstone beneath his bed, and the bag containing the homing device between his feet on the floor of the tractor, Father Gilbert set off. He was to follow, as closely as possible, the direction of the road below the monastery for two or three kilometers, and leave the bag under a bush before coming back.

As soon as he saw the tractor's single dim headlight reach the far end of the vineyard, Bennett began to walk slowly down the track, Anna fifty yards behind him, driving almost blind in the darkened car, navigating by the white blur of Bennett's shirt.

———

Gérard zipped up his fly and stretched before getting back behind the wheel. It had been a long, hot day, and it looked like he was beginning another long night in a string of long nights. His partner, head back and mouth gaping, was snoring at a level loud enough to drown the sound of anything less piercing than a siren. Gérard shook him awake, then leaned forward to the receiver. Was it his imagination, or was the signal getting weaker? He turned up the volume, cocked his head. *Merde.* It was definitely fading. So they couldn't be coming down the track, and there were no roads leading anywhere else—at least, not on the map. They must be going across country, to pick up the road farther along. Left or right? He'd soon know. He started the engine and pulled away to the right.

From the slight rise halfway down the track, Bennett saw headlights come on, move off down the road, and round a bend, following the general direction taken by Father Gilbert's tractor. He ran back to join Anna in the car. They coasted down to the road, lights still off, and waited until the last of the other car's glow had gone from the sky.

———

Bennett had suggested they catch a few hours' sleep in Cavaillon before taking the long drive down the autoroute to Italy, but he had misjudged the eagerness of provincial hotel owners to provide hospitality to late arrivals. It was past midnight, and Cavaillon was not receiving visitors. After trying unsuccessfully to raise a sign of life from every hotel they could find, they resigned themselves to spending the night in the municipal parking lot.

Anna settled her head on Bennett's shoulder. "You really know how to spoil a girl, don't you?"

Bennett stroked her hair and smiled in the darkness. Tomorrow would be different.

———

Cavaillon is a *routier* town and a market town, and several of the cafés are open at dawn to provide an early jolt of caffeine for the truckers and a breakfast Calvados for the all-night market workers. Anna and Bennett unfolded themselves from the car and eased the stiffness from their backs in the cool morning air. From the parking lot, they could see a café in the Cours Bournissac, almost opposite the *gendarmerie,* that was already crowded. Bennett found a table while Anna went to experiment with the sometimes complex arrangements of café plumbing.

A few more hours, Bennett thought, and they'd be home and dry. He wondered how long Poe's men would lie in wait for an empty bag under a bush. They'd been lucky that Anna had found the homing device, luckier still that she knew what it was. Fate seemed to have changed sides.

At the next table, a crew-cut man with forearms like miniature thighs was turning to the sports section of that morning's edition of *Le Provençal*. Bennett glanced casually at the front page that was held up four feet away, expecting to see the usual early-summer mixture of Tour de France news, *boules* championships, and local politics. Instead, he found himself transfixed, staring with horror at a photograph of his own face.

Anna's was there, too, under a headline in large, screaming type: HAVE YOU SEEN THIS COUPLE?

Bennett jerked his eyes away, fighting the urge to run, forcing himself to stay calm, willing the man to fold the front page back. He put on his sunglasses and kept his head down. Where the hell was Anna?

She emerged from the back of the café, shaking her head as she sat down. "Boy, I thought the monastery bathroom was medieval. You should see this place. Unbelievable." She noticed Bennett's strained, fixed expression. "What's the matter?"

He leaned close, and whispered. "Keep your voice down. Put on your sunglasses. We've made the front page. Let's go."

They stood for a moment outside the café. Across the road, the morning shift was arriving at the *gendarmerie*. Keeping their heads averted, Bennett and Anna walked quickly back to the parking lot. He left her in the car, summoned up his nerve, and stepped briskly into a *bar-tabac,* feeling as though he were wearing a foot-high Wanted sign across his chest. The woman behind the bar, bleary-eyed and surly, took his money for the newspaper without looking up, shrugging as he left without his change.

They sat in the car and read the article. After the breathless excitement of the opening—foreign couple sought to assist in official inquiries concerning an important robbery, police mobilized *partout*—there was a paragraph of padding about the crime rate in Provence, and then a number to call. Anyone with information would be put straight through to Captain Bonfils in Cannes, who was in charge of the investigation. There were vague hints of an unspecified reward.

For once, the journalists had succeeded in getting the details correct. All the details: their names, ages, height, color of eyes and hair, the make and color of the car, the registration number.

"Jesus," said Anna. "Where did they get all this stuff?"

"Our passports and my car papers. Tuzzi must have given them to the police." Bennett stared out across the parking lot. Cavaillon was waking up. Outside the corner vegetable market, a woman in slippers and an apron arranged her produce in neat, multicolored pyramids, and wound down the awning to shade them from the sun. A traffic policeman yawned as he checked his first parking meter of the day. "Well," said Bennett, "we can't stay here. The autoroute's five minutes away. Do you feel like risking it?"

"Do we have a choice?"

They drove out of Cavaillon, crossed the bridge over the Durance, and started the descent to the autoroute. Bennett could see trucks lining up to pass through the tollbooths and—just beyond them—a sight that made him brake violently and wrench the car onto the shoulder.

"Shit and disaster. Look at that."

There were six tollbooths marking the entrance to the autoroute. Opposite each booth stood a *gendarme,* arms folded, facing the oncoming traffic. An orderly, sinister row of six of them, identical in their *képis* and sunglasses and short-sleeved blue shirts.

"They may not be looking for us," said Bennett. "They do this a lot in the summer. But it's too much of a coincidence. We can't take the chance."

Anna stayed silent as Bennett committed an illegal U-turn and drove back toward Cavaillon. Poe was looking for them. Tuzzi was looking for them. Now the police were looking for them. Dinner in bed at the Villa d'Este seemed a long way away.

19

MOREAU knocked the dottle carefully from the Cogolin briar that his daughter had given him on his last birthday, the pipe that would see him into retirement. Once again, as he tamped down a refill of fresh tobacco, he went over the notes that he had made during the briefing from Captain Bonfils (Polluce having been forthcoming after the captain described his predicament). Yes, he thought. It was possible. It was entirely possible. He remembered reading somewhere that the government had been trying for years to find exactly what Bonfils had described to him.

He lit his pipe and stared through the grimy window of his office into the bright sunlight that, according to the bureau of tourism, warmed the streets and beaches of Cannes for three hundred days a year. How he disliked the south—the violent colors, the preposterous vegetation, the lack of snow, the smiling, slippery, *swarthy* Mediterranean character. He was counting the months until he could retire to the house his mother had left him in the Charente, where both the climate and the inhabitants were altogether more temperate and reasonable. And to retire with distinction, to retire after a successful *coup*—that would be a bonus.

He opened his address book, flicking through pages covered in his cramped, meticulous script until he found the number of his old friend Chevalier, another Charentais. Chevalier was a civil servant, a senior mandarin in the Ministry of Agriculture, a man whom Moreau knew to have high and serious connections.

After the customary regrets that they hadn't seen each other for far too long, Moreau came to his reason for calling. "It appears," he said, "that someone might have succeeded in producing a formula for truffle cultivation. I'm told that it has been thoroughly tested and that results have been achieved, very convincing results. Now, *mon vieux,* in your opinion— your expert opinion—is this likely?"

There was a moment of consideration before Chevalier's measured, politician's response. He always spoke with qualifications, as though what he said might be taken down and used in evidence. *"En principe,* there is no reason why such a discovery could not have been made, although I must tell you that we here in the ministry have sanctioned many experiments of a similar nature in the past." He made a daring concession to candor. "All of them have been disappointing." He paused for a moment, to recover from making such an uncharacteristic admission. "That, however, does not preclude the possibility that such a formula might be developed by, let us say, an unauthorized specialist, working independently of the government. And naturally, if that were the case, we would be most interested." Another pause, this time for emphasis. "Should it be genuine, this formula, it is crucial that it falls into the right hands."

Moreau had no difficulty guessing what that meant. "Yours, for instance."

There was a chuckle from Chevalier. "Indeed, my dear Moreau, indeed. If we were able to regulate the production of truffles, there would be considerable interest at the very highest level." The final words were spoken in capital letters. "As you know, our president is from Corrèze—one might almost say a country lad, as long as one says it very quietly—and I think he would be more than happy to see the exploitation of one of France's natural treasures come under official control. There would be feathers available for various caps, Moreau. Principally yours and mine. When could you let me have the formula?"

Moreau explained the circumstances, with Chevalier interrupting occasionally to ask for clarification, or more detail. Moreau could sense that the ministry man was becoming increasingly excited—as far as career politicians ever allow themselves to be—and their conversation ended with Chevalier's promise to call back after dipping in a toe, as he said, to test the presidential waters.

To Moreau's astonishment, this happened within an

hour. The president was intrigued. No, more than intrigued; he was adamant that this agricultural secret
weapon should not be allowed to escape the clutches
of Mother France. Every effort was to be made,
Chevalier said, to find and apprehend the two fugitives and recover the formula. French gastronomy
could be at stake here, and every conceivable re-
source—including, if necessary, the entire garrison
stationed at the army base in Draguignan—was to be
put at Moreau's disposal.

Bonfils was summoned to Moreau's office and
given his instructions. More police must be brought
in, priority directives and photographs distributed to
all *gendarmeries,* additional checks on every major
road, vigilance everywhere, and promotion for those
making the arrest. As Bonfils got up to leave, Moreau,
his pipe sending up a string of smoke signals, put
through a call to Draguignan, and Bonfils heard him
ask for the commanding officer.

Bonfils was a worried man. This was getting out of
hand, and well beyond his control. He sat at his desk,
shredding cigarettes, putting off the moment when he
would have to report back to Polluce. The *army,* for
Christ's sake. All available police in the Midi. Heli-
copters, roadblocks, red alerts. There hadn't been a
manhunt like this on the coast since the legendary
bank robber Spaggiari had jumped out of the judge's
office window onto a waiting motorcycle and escaped
from Nice. They never did catch him, Bonfils thought,

with a most unprofessional twinge of admiration, as he picked up the phone.

Polluce was far from sympathetic. His voice, never warm, today was arctic. "I am relying on you, Bonfils. My colleagues also. I must know everything that happens. As soon as you know it, *d'accord?* As soon as you know it."

Merde. What the hell was he supposed to do now? Whatever happened was certain to cause him grief, either with Polluce or with Moreau. He was in the chocolate up to his eyebrows. As he started to carry out his instructions, Bonfils couldn't help but hope that the *putain* Englishman, his *putain* girlfriend, and the *putain* formula were all safely out of France.

———

The countryside around the hamlet of Buoux, to the north of Bonnieux, is remarkable for the beauty of its secret valleys and vast horizons, its solitude, and the uncounted dozens, possibly hundreds, of abandoned *cabanons* and *bories*—the small stone shelters that were used by goatherds and hill farmers before the arrival of mechanized agriculture. Many of them are now not much more than walls (a building with a roof being subject to tax), or beehive-shaped piles of stones, and it was midmorning by the time Anna and Bennett found what they had been looking for.

They had driven up an overgrown track that led to a clearing where, some centuries before, a low stone hangar had been constructed, extended, patched up, and eventually left to fend for itself against the elements. Half the roof had collapsed, and the walls were bandy with age, sections of them held together only by spiky coils of brambles. But there was space at one end to hide the car, there was shade from the sun, and they were a comfortable few miles away from the nearest *gendarme*.

Ever since seeing the roadblock on the autoroute outside Cavaillon, Bennett had been preoccupied, scraping his mind for ways of escape that didn't depend on a car, or expose them to checks at airports or train stations. Earlier, he had joked about walking to Italy. Now it had to be considered as a possibility. What would it be like—skulking around villages, keeping off the main roads, ducking and diving, sleeping rough? It wouldn't be easy walking, either. They'd be doing well if they covered twenty miles a day. God, it would take them weeks. He was staring at the map when he felt Anna's fingers, kneading the knot of tension that had settled at the back of his neck.

"You know something? You haven't said a word for ten minutes."

"Sorry." He made an effort to smile. "Not my usual sparkling self, I know. But we are in a bit of a jam."

Anna looked at him with wide, serious eyes. "Bennett, I know this may not be the best moment to tell you." She leaned over and kissed the frown on his forehead. "But I'm starving."

When had they last eaten? Bennett couldn't remember, and now he became aware of the void in his
own stomach. "You're right," he said. "We'd better
get something." The prospect of activity, however
trivial, made him more cheerful. "Come on. We'll go
to Apt. Don't forget your false mustache."

They went over to the car. Bennett squatted down,
took a handful of earth, spat in it, and rubbed the
muddy paste over both number plates until the white
letters and numerals were less prominent. As he was
getting in, his eye was caught by the bag on the back
seat, the million-dollar bag. He reached over and
pulled it out, took it into the hangar, and buried it
under a pile of rubble in a dark corner, a puzzled Anna
looking on.

He came back, wiping earth and cobwebbed dust
from his hands. "I don't want to carry it around Apt,
and it's safer here than in the car. Do you know," he
said, as he started the engine, "in the summer, there's
a car stolen in the Vaucluse about every five minutes.
The crooks can't wait for September, so they can take
some time off."

His mood had changed. Something would turn up,
as it always had at the right moment over the past few
days. He was feeling lighter, more hopeful, lucky. He
rested one hand on Anna's thigh and squeezed gently. "Right. I'm taking orders for breakfast, lunch, and
dinner. What are you having?"

"Croissants," she said. "Two ham sandwiches,

pizza, some of that great greasy roast chicken they do here, french fries, cheese, a bottle of red wine—"

"No sausage?"

"Saving that for lunch."

They crossed the D232 and dropped down the twisting back road that led into Apt from the south. The outskirts of town were thick with cars and vans and the underpowered, undersilenced, maximum-decibel motorcycles so dear to the hearts of French teenagers. It was Saturday, Bennett realized, Apt's weekly market day, a good day to get lost in the crowds.

He disputed possession of a parking space with a florid couple in an English car, and heard their squawks of indignation as he nosed in ahead of them. *"Typical!"* said the woman, in a voice like an irate bugle. "Just typical! We saw it first. *Dreadful* little Frenchman, pushing in." Bennett nodded and smiled at her as he turned off the engine. Another nail in the coffin of the *entente cordiale.*

They made their first stop, on Anna's suggestion, at a small shop behind the market, which sold espadrilles, baskets, cheap and almost authentic Provençal pottery made in Taiwan, corkscrews with twisted olive-wood handles, and a variety of hats. Anna's theory was that hats would provide at least some element of disguise, something to distract the eye from the two faces that were displayed so prominently on the front page of newspapers. She chose a modified straw fedora; Bennett, a flat cotton cap of the kind worn by almost every old *boules* player in France. With their new purchases pulled down over their sunglasses, they went in search of nourishment— hand in hand, the young couple enjoying their summer vacation.

The Apt market stretches and sprawls from one side of town to the other, spilling into small *places* and tight streets, offering everything from postcards and souvenirs to lawnmowers and wasp traps. And on stalls, on trestle tables, in tiny aromatic shops, there is food. Anna had never seen anything like it. There were goat cheeses, moist and mild and milky white, or hard and pale yellow from months in an olive oil marinade. There was fresh tuna, cut to order in thick, bloody slices from an entire fish the size of a young boy's body. There was bread—*fougasses, ficelles, boules, pompes à l'huile*—made with olives or rosemary or cheese or pork scratchings. There were rainbow displays of fruits and vegetables. There were butchers who specialized in the cow, the pig, or the horse. And, strolling through this pleasant abundance in the Saturday sunshine, grim and alert, there were the police.

Bennett noticed that the local *gendarmes* had been reinforced by men normally reserved for use against rioters and terrorists, men from the CRS: hard faces, silent-soled boots, and dull black guns. He also noticed something that made him stop short, before steering Anna abruptly into a café.

"I'm an idiot," he said. "I should have thought of it before." His fingers drummed an excited tattoo on the table as he looked through the café window. "Over there, the other side of the street. See that bus? It's going to Spain. There's a regular service in the summer."

They watched as the bus pulled away from the curb. "Next stop Barcelona," said Bennett. "No passports required. I knew someone who did it once. The lavatory blocked up outside Perpignan, but otherwise he said it was fine. What do you think?"

Anna looked at the enthusiastic, grinning face under the blue cap, a schoolboy with two days' stubble. She grinned back. "I'll pack my castanets."

Bennett went off to the tourist office, leaving Anna to order. It was strange to think that a week ago she didn't know him; now she felt they were joined at the hip, a pair. She asked the waiter for coffee and croissants, and watched the slow swirl of humanity outside. No bustlers there, whatever the guidebooks said. She tried to imagine Bennett in New York, in her small apartment on Wooster Street. Was he house-trained? Probably not. From what she'd seen, he was a domestic disaster. Did it matter? Not a bit.

Ten minutes later, he was back, less happy than when he'd left. There were no more buses today, none on Sunday, and as Monday was devoted to a particularly well-regarded saint and was therefore a public holiday, there were no buses on Monday—not from Apt, not from Avignon, not from Cavaillon. There was nothing to do but hide out in the ruin and wait until Tuesday. They made up a shopping list on the back of a beer coaster, and went to join the rest of the world in the market.

————

Bennett followed Anna up the steep side street to the *place* where they'd parked the car, holding several blue plastic shopping bags that contained enough food and wine for an extended three-day picnic. The delay was a disappointment, but nothing more, and at least they wouldn't be on the run. As he watched the swell of Anna's buttocks under their tight skin of denim, he thought of the river that ran along the bottom of the valley below Buoux. Once it was dark, they could go down there and bathe, take the blanket from the car and a bottle of wine, lie naked under the stars— yes, he thought, there's something to be said for a weekend in the country. He was humming softly as he quickened his pace to catch up with her.

They put the plastic bags on the roof of the car. Bennett smiled at her as he dug in his pocket for the keys. "You're doing it again," she said.

"What's that?"

"Leering."

He pulled his sunglasses down his nose and winked at her. "Inspired by your spectacular *derrière,*" he said, "I was planning a moonlit swim, naked as nature intended, followed by a midnight picnic. Unless you have a previous engagement."

Before she had time to answer, the side door of the nondescript, unmarked van parked opposite slid open. They looked around, and found themselves staring at four *gendarmes*.

20

"THE glasses and hats. Take them off."

The *gendarmes,* brawny in their summer blues, stood in a loose semicircle in front of the car. The opaque mirror lenses of their sunglasses—motorcycle cop sunglasses, impenetrable and sinister—glinted beneath the peaks of their *képis.* As Anna and Bennett stood bareheaded and blinking against the glare, one of the *gendarmes* took a sheet of paper from his shirt pocket, unfolded it, compared the photographs with the faces, and grunted.

"Bon. No doubt about it. Make sure they're clean." Probing, suspicious hands, moving slowly and methodically, made their tours of inspection, and came up with nothing more lethal than Bennett's car keys. The senior officer jerked his head in the direction of the van. "Get in." He turned to the youngest *gendarme.* "Desfosses—you follow us in their car."

The van was a Saturday-night-roundup special, with a heavy steel-mesh partition separating the front compartment from the passengers. There were no seats in the rear. A bar ran down the center of the ceiling at head height, to which anyone considered dangerous or unruly could be handcuffed. As the driver pulled away, Anna stumbled, and caught hold of Bennett's arm for support. They looked at each other, eyes glazed with shock. It had happened so quickly. Now it was all over. Above the crackle and whine of static, they could hear the driver talking to headquarters. "The Englishman and the girl, we just picked them up. No problems. Get the medals ready, eh? Tell the captain. We'll be there in ten minutes."

The van picked up speed as it left Apt and took the N100 heading west. The three *gendarmes* in the front lit cigarettes and started to argue about Marseille's chances in the next soccer season. Anna and Bennett might have been two sacks of potatoes in the back, bundles of no particular interest to be delivered.

"What are we going to say?"

Bennett shook his head. "I wish I knew. As little as possible, I suppose. Plead ignorance. Demand to see the British consul. I don't know."

"How about telling them the truth?" Anna thought for a moment. "All we've done is try to recover stolen property and give it back to the owner."

"Give it?"

"Well, something like that."

They fell into a dejected silence for the remainder of the journey, and there was nothing cheering about their destination. The *gendarmerie* at Les Beaumettes, despite its window boxes bright with flowers, had the same effect on Bennett as all official institutions. It made him feel guilty. And this time, he was.

They were taken to a windowless room at the back of the building, where they were asked to confirm that their names were Hersh, Anna, American, and Bennett, Luciano, English. Their monosyllabic answers were noted down. They were locked in and left alone to wait. An uneasy hour passed.

For the captain of the *gendarmerie,* it had been an hour of triumph, an hour to be savored. Moreau, over in Cannes, had been most generous with his compliments about the diligence and alertness of the men from Les Beaumettes. The captain had done his best to be modest. Part of it was always luck, he'd said, but he allowed himself to admit that he'd trained his lads well: check, check, and check again. There was no substitute for dogged, routine police work. And young Desfosses, barely dry behind the ears, had proved it. After examining the plates of every white Peugeot 205 he could find, more than thirty of them, he'd hit the jackpot.

Best of all, from the captain's point of view, a helicopter was on the way from Cannes to pick up the two suspects and relieve him of any further responsibility. An uncomfortable thing, responsibility, particularly if foreigners were involved in what seemed to be an important case. One never knew. He looked at his watch, glad that he'd tipped off the boys in Cavaillon. The photographer and the reporter should have arrived by now, ready to record a dramatic moment in the fight against crime.

The captain was well aware of the stimulating effect of publicity on a police officer's career, and this, no doubt about it, would be front-page stuff. Pity it was going to be too late for the Sunday edition. He went over to the small mirror hanging on the back of his office door. Should he wear his uniform jacket? Perhaps not—best to be seen as the working cop, indifferent to appearances. He made some minor adjustments to his mustache, and went outside to add his authority to the controlled chaos taking place on the N100.

The problem had been finding somewhere for the helicopter to land. The hill behind the *gendarmerie* was impossible, the vineyard on the opposite side of the road being sacred and untouchable. And so the decision had been made to block off the road in both directions so that the helicopter could touch down within twenty yards of the building. The N100 being an important trunk road, and Saturday being a market day, the ensuing dislocation of traffic was, as the captain noted approvingly, *impressionant.*

Lines of cars and trucks and mobile homes stretched away in both directions under a wavering cloud of fumes. Several drivers had left their cars and walked up to the cordon of bright-orange cones that blocked the road, hopeful of seeing the remains of a spectacular accident. On finding the tarmac disappointingly free of bloodstains and wreckage, they demanded information from the *gendarmes,* who took considerable officious satisfaction in telling them nothing. There was much gesticulating. Shoulders, hands, and voices were raised. Tempers frayed audibly.

All of which was recorded by the reporter and photographer, who, acting under instructions from the captain, had installed themselves on the roof of the building, the better to appreciate the *vue panoramique* of the great clog of vehicles that extended as far as the eye could see. And now, right on time, thrashing its way in from the east, came the helicopter.

It hovered, dropped, and settled itself gingerly, as if it were testing the temperature of the tarmac. With a nod in the direction of the photographer—it would be tragic if he missed the moment—the captain gave orders for the suspects to be brought out. He personally led the escort group, giving the camera a long, tough, crime-fighting glare *en passant.*

Anna and Bennett felt as though they had stumbled into a war zone. Surrounded by armed and uniformed men, they walked to the squat military helicopter, its olive-drab paintwork flat and dull in the sunlight. Inside, more armed and uniformed men directed them to two steel-framed seats in the back and strapped them in. The helicopter lifted off, and tilted back toward the east. Below them, they could see the diminishing figures of *gendarmes* removing the road cones and beginning to wave the traffic through. Nobody had spoken to them. They had barely spoken to each other. There was nothing much to say.

———

The front page of Saturday's edition of *Le Provençal* had attracted greater interest than usual among certain of its readers in the Vaucluse. The entire village of Saint-Martin was in a stew of speculation about the activities of its English resident. The table of old men in the café had clubbed together and, for the first time in Léon's memory, actually paid for a newspaper. They huddled over it like buzzards around dead meat, shaking their heads and sucking what remained of their teeth. *Foreigners.* An unpredictable bunch, foreigners, more than likely up to no good. What had he stolen, this Bennett?

Papin at the post office, the one-man intelligence bureau, had his theories, which he was more than happy to share with his clientele, who were more than happy to listen. Drugs, he said, with the conviction that comes from total ignorance. A quiet enough fellow, the Englishman, but appearances were often deceptive. Still waters ran deep. *Beh oui.* It was undoubtedly an affair of narcotics. Ordinary, everyday burglary, of the kind that flourished in that sink of iniquity, that cesspit of depravity on the coast, would never have made the front page.

Georgette, of course, her intimate domestic connections with the fugitive giving her a certain cachet, was assumed to know more than anyone else, which she did. The case buried under the gravel in her *cave* was, she was certain, the stolen item. Having closed her shutters and locked her door against the insufferable curiosity of her neighbors—why couldn't they mind their own business?—she disinterred the case and spent an extremely frustrating half hour trying to find the combination that would reveal the secret. She was quite sure that her Englishman, her little *milor,* hadn't committed anything more serious than a misdemeanor; it wasn't in his nature. And yet . . . well, there was never an omelet without some broken eggs. She shook the case in frustration, hoping to hear a clue—the chink of coins, the rich rattle of jewelry— but the contents, whatever they were, had been too tightly packed. She knelt on the floor of the *cave,* put the case back in the shallow depression she had scooped out, and smoothed the gravel level. She would try again later, when there was less chance of being disturbed by people with nothing better to do than pry.

———

Julian Poe, whose taste in newspapers ran more to the *Wall Street Journal* than *Le Provençal,* had read the piece on Anna and Bennett with great interest but no particular alarm. After all, he knew where they were. He had them bottled up in Haute-Provence, under close surveillance. Gérard had called in to say that the signals from the homing device were still coming through, regular as a heartbeat. Nevertheless, this waiting was tiresome. If they hadn't made a move by nightfall, he'd send Gérard in to pick them up and bring them in. As a rule, he avoided violence, which he considered a crude last resort. But his patience wasn't infinite, and he had decided that Bennett should spend a few hours with Shimo, an irresistibly persuasive man when he put his mind to it. By this time tomorrow, both the case and the money would be back where they belonged. With the sense of satisfaction that comes from a problem neatly solved, Poe turned his attention to Tuzzi, and revenge. That Italian clod needed to be taught a lesson.

————

Two police cars were waiting at Mandelieu airport to meet the helicopter, and the ride into Cannes, with traffic melting away in obedience to the blare of klaxons, was brief. Anna and Bennett, still dazed by the speed with which they had become official captured criminals, still bewildered by high-security treatment more suited to terrorists than to amateur thieves, clutched hands for comfort in the back of the car, their emotions deep-frozen. They might have been driving to their own execution.

They were taken into what is euphemistically known as the reception area of police headquarters in

Cannes—hard-edged and hostile, with a whiff of fear hanging in the air—and booked. Pockets were emptied, prints taken; they were processed like two pieces of human flotsam. The desk sergeant reached up to the bulletin board where their photographs were on display, ripped the sheet down, and tossed it into a bin. Another hunt over, another case solved.

Captain Bonfils, casual in blue jeans and open-neck shirt, came through from his office in the back and stood scowling at them. If the cretins had to be caught, why couldn't they have let it happen on a *sacré* weekday, instead of screwing up his weekend? He motioned them over with an irritable flick of his hand, and led them down the corridor to Moreau's office.

———

Moreau thought of himself, with some justification, as a man with a gift for cross-examination. Over the many years and thousands of hours he had spent squeezing information out of criminals, sifting lies from half-truths, coaxing confessions, he had developed his technique, refined the rhythm of his questioning, sharpened his skills of observation. The instinctive clenching of a hand, the sudden blink of an eye, the involuntary shift of position in a chair—these said as much to him as words. He thought of interrogation as a form of chess, a gradual, often indirect, series of moves that ultimately led to a position of no escape. Checkmate. He liked to take his time, something Bonfils seemed incapable of learning. Bonfils, now sitting over to one side, notebook on one knee, was essentially a shouter, a threatener, a man who wore his violence on his face.

Moreau studied the couple sitting opposite him. Good-looking, he thought, both of them, but showing signs of strain around the mouth and eyes. That was encouraging. He took his pipe from his mouth, and smiled.

"So, Monsieur Bennett. It appears you no longer have the Rolls-Royce."

Bennett hadn't known what to expect, but certainly not this. "The Rolls-Royce?" His mouth was dry, his voice thin and defensive. "What Rolls-Royce?"

Moreau pointed with the stem of his pipe at the objects arranged on his desk: passports, cash and credit cards, and, attached to a well-worn leather-and-enamel fob decorated with the RR symbol, Bennett's car keys.

"Oh, that. Just a present from someone in London, a long time ago."

Moreau turned to Anna, and his expression became sympathetic. "I must offer you my condolences, mademoiselle. I understand that your mother is not at all well."

Anna felt exactly what Moreau wanted her to feel: wrong-footed, shaken. "How do you know?"

"We have telephones. I have very helpful colleagues in New York. Information is so easy to obtain nowadays, now that the world has shrunk. Personal privacy hardly exists anymore. It's terrible—isn't that right, Bonfils?" The master glanced over at the novice.

Shut up and get on with it, you pompous old *connard*. "That's right, chief. Terrible."

Moreau suddenly seemed to find the contents of his pipe engrossing, scraping the bowl with a tool the shape of a narrow spoon, tapping the charred fragments into an ashtray, blowing gently through the mouthpiece. Apart from the small sounds he made, the room was still. Bonfils glowered in his corner. Anna and Bennett exchanged puzzled looks. Was this why they'd been rushed to Cannes—to watch a police inspector servicing his pipe? Bennett cleared his throat. Moreau ignored him and began feeding his pipe with tobacco from a wrinkled oilskin pouch.

At last, Bennett could stand the silence no longer. "Could you tell us why we've been arrested? What have we done?"

Moreau looked up with an air of faint surprise, as though he'd forgotten they were there. "Why don't you tell me?"

Bennett thought for a moment before giving what he hoped was a harmless answer. "Well, we were asked to pick up a case from this boat."

"Asked by whom?"

"An old chum of Mademoiselle Hersh. Actually, it was a job. We were going to be paid."

"By the old chum."

"That's right."

"And the old chum, who is this?"

"A man called Poe. Julian Poe."

"Ah yes." Moreau returned to his pipe, using three matches before he was satisfied the tobacco was drawing evenly. "And this case that was on the boat, the case that Monsieur Poe was paying you to collect. What was in it?"

Bennett hesitated before the first lie. "It was locked. I don't know."

"You don't know." Moreau picked up the two passports. "You left these on the boat." He put them in a drawer of his desk. "Careless of you. Did you leave the boat unexpectedly? In a hurry?" He took a bunch of keys from his pocket and locked the passports in the desk drawer.

"Must have forgotten them." The second lie.

"I see. What time was it when you left the boat? Approximately."

"Oh, I don't know. After dinner sometime."

"With the case?"

"Yes."

"Now, that would have been—what? Two days ago? Three days ago?"

Bennett honestly couldn't remember. "Something like that, yes."

"And then, of course, you took the case to Monsieur Poe, and he paid you."

"Well, we haven't actually had a chance to—"

"Bennett." Anna interrupted him, shaking her head. "Forget it. This is crazy. It won't work."

Moreau peered at her through a cloud of smoke and nodded with approval. "What a very sensible young woman you are. Now then, Monsieur Bennett, we'll start again. Before you do, I'm going to tell you certain things that should influence your statement." He took the pipe from his mouth and pointed the stem at Bennett. "One: the case contains a formula for the cultivation of truffles, which I'm sure you know. Two: you stole the case."

"But it had already been—"

Moreau held up his hand for silence. "I'm simply telling you the facts as we know them. You can add to our knowledge, and for your own sakes, I hope you will. At the moment, both of you are under suspicion of robbery. I have no doubt we shall be able to prove the case against you, but the preparations will take several months, and naturally during that time you will be in jail." Moreau fussed with his matches, and relit his pipe. "Then you will be sentenced—and here there are circumstances that are not in your favor. Once the French government takes an interest in a case, as it has done on this occasion, it is no longer a

simple question of common theft. It becomes more serious and will obviously carry a more serious
sentence."

"But that's outrageous. It's got nothing to do with
the government."

"It has now." Moreau smiled, a thin-lipped, hu-
morless smile. "I see from your records that you've
lived in France for many years, Monsieur Bennett. I'm
sure you will have noticed that the authorities here
have considerable powers—powers which some foreigners feel are quite extreme. Very useful to us in the
police, I must admit."

Moreau allowed the threat a few moments to sink
in. He had exaggerated a little, but only a little. The
two faces opposite him were looking drawn and
dispirited. He felt he was almost there. Now for the
promise of a more pleasant alternative.

"Should you decide to cooperate with us fully, it
can be arranged for charges to be dropped. Misunderstandings occur from time to time, as we all know,
and this would be treated as an unfortunate case of
mistaken identity, with official apologies for any inconvenience."

Bennett looked at Anna. All he wanted to do was
take her away, and leave Poe and Tuzzi and the bloody
French police to argue among themselves. "Well?
What's it to be?" He touched her cheek with his hand.
"I'll go along with you."

All the air seemed to leave her body in a single, sobbing sigh. She leaned over, turning away from Moreau, and rested her head on Bennett's shoulder, the picture of defeat. Faintly, very faintly, he heard— he thought he heard—her whisper, barely louder than breath against his neck: "Don't tell him about the bag."

21

BENNETT started at the beginning, gaining slightly in confidence as he recited the early, innocuous details of his search for employment. Moreau leaned forward on his desk, chin supported by a steeple of fingers, muted plumbing sounds coming from the pipe clenched between his teeth. Anna remained silent, head bowed, willing Bennett to have heard the whispered sentence. Bonfils sulked and took notes. His preferred methods of interrogation involved truncheons and kidneys, not this interminable talking.

Bennett's account of his first days in Monaco and the loss of the case prompted no more response than the occasional lifting of a Moreau eyebrow. It was not until he reached the point of his recall to the Domaine des Rochers, and Poe's description of the contents of the case, that Moreau's pipe came out of his mouth, followed by a question.

"This man," said Moreau, "this *expert de truffes* employed by Poe—what is his name? What is his background?"

Bennett shook his head. "I was never told his name.

He worked somewhere official before Poe found him, the department of something—agriculture, I suppose. I'm not sure."

"A civil servant?"

"That's right. I remember Poe mentioning a ministry, people not appreciating his work, things like that. Apparently, that's why he left."

"You never met him during your visits to Monsieur Poe's property?"

Bennett shrugged. "Not a chance. He's dead. Poe told me it was a car accident. Brake failure."

"How very convenient that he finished his work first." Moreau turned to Bonfils. "Check with the Ministry of Agriculture on Monday—resignations from the research department over the past four years, their *dossiers de travail*, the usual." He turned back to Bennett. This was better than he'd hoped. Any research carried out on government time, and—stretching the point a little, but not too far—any results coming from that research, were the property of the state. The lawyers would make sure of that. *En plus,* the man was dead, so he wasn't in a position to argue. It was working out very nicely. Moreau began to have visions of a minor decoration accompanying him into retirement. Services to France. That would go down well in his village in the Charente, establish him immediately as an *homme sérieux,* even a possible candidate for mayor. "Continue, monsieur."

Bennett described being given the fake case, meeting Anna in Nice, and their arrival on board the *Ragazza* for the floating auction. Bonfils was scribbling away diligently, and Moreau now started to take notes. "Give me names," he said. "Everyone you can remember."

"There was Tuzzi, the owner, and his partner, Lord Glebe. An American called Penato, Kasuga from Tokyo, and an older man, I think he said he was from Corsica. Polluce? Something like that."

The mention of Polluce caused Bonfils to crouch even more diligently over his notes. His mind was churning with a number of possibilities, none of them pleasant. He could see his chances of promotion dwindling, but that was nothing compared to the other consequences of failing to deliver the case to Polluce and his friends. They could have him put back on the beat, dishing out parking tickets. Or worse. The Union Corse was not noted for its benevolence toward those who had fallen down on the job. *Merde.*

"Bonfils?" Moreau's voice made him start. "One of your compatriots. Know anything about him, this Polluce?"

"Never heard of him, chief. I'll check him out." *Merde* again.

"So, Monsieur Bennett." Moreau looked at his notes. "There you were, on the *Ragazza,* with your bogus valise. Then what happened?"

Bennett skated as quickly as he could through the events leading to the taking of the case and their escape from the boat. "And then, when we got to Cassis, we . . . well, we borrowed a car and—"

"Borrowed a car?" Bennett said nothing. Moreau added automobile theft to Bennett's transgressions, which were mounting up in a most satisfactory manner: complicity in a tax evasion scheme, impersonation with intent to defraud, robbery—he read the list out loud in a quiet, reflective voice and watched Bennett move uncomfortably in his chair. After a pause while he attended yet again to the combustion of his pipe, Moreau continued. "It seems to me logical," he said, "that you would then have driven in your borrowed car directly to Monsieur Poe, delivered the case, and received your payment. But you didn't. Why was that?"

For the first time since Bennett had started his story, Anna spoke up. "That was my idea. I didn't trust Poe to pay us. He's not . . . well, he's kind of . . ."

Moreau's eyebrows climbed up his forehead. "Dishonest, perhaps? Would that be the word?"

Anna nodded vigorously. "You said it. The guy's a complete snake."

"*Tiens.* And yet you worked for him. How trusting of you." Moreau looked at Bennett. "So he hasn't paid?"

Anna held her breath. Don't blow it, Bennett. Think of getting out of here with a million dollars. Think of room service at the Villa d'Este. Think of anything you like, but just don't blow it.

"To tell you the truth," said Bennett, "we haven't even seen him—too busy making sure we keep out of Tuzzi's way. We've been hiding out, trying to decide what to do." Anna breathed a silent prayer of thanks.

"Then you haven't given him the case."

"Good God, no." In his relief that Moreau had not pursued the question of payment, Bennett plunged ahead. "I know it's safe, of course. Quite safe. Hidden. We managed to arrange that. Didn't want to leave it in the car, what with all the stories one hears about cars being broken into. Shocking, really—nice place like the south of France—"

Moreau cut him off. "Where is the case?"

Bonfils leaned forward, his pen poised over his notepad. If he could get the information to Polluce quickly enough, he might be off the hook.

Bennett took a moment to think. Best to keep Georgette out of this, not get her involved with the police. The old girl would have a heart attack. "Actually," he said, "I don't know, not exactly. It's with a friend. But if I could make a phone call, I could get it dropped off at my house in Saint-Martin in no time."

"*Bien.*" Moreau sat with his head down, calculating his options, his pipe growing cold. Getting the case back, that was crucial. Gratitude would follow, gratitude from the highest level. But there might be a bonus, maybe a more important decoration for services to France. This Julian Poe, certainly a tax dodger, liable to charges of filching vital agricultural secrets from the state, possibly involved in a murder conspiracy—to pick him up in the act of receiving what were technically stolen goods, well, that would be a fitting end to a highly successful operation. *"Bien,"* he said again. "This is what we'll do."

He looked at his watch and saw that the afternoon had gone. It would take some time to put everything in place—the net must be secure, with no way of Poe's slipping through. But there was no rush. The case was safe and hidden. Tomorrow would be soon enough. He pushed one of his phones across the desk toward Bennett.

"I want you to make two calls. First, to arrange for the case to be delivered to your house and left there tomorrow morning. That is possible, yes?"

Bennett nodded.

"The second call will be to Monsieur Poe, instructing him to pick up the case. Shall we say ten o'clock? It will be Sunday, after all. We don't want to get him out of bed too early." Moreau rubbed his hands together, a dry, leathery sound, and smiled. "It may be his last comfortable night for some time." He gave the phone another nudge. *"Allez,* Monsieur Bennett. Remember that these calls will give you your freedom."

Georgette picked up on the second ring. Bennett could hear the blare of her radio in the background.

"It's me, Bennett."

"Eh, alors! Have you seen the paper? What's going on? Where are you?"

"I'm fine. I'm in Cannes. Listen, I have to ask you to do something for me."

"Attends." Georgette put down the phone and went to turn off the radio. Bennett heard hurried footsteps going and coming across the floor. "So. It is without doubt the affair of the case, *non?* The whole village asks me what I know—the *salaud* Papin, Madame Joux, everyone. To them I say nothing. I am silent like an oyster. When will you return here?"

"Soon. But before I do, I'd like you to take the case tomorrow morning, and leave it in my house, on the table in the sitting room. Leave the front door unlocked, OK? Someone is coming at ten to pick it up."

"Ah bon? And then you will be back?"

"I hope so. Don't forget. Ten tomorrow morning, and then get out of the house. Go home."

"Of course," said Georgette. And of course she had no intention of missing such a dramatic moment, one that she would be able to describe later to *le tout village.* But Bennett didn't need to know that. "I shall do as you ask."

"Thanks. Thanks a lot," said Bennett. "I'll explain everything when I see you."

He put down the phone and looked at Moreau. "The case will be there."

Moreau had noticed that Bennett had been careful

not to mention a name. Some crony in the village, probably. He decided to let it pass. "Excellent. And now for Monsieur Poe."

Shimo answered and put Bennett through. Poe didn't bother with any preliminaries. "Where is it?"

"It's on its way to my house in Saint-Martin. Number three, Allée des Lices. Shimo knows where it is. The front door will be left unlocked. The case will be on the sitting-room table. Ten o'clock tomorrow morning, OK? It'll be there at ten."

"It had better be." Click.

Bennett pushed the phone back to Moreau. Bonfils fidgeted on his chair, then stood up and started toward the door. "Chief? *Pipi.* I'll be right back."

Moreau ignored him, immersed in his preparations. He gave Bennett a sheet of paper and a pencil, and asked him to make a rough plan of the village. It all appeared to be going on wheels. He could hardly wait to call Chevalier and bring him up-to-date. How many men would he need? Half a dozen should be enough, plainclothes, helicopter on call if necessary. He looked up to give Bonfils some instructions, and frowned. How long did the man need to empty his bladder, for God's sake?

———

Bonfils stood by his desk, the phone to his ear, his eyes fixed on the glass door of his office. He felt the sweat trickling down his chest, soaking into his shirt.

Come on, you bastard, pick it up. Finally, he heard the familiar cold voice.

"Monsieur Polluce? Bonfils. I can't be long. The case is being delivered to a village called Saint-Martin; the address is number three, Allée des Lices. It's coming in at ten tomorrow morning. What? No, impossible. Moreau's got his eye on me. He's making a meal of it, an operation. I have to stay with him. I know. I'm sorry, it's the best I can do." Bonfils hurried back to Moreau's office, his shirt clammy against his stomach.

———

Polluce took a sip of Cynar and looked out toward the sea, now polished with light from the evening sun. This was turning into a shambles—messy, possibly dangerous, and not a situation he wished to involve himself in personally. His influence with the police, although well distributed among the Corsicans, had never extended as far as Moreau. Overtures, discreet and delicate, had been made in the past, but the self-righteous old *schnoque* had never even accepted a free lunch, let alone an honest bribe. And he was in charge of the operation. Maybe there was a chance that something could be done, but the odds would be long. It wasn't worth putting a valuable man at risk. Luckily, thought Polluce, there was someone suitable close at hand, someone totally expendable. He put through a call to the *Ragazza,* lying at anchor less than a mile away.

"Tuzzi, I have good news. Our people have been working hard, and various arrangements have been made." A sudden thought crossed Polluce's mind. If Tuzzi did recover the case, it would only be fair and businesslike to make him pay for the information. "These arrangements have not been without some cost, but I can tell you that the case is being delivered tomorrow morning. And I can tell you where."

"*Bene, bene,* my friend. I am very happy for you. I am in joy."

"But there are some details to be agreed. In getting this information, we have spent a certain sum of money, which I think should come off the price. A little discount between friends."

Tuzzi was silent. How he hated to part with other people's money.

"A hundred thousand dollars."

Tuzzi drew in his breath. Greedy, double-crossing pig of a Corsican. But what could he do? "My friend, that seems very reasonable. You shall have a check on Monday morning, on my mother's head. I love that this has ended so well for us."

"*Bon,*" said Polluce. "You can bring the check with the case."

"The case? Me?"

"Part of the arrangement is that it will only be handed over to you. There is nobody more reliable. You have my trust. Now listen carefully."

Five minutes later, Tuzzi was reporting the conversation to Lord Glebe, who, his nose finely tuned to such matters after many years of duplicity, smelled a rat. He hastened to distance himself from the expedition.

"Wish I could come with you, old boy," he said. "But duty calls in London, I'm afraid. I sometimes wonder how the House ever gets a day's work done without me." He leaned over and patted Tuzzi's arm. "Don't need me, anyway. Simple errand. Take young Benito."

"You think it is a square deal? No hanky-pinky?"

"Panky, old boy. No—I think Polluce has called in his markers with all his unsavory friends, and it's paid off."

"So why not they to pick up the case?"

Glebe pulled out a cheroot, while he tried to think of one good reason. "Funny lot, Corsicans," he said finally. "They attach a great deal of importance to respect—as indeed do you Italians, eh?—and Polluce feels, I suppose, that it's up to you to make up for the . . . inconvenience he's suffered."

"Ah," said Tuzzi. *"Rispetto."*

"The very word I was searching for. Wish there was more of it in England. There's always some clown of a politician being caught with his trousers down, and the bloody press turn it into a national emergency. No respect for the governing classes. Between you and me"—Glebe's voice took on a confidential note—"that's why I've got to go to London tomorrow. All hell's broken loose. Distinguished backbencher, eminent man, found in Hyde Park wearing a miniskirt and high heels. Dreadful business. Dreadful. Wrong school again, you see? Always comes out in the end."

———

Moreau had a busy evening ahead of him. Certain arrangements could be left to Bonfils, but the subtleties, the important details—not to mention the calls to those in high places in Paris—all of that he would deal with himself. He looked at the sketch Bennett had given him of Saint-Martin. Like in many of the little hill villages in the Vaucluse, there was no through road. It could have been designed specifically with this operation in mind. Half a dozen well-positioned men could stop the whole place up like a bottle. Excellent.

Anna and Bennett, sitting in silence opposite him, were showing the effects of a long, draining day—they were pale-faced, hollow-eyed, and clearly tired. Moreau found himself warming to them; they had been unusually cooperative, and it was thanks to them that his career was going to end on such a high note. He might even mention their usefulness to the authorities in Paris.

"Bien," he said. "I think that will be all for today, but we shall be making an early start tomorrow. As for tonight"—his shoulders went up in a shrug of apology—"I must ask you to be our guests here. Bon-

fils will make you as comfortable as possible. The quietest cell for them, Bonfils, as this is Saturday night, and arrange for the restaurant on the corner to bring them something to eat." With a nod of dismissal, he reached for the phone.

Bonfils led the way down to the cells, rigid with irritation at being treated like a *putain* hotel clerk, and him a captain of police. He pushed open the cell door—two bunks, barred window, the stinging smell of disinfectant—and stood aside to let them in. "Someone will bring food," he said, and turned to leave.

"Captain?" Bennett's voice stopped him. "We'd like to see a menu." He inclined his head. "Please."

Bonfils struggled with the impulse to kick the Englishman in the tripes and beat him senseless, and went off to snarl at the desk sergeant. A menu, for Christ's sake!

Bennett put his arms around Anna and felt her body fit into his, relaxed and limp. She looked up at him, her eyes wide and deep and serious. "It's nearly over, isn't it?"

Bennett nodded. "As long as we don't pass out from starvation."

————

It was a meal they would never forget, more because of the circumstances than the food. The waiter from the restaurant, a young Algerian who was working in France without the benefit of formal papers, was in evident terror at finding himself serving dinner in a police station. His agitated hands shook, the tray clattered, he missed the neck of the wine bottle with his corkscrew and speared a finger. When Bennett apologized for not being able to give him a tip, he backed out of the cell sucking his wound, his eyes rolling in astonishment. Was this how criminals were treated in France? It was in truth a strange and wonderful country, just as he had been told by his father in Oran.

Bennett raised his glass to Anna. "I promised you room service, didn't I?"

While they ate, they were conscious of the sound of feet stopping outside their cell, curious eyes looking in through the bars as the night shift inspected these two ex-fugitives, now privileged inmates. A young *gendarme* came in to clear away, gave them coarse, prison-issue towels, and showed them to the carbolic-scented heaven of hot showers. Full, clean, and exhausted, they collapsed on their bunks. By the time the first batch of Saturday-night drunks and walking wounded were being tossed into the other cells, they were sleeping like bones.

22

ANNA and Bennett followed Bonfils along a corridor lined with cells, unable to resist glancing through the bars at their neighbors of the previous night. Huddled bodies in varying degrees of dirt and disrepair snored and twitched on bunks, or sat disconsolately, heads in hands, contemplating the floor and the prospect of punishment. Sunday morning in the slammer—malodorous, squalid, despairing. The sweet sea air out on the street came like a rush of clean water to the head. It was six o'clock.

Three large unmarked Citroëns of that smoky-blue color preferred by the French police when traveling incognito were parked outside headquarters. Moreau, Anna, and Bennett joined the driver of the lead car. Bonfils checked the passengers in the other two vehicles—seven *gendarmes,* in their weekend plain clothes of jeans, *blousons,* and sunglasses, which, with their regulation short haircuts, gave them the appearance of a group of young soldiers on leave. They were in high spirits, delighted at the thought of a day off from the drudgery of the beat, doing undercover work on double pay. Bonfils, surly and nervous, got in the second car, and the convoy turned onto the Croisette and made for the autoroute.

Moreau, adrenaline high and pipe agurgle, sat in the front seat, making lavish and rather superfluous use of the car phone as he went over details that had been discussed at length the night before. He reminded the commanding officer of the air force base at Salon to have a helicopter on standby. He reminded the captain of the *gendarmerie* at Les Beaumettes to keep his men on their toes—"but discreetly, *mon vieux,* discreetly. We mustn't frighten off the pigeons, eh?"— in case local reinforcements might be needed. He woke Léon at the Café Crillon in Saint-Martin, to remind him that a command center would be set up in the storage room behind the bar. And when he'd run out of legitimate targets, he called Bonfils in the second car, to nag him once again.

Yes, chief, the men are armed. Yes, chief, they know the drill. No, chief, there are no problems. Bonfils cradled his phone and stared gloomily at the car ahead. What a pig's breakfast this was turning into. Suppose Polluce turned up? Surely he was too smart for that. But what if he wasn't? What if his determination to get the case made him take the chance? He'd be arrested on suspicion and in a cell so fast his feet wouldn't touch the ground. And that would be the end of a promising career for Captain Bonfils. He turned around and told the men in the back to shut up. Babbling away like a bunch of schoolgirls. Anyone would think this was a *putain* picnic.

The three cars, unhindered by the civilian restraints of speed limits, were keeping to a steady one hundred eighty kilometers an hour, racing the sun as it rose slowly behind them. Anna and Bennett were finding it difficult not to let their elation show. In a whispered conference before dawn, they had agreed to act as though normally apprehensive at being involved in a police operation. But it was hard. Every time they looked at each other, glances of delicious complicity, they had to fight the urge to smile. They locked hands, and forced themselves to turn away from each other and study the landscape.

The convoy passed the exit to Marignane airport and flashed through countryside that was becoming increasingly jagged and untamed, a severe contrast to the soft lushness of the palm trees and barbered grass they had left behind in Cannes. Moreau looked at his watch for the twentieth time, and then, nodding to himself in satisfaction, called the other two cars and ordered a brief stop at Cavaillon. Newspapers were to be bought and issued to the men. Camouflage, to give them a touch of Sunday-morning authenticity as they waited in Léon's café to spring the trap. But not the same newspaper, *comprenez?* A selection. It wouldn't do for everyone to be hiding behind *France-Dimanche.* How true it was, thought Moreau, that God was in the details. God and police work.

They made Cavaillon by eight. The men got out to stretch their legs, while Bonfils supervised the choice and purchase of newspapers. Requests for coffee were refused; Moreau was impatient to reach Saint-Martin and establish himself in his café headquarters. There would be coffee then, he told the men, coffee and fresh croissants. With a growing sense of excitement, Moreau directed the driver—who had no need of directions, having memorized the route already, according to his chief's instructions—to take the D2 out of Cavaillon. They would be in Saint-Martin in fifteen minutes.

————

Enzo Tuzzi had gone to bed in his cabin with a problem and woken up with a solution. The $100,000 discount demanded by Polluce rankled. It was unreasonable and excessive. Just the thought of it at dinner had given Tuzzi indigestion and heartburn, most unusual for a man who took pride in the robust efficiency of his bodily functions. But by morning, the heartburn had disappeared and a simple scheme had presented itself. He would charge Polluce a delivery fee of $100,000, and if the miserable Corsican *stronzo* didn't like it, Tuzzi would sell the formula elsewhere. *Bravo,* Enzo, *bravo,* he said to himself as he applied pomade to his hair before securing it carefully in a glistening tuft at the nape of his neck.

And now for the wardrobe, but nothing too conspicuous. He selected a loose-fitting checked shirt, which he wore outside a pair of dark-blue cotton trousers. From his bedside table—an unnecessary precaution, he was sure—he took the nickel-plated .38 in its chamois holster and clipped it to his waistband, under the shirt. A generous dab of cologne, a final flick to the mustache, one last admiring preen in front of the mirror, and he was ready. Glebe was right. This was a simple errand. Perhaps he would take young Benito to lunch afterward to celebrate. The boy tried hard, and had a useful uncle in the construction business in Naples.

He arrived on deck to find Lord Glebe, in his traveling outfit of dove-gray linen suit and slippers of embroidered velveteen, giving the steward detailed instructions about the care and feeding of Genghis during his master's absence. Tuzzi took him aside to explain his $100,000 idea.

"It's worth a try," said Glebe. "But I think we should expect a little resistance from Polluce. He won't be a happy man."

"So?" Tuzzi dismissed the unhappiness of Polluce across the deck and into the Mediterranean with a flick of his hand. "We will have the case. He wants it, he pays for it. Or we go somewhere else." Tuzzi grinned, and massaged Glebe's shoulder in his enthusiasm.

Surveying the wrinkled damage to the linen of his suit, Glebe moved out of arm's reach. "Well, as I said, it's worth a try. Every little bit helps. But if I were you, old boy, I'd wait until you're back on board before you make the call. Hotheaded lot, those Corsicans."

"What is this hothead?"

Glebe sighed. It would be a relief to spend a few days in a country where people spoke English, or what passed for English nowadays. "It means excitable, old boy. Quick-tempered, fiery, that sort of thing."

"Ah," said Tuzzi. *"Vulcanico."*

"The very word. Well, I must fly. Good luck—or maybe I should say *buona fortuna."* Glebe walked aft, to the launch that waited to take him ashore.

Tuzzi called after him. "I count the days for your return, my friend."

Dear God in heaven, Glebe thought to himself as he waved his cheroot in a languid farewell, he manages to make everything sound like a second-rate aria.

Tuzzi called for coffee, and Benito.

"Don Tuzz', I am ready." The burly young man stood in front of Tuzzi, his chest swelling with enthusiasm. Tuzzi flinched as he read the message that stretched across Benito's T-shirt: *Per favore, non mi rompere i coglioni.* It brought back painful memories. Besides, the sentiment was inappropriate for Sunday morning, a churchgoing day. Please don't break my balls. Tuzzi shook his head. Young people needed guidance. He sent Benito off to change, and sipped his coffee. Tomorrow he would make for Ibiza, and some

well-earned rest and diversion with those young Spanish girls, plump as ripe figs.

———

    Julian Poe stood on his terrace, admiring the morn-
ing light as it spilled over the peaks of the Grand
Lubéron. He had been tempted to get to Saint-Martin
early, but had finally decided against doing anything
that might spook the messenger with the case. Amateurs scared easily. Bennett and the girl would certainly scare easily, he thought, once Shimo got his
hands on them in that cold, bare room next to the cellar. Gérard—poor Gérard, stuck in a car for days on
end—had been told to move in and pick them up at
ten, and not to be too gentle about it.
    All in all, it promised to be a most pleasant day—
the formula recovered, the money returned, and the
bonus of vengeance. Poe looked at his watch and saw
that there was ample time for a civilized breakfast, an
English breakfast. This morning, he was having the
last of the Cumberland sausages from Harrods, and
then he would call Chou-Chou in Paris to make
arrangements for her return. Or maybe she'd like to
meet him in London, for a few days at the Connaught.
Yes, it was going to be a fine day. He turned back to
the house and saw Shimo waiting like a statue inside
the doorway.
    "Morning, Shimo. In your Sunday best, I see." For

once, the Japanese had put aside his suit, and was dressed in baggy black cotton trousers and top, black shoes with thin crepe soles. His fighting clothes—the trousers loose enough for kicks, the crepe soles for grip. Poe didn't anticipate trouble; Shimo always did. It was one of the reasons he'd lasted so long.

He inclined his head. "Good morning, Mr. Julian. Breakfast is ready."

"Splendid." Poe patted Shimo on the shoulder, feeling the hardness of highly trained muscle under the cotton. "I couldn't tempt you into a sausage, could I? They're very good."

Shimo shook his head. "I ate at six. Rice and miso soup. Healthy food."

Poe sensed faint disapproval, as he always did where his diet was concerned. Shimo would be happier if he made do on bean sprouts, but the smell coming from the kitchen dispelled any guilt. "You're right," Poe said. "I know you're right. But I do love a good sausage." He sat at the table, reveling in the feel of the linen napkin, the delicacy of the almost translucent Limoges china, the heft and balance of the antique silver cutlery, the wonderful, luxurious, orderly texture of his privileged existence. And they say crime doesn't pay, he thought. Idiots.

————

Georgette had left her bed shortly after dawn, woken by anticipation and curiosity and unable to get back to sleep. She had dressed quickly and gone round to Bennett's house, to make sure that no dead flies or errant motes of dust had fallen during the night to blemish the buffed perfection of tiles and glass and wood. She was determined that whoever was coming this morning—be it the president of the Republic himself—would find the Bennett residence immaculate, a credit to her and to the village. And so it was.

She returned home and took the case from its bed under the gravel. After one final fruitless attempt to unravel the mysteries of the combination lock, she scoured and polished the ribbed aluminum until it gave off the subdued gleam of old pewter. The case joined her for breakfast, sitting there on the table as she dipped a toasted slice of yesterday's baguette into her *café crème,* watched the slow crawl of time around the face of the clock, and thought with pleasure of how she would impart the morning's news to Papin and the others. She would drip it to them, detail by fascinating detail, saving the best—whatever that might be—for last. Finishing breakfast, she washed the dishes, and waited.

———

One by one, the early regulars were drifting into the Café Crillon. Anny and Léon, alert and expectant behind the bar, were trying to give the impression of business as usual, just another Sunday. But they failed to convince the oldest of the old men, the grandfather in chief, the old despot whom Léon called the *chef des pépés.* He was, after all, the self-appointed chairman of the table in the back.

And he sensed that something was up. He stopped just inside the threshold and looked around him with deep suspicion, an old hound picking up the scent of a hidden cat.

Ever since his doctor had told him to give up the after-dinner tots of *marc,* he had been an early riser, and deprivation of rough alcohol and the consequent insomnia had made him crusty. He stood, leaning on his stick, head thrust forward, the wattles on his neck tensed with the expectation of unpalatable news. *"Eh, alors,"* he said. *"Eh, alors.* What's going on?"

Anny feigned innocence. "What do you mean, *pépé?"*

The old man shook his stick at the vase of flowers on the bar, the unusual neatness of the tables and chairs, each table decorated with a single bright nasturtium in a miniature brandy snifter.

"All this," he said. "Flowers. Folderol." He moved slowly to his table at the back, the ferrule of his stick a tapping counterpoint to the shuffle of his carpet slippers. "And the prices," he said. "No doubt they have been augmented to pay for this *friperie."* He put one hand to the approximate area of his liver, grunted, and eased himself into his chair.

"Not at all," said Anny. "Flowers brighten the place up. Besides, it's Sunday."

"*Bof,*" said the old man. "Expecting the Almighty to drop in after Mass, are you?" He snorted. "Flowers. Soon it will be chandeliers, no doubt. Bring me a little *rosé*. Where are the dominoes?"

The hunt for the dominoes was cut short by the sound of cars pulling up outside the café. "It's them!" Léon ducked around the bar and through the door.

"It's who?" The old man banged his stick on the floor as he watched Anny follow Léon out of the café. "*Dieu et Jésus,* must one die of thirst?"

Léon directed the three cars to the yard behind the café, where the beer trucks from Mutzig and Kronenbourg made their deliveries. He embraced Bennett, shook hands deferentially with Moreau, and led the way through the back door into the storage room. "*Voilà,*" he said. "It's not comfortable, but it's private. And from here"—he pushed open the shutter of a tiny window—"you can see everyone who comes to the village." He invited Moreau to inspect the view of the main street and the parking area. "You see, monsieur? It is as I told you on the phone. I hope you find it satisfactory?"

Moreau peered through the window, his lips making faint popping sounds around the stem of his pipe. He nodded. It was satisfactory. "Bonfils, get the men out of the cars. We'll put four of them at the tables outside—not together, mind—and the rest inside, at the front." He turned to Anna and Bennett. "You stay with me, in here." He paused, his head cocked. "What's that?"

The steady thump of the old man's stick on the floor had become louder and more insistent. Léon opened the door that led to the bar. *"J'arrive, j'arrive. Anny,* see what our friends would like—*pastaga,* maybe a little *Calva."* The thumping continued. Léon shook his head. *"Merde! J'arrive!"*

The *pépé,* all thoughts of dominoes forgotten, glared at the sudden influx of young men with newspapers, who were seating themselves in the front of the café. Strangers, every one of them. He grunted as Léon placed a tumbler of *rosé* in front of him. "Crowds," he said. "One cannot even have a quiet drink on a Sunday. Who are they?"

"Tourists," said Léon. "Just tourists."

"Foreigners."

Saint-Martin's watch committee of elderly ladies, now settled on chairs in front of their houses around the *place* to keep an eye on the comings and goings of the morning, were finding the clientele of the café unusually absorbing. All these clean young men, and so early. And why was it that each time a car pulled into the village, their newspapers dropped in unison? It was not normal. It was not at all normal.

Anna and Bennett stood at their post by the window

in the storage room, drinking coffee and trying to ignore the agitated splutter of Moreau's pipe and the
glowering presence of Bonfils. Moreau was seated
on a beer keg, two wine cartons serving as a makeshift
desk, his notes and his tobacco pouch arranged in
front of him, his eye returning constantly to his watch,
his hand hovering over his cellular phone until he
could restrain himself no longer. He put through a call
to Chevalier.

After a brief but evidently successful conversation—excitement mounting with every *"Ah bon?"*
until his voice approached falsetto—he came over to
the window to share his good humor with Anna and
Bennett. "Paris is pleased with the progress of this affair," he said. "Extremely pleased. The highest level
is taking a close personal interest. He will be at his
desk to hear our news. An amusing connection, don't
you think? The back room of a country café, and the
Elysée Palace." He looked at his watch and hummed
softly to himself. Any minute now.

———

Georgette's head emerged from her front door with
infinite caution, her eyes checking the windows of her
neighbors' houses. All was still, the lace curtains
hanging motionless. In fact, most of her neighbors,
drawn by the magnet of speculation coming from the
ladies around the *place,* had discovered a pressing

need to visit the café, where Anny and Léon were having their busiest Sunday morning in years.

Satisfied that her journey would pass unnoticed, Georgette pulled her cap down over her eyes, picked up the plastic shopping bag containing the case, and scuttled around the corner to the Allée des Lices. She let herself in and put the case on the table as Bennett had told her, taking care not to scratch the waxy mirror shine of the wood. She made sure the front door was unlocked. She ran her hands over the couch, smoothing away nonexistent wrinkles, and went into the kitchen. There she waited.

———

The dark-green Range Rover swung into the village and parked by the side of the monument to the dead of the First World War. Outside the café, the newspapers were lowered to half-mast. Around the *place,* the elderly ladies paused in their muttered conversations to inspect the passengers. The church clock began to wheeze and whir and count the strokes to ten.

Bennett watched the car doors open, saw Shimo get out, then Poe, and nodded to Moreau, standing just behind him. "That's Poe." Anna looked at her former lover, elegant in beige and black, and reached for Bennett's hand. He smiled at her. "Punctual bastard, isn't he?"

Moreau kept his eyes on Poe. "Bonfils? We give

him five minutes, and then we pick him up. I want him with the case in his hands, *d'accord?*"

———

Poe and Shimo, dismissing the undisguised stares of the villagers as normal rustic nosiness, walked up the street and turned into the Allée des Lices. Shimo pushed open the door of number 3, and they stepped inside. In the kitchen, Georgette held her breath, listening to the soft sounds of their footsteps on the tiled floor.

Poe bent over the case. "Let's make sure it's all there, shall we?" He spun the tumblers on the lock, snapped up the two fastenings, and opened the case, laying it flat on the table.

Georgette, her ears straining, heard the succession of clicks, the faint squeak of hinges. *The case was being opened.* Not ten feet away, the secret was being revealed, the secret that she alone in the entire village could see, and later describe in all its fascinating detail. How could she resist?

"Bonjour, bonjour, bonjour!" She burst from the kitchen, her eyes darting toward the open case. *"Un petit café pour les messieurs?"*

The two men spun around, Shimo falling instinctively into a position of combat readiness until he took in the short and decidedly unthreatening figure in the yellow baseball cap.

"Who the hell is she?" said Poe.

Shimo relaxed. "The *femme de ménage.*" He moved

to block Georgette's view of the case. "No coffee." He nodded toward the kitchen. "Go in there."

Eyes wide, Georgette backed through the door. Poe resumed his study of the contents of the case.

———

"Bon," said Moreau. "Let's go." The gendarmes put down their newspapers and rose as one, and the group began to move out of the café and into the main street, the eyes of Saint-Martin upon them. Truly, this was a most irregular Sunday.

———

Tuzzi's Mercedes, driven with enormous brio by young Benito, swept up the village road and swerved over to the café.

"You!" called Tuzzi from the car. "Where's the Allée des Lices?"

The startled *gendarme* barely had time to point the way before Benito applied a heavy foot to the accelerator and took off, leaving rubber scars on the road and Bennett with his jaw dropping in surprise. "But that's Tuzzi," he said to Moreau. "What the hell is he doing here?"

———

Benito stopped the car at the entrance to the alley and shrugged. Too narrow. "Stay here," said Tuzzi.

"I'll be two minutes." In his haste, he left the passenger door open, and as Benito leaned across to close it, he saw, reflected in the rearview mirror, a group of figures coming up the street. What a busy place it was for a little village. He tuned in to Radio Monte Carlo and thought about girls.

———

The door to number 3 was ajar. Tuzzi pushed it open, paused in the hall, and moved through to the living room, his feet, in espadrilles, soundless on the floor. He was almost in the room before Poe and Shimo were aware of him.

For a second, maybe two, they all were motionless—Poe standing with the case in his hand, Shimo to one side, Tuzzi's bulk filling the doorway. Poe was the first to move. With a sideways chop of his free hand, as if to push away an unwanted dog, he spoke. "Deal with him, Shimo."

The Japanese crouched and turned. His preference—a foot-administered frontal lobotomy achieved by a roundhouse kick to the temple—was impossible. Tuzzi was protected by the frame of the doorway. It would have to be *mawashi-geri-gedan,* foot to pubic bone, followed by *hadaka-jime,* the naked strangle. He took two steps forward, seeing as if in slow motion Tuzzi's hand coming up from his hip, holding a gun.

———

Later, for many years and to many rapt audiences, Georgette would describe the events of the next few seconds, as seen from the kitchen door. Shimo's foot, with the unimaginable velocity developed by years of training, struck the Italian on the appointed spot. There was an explosion as Tuzzi doubled forward, the bullet released by the involuntary spasm of his trigger finger passing within inches of Shimo's shoulder, its trajectory rising before it reached its accidental destination. Poe grew a third eye in his head, and died without losing his astonished expression.

The *gendarmes* entered the house like a torrent, pointing their weapons at everyone in sight. Shimo stood with his back against a wall and folded his arms. Georgette raised her hands. Poe bled silently onto the carpet. Tuzzi, an oversized fetus, whimpered on the floor.

Moreau could hardly have wished for a more dramatic climax to the operation. His pipe forgotten, he moved to the center of the room and knelt by Poe's body. "Bonfils, call homicide in Avignon. Photographer. Ambulance. The usual."

Georgette, now that the shock was beginning to subside, saw a further opportunity to take part in the proceedings. "Monsieur? Aristide my cousin is the village *ambulancier*. He can arrange the dead one.

Also that other, he who moans on the floor. It is very large, a four-body ambulance."

Moreau got to his feet and looked down at Poe. "He is evidence, madame. He must under no circumstances be moved until photographs and measurements have been taken."

Georgette came over to take a closer look at the body. "And my carpet? What of my carpet? See how it stains."

A sigh of exasperation from Moreau. "Calm yourself, madame. The state will replace it. Bonfils! Make a note of the carpet." He looked across the room at Bennett. "Now, monsieur. To the best of your knowledge, is this the genuine case?"

Bennett left Anna at the doorway and stepped over Poe's body. "I think so. May I open it?" Georgette craned her neck for a better view as he fumbled with the lock. Thirty-six twenty-four thirty-six. The vials, snug in their beds of foam rubber, the folders and printouts—everything was as he remembered seeing it before he'd left it with Georgette. He looked up and nodded at Moreau.

Leaving two men to guard the corpse, they left the house. The villagers of Saint-Martin were then treated to the sight of a slow-moving procession headed by the bent, shuffling figure of Tuzzi, supported by Benito and followed by Shimo, the three of them covered by the guns of the *gendarmes*. Sunday-morning business was abandoned as the butcher, the baker, and Madame Joux from the *épicerie* attached themselves to the rear of the group, showering Georgette with questions, which, with enormous pleasure, she declined to answer.

———

Bennett put his arm around Anna and felt the ridge of tension in her shoulders. "Are you OK?"

"I'll be fine. He didn't know what hit him, did he?"

Bennett thought of the expression of disbelief on Poe's face, the neat hole above one eyebrow, the surprised gape of his mouth. "No. He didn't."

"Can we get out of here? I've just about had it with guns and policemen."

But there were, as a jubilant Moreau said when they reached the café, certain formalities to complete, the first of which was a call to Chevalier. He left Georgette, Anna, and Bennett at the bar, where Léon, with great ceremony, insisted on pouring them glasses of his second-best champagne.

The café had never seen such a crowd, and a knot of villagers soon formed around Georgette, who, in her starring role of eyewitness, was rationing her answers rather more carefully than her consumption of champagne. The old men at the back couldn't hear, and shouted for her to speak up. Anna and Bennett escaped to the comparative peace of an outside table.

Moreau came out to join them, glowing with satisfaction. "I don't think we need detain you any longer."
He put the car keys and their passports on the table.
"A driver will take you to Les Beaumettes to pick up
your car. All that remains for me to say—"

"Monsieur Moreau?" Léon, wide-eyed and flus-
tered, called from the door, his hand up to his ear
making the shape of a telephone. "It's the office of the
president."

The café fell silent, every ear straining to listen as
Moreau took the call. He stood to attention. He nodded several times. By the time he put down the phone,
he seemed to have grown several inches.

"Well!" he said to Anna and Bennett. "I must tell
you that the president of the Republic is pleased. Not
only with the total success of the operation"—he
paused for a self-effacing shrug—"but also with your
helpful part in this affair." He dropped his voice. "*Entre
nous,* there is talk of official recognition for your services to French agriculture. Be sure to leave an address
with the captain at Les Beaumettes." He looked at his
watch and gave an exaggerated sigh. "You must excuse
me. There is still much to do. Dead men make paperwork, you know." After shaking hands with them both,
he returned to the melee around the bar, where Georgette, her cap now slightly askew, was describing how
she had felt against her cheek the wind—the deadly
breath—of the fatal bullet as it passed.

———

Anna and Bennett drove away from the *gendarmerie,* half expecting to hear the sound of a police siren. Bennett's eyes flicked constantly to the mirror, the guilty tic of a fugitive. It wasn't until they reached the ruin above Buoux that they began to believe their liberty.

Bennett dusted off the bag and tossed it onto the back seat. A million dollars, less the price of a tractor. "We've got enough for lunch," he said. "I think we've earned it."

He'd thought about it often, during the past few days—where they'd go, how it would feel to be together and safe—until it had assumed the importance of much more than a meal. It would mark an ending and a beginning, a celebration and a reward. And for such an occasion, there is nowhere in the world quite like France at noon on a fine summer Sunday. The only problem is an embarrassment of choice. Bennett had eventually decided on an old favorite, Le Mas Tourteron, a substantial stone farmhouse on the road below Gordes, its cooking and its courtyard an irresistible combination.

He turned into the parking area and squeezed the Peugeot in between a Jaguar with Swiss plates and an unkempt local Renault 5. Anna got out of the car and looked through the entrance to the courtyard—tables dressed in white and blue, dappled light, huge pots of flowers against the walls, the clients studying their menus like prayer books. She pushed a hand through her hair, glanced down, and shook her head.

"A place like this. They'll never let me in."

Bennett looked at her dust-caked boots, her rumpled jeans, her T-shirt, which showed signs of great fatigue. And then her face, and the glow of her eyes. You'd have to be blind to resist, he thought.

"You look hungry," he said. "They'll let you in."

He picked up the bag and took her hand. They were greeted in the courtyard by the smiling husband of Elisabeth, the chef, who showed them to a corner table where their closest neighbors were geraniums. "Would you like me to take the bag while you have lunch?"

Bennett grinned at Anna. "No," he said. "Thank you. I think we'll hang on to it."

Peter Mayle spent fifteen years in the advertising business, first as a copywriter and then as a reluctant executive, before escaping Madison Avenue in 1975 to write books. He is the author of *A Year in Provence* and *Toujours Provence,* as well as the novels *A Dog's Life* and *Hotel Pastis.* He and his wife live in Provence and Long Island, New York.

(continued)

Grimes, Martha, *Rainbow's End*
Grimes, Martha, *Hotel Paradise*
Hepburn, Katharine, *Me*
James, P. D., *Original Sin*
Koontz, Dean, *Dark Rivers of the Heart*
Koontz, Dean, *Intensity*
Krantz, Judith, *Lovers*
Krantz, Judith, *Spring Collection*
Landers, Ann, *Wake Up and Smell the Coffee!*
Lindbergh, Anne Morrow, *Gift from the Sea*
Mayle, Peter, *Anything Considered*
McCarthy, Cormac, *The Crossing*
Michener, James A., *Mexico*
Michener, James A., *Miracle in Seville*
Michener, James A., *Recessional*
Mother Teresa, *A Simple Path*
Patterson, Richard North, *Eyes of a Child*
Patterson, Richard North, *The Final Judgment*
Phillips, Louis, editor, *The Random House Large Print Treasury of Best-Loved Poems*
Pope John Paul II, *Crossing the Threshold of Hope*
Pope John Paul II, *The Gospel of Life*
Powell, Colin with Joseph E. Persico, *My American Journey*
Rendell, Ruth, *Simisola*
Rooney, Andy, *My War*
Shaara, Jeff, *Gods and Generals*
Truman, Margaret, *Murder at the National Gallery*
Tyler, Anne, *Ladder of Years*
Tyler, Anne, *Saint Maybe*